ANNE TAYLOR

# With Great Power

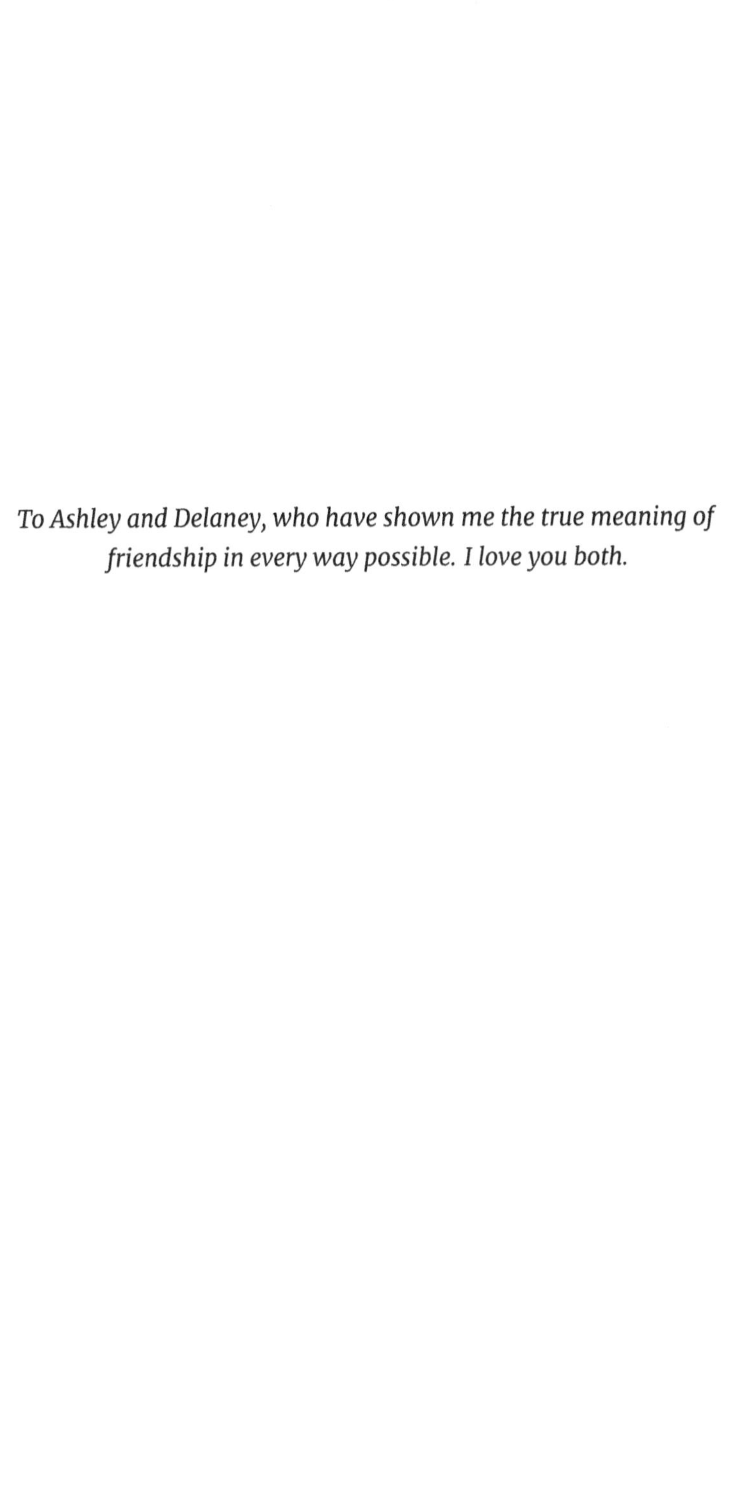

*To Ashley and Delaney, who have shown me the true meaning of friendship in every way possible. I love you both.*

# Contents

# 1

# Lani

Lani's hands were shaking. She scanned through the letter one more time to make sure she hadn't missed anything.

"Oh my gosh," she breathed.

Her roommate, Lucy, looked up from her computer.

"What?"

Lani held out the letter.

"Are you okay?" Lucy asked, glancing at the piece of paper. "I can't tell if this is good news or bad news."

"The contest!" Lani stumbled out. "The essay I wrote—it won!"

Lucy's eyes widened.

"The contest for that retreat you told me about?"

Lani nodded furiously and shoved the letter at Lucy.

"Look!"

Lucy took it and started reading out loud.

"Ms. Lani Chambers, we are happy to inform you that you have been selected as a winner to attend Dr. Theodore Arnold Fredricksen's exclusive week-long writing retreat. We found your essay to be touching and feel you are just the type of person Dr. Fredricksen would like to mentor during this event. He sees a great amount of potential in you and your writing."

Lucy paused and stared at Lani with her mouth open in a smile.

"That's so exciting," she said. "He's like, one of the most famous authors in the world."

"Keep reading," Lani said eagerly.

Her heart was pounding.

"You are invited to visit Dr. Fredricksen's home for a week-long retreat with the other essay contest winners," Lucy went on. "There, you will attend a series of lectures and workshops dedicated to helping you become a better writer. You will also receive one-on-one mentoring from Dr. Fredricksen throughout the week. At the end of the event, one attendee will be chosen to receive a $100,000 grant to help them pursue a full-time writing career."

Lucy paused and looked up at Lani with her mouth hanging open.

"You didn't tell me you could win 100 grand!" she said.

"I didn't think I even had a chance," Lani admitted.

Lucy rolled her eyes with a smile.

"There you go doubting yourself again," she teased.

"I mean, I still don't know why I was picked," Lani said, reaching for the letter.

Lucy pulled it back.

"Wait, what does the rest say?" she asked.

"Just that I have to call to confirm, and that they'll cover all the expenses," Lani said, pulling the letter out of Lucy's hands. "And I'm not supposed to tell anyone besides friends and family."

"Ooh, why?"

"They said they want to avoid a media frenzy for as long as they can, so don't tell anyone, okay?"

Lucy nodded, and the two sat in silence for a few minutes to take everything in.

"This is so crazy," Lucy finally said. "A $100,000 grant? That would cover all four years of tuition. How do you think he'll pick the winner?"

"I don't know. I don't even know how many people will be there."

"Oh yeah...probably no more than, like, twenty people though, right? It said you'll get one-on-one time with him, so there can't be that many."

"Yeah," Lani said.

She exhaled.

"I can't believe they picked my essay."

"What did you write about?" Lucy asked.

"I mostly talked about volunteering at the women's shelter last year. I honestly didn't think it was that great."

"Well, apparently it was. When are you going to call them?"

Lani shrugged.

"Might as well do it right now," she said.

Lani grabbed her phone and dialed the number on the letter. She heard two rings before someone picked up.

"Hello," a cool voice answered. "This is the Estate of Dr. Theodore Arnold Fredricksen. My name is Barbara. How can I help you?"

"Hi, my name is Lani Chambers, and I just received a letter from the estate confirming that I'm one of the winners of Dr. Fredricksen's essay contest for the writing retreat."

"Oh, congratulations," Barbara said.

She sounded like she was older, maybe in her 60s.

"Thank you for calling. Yes, I can see you right here. Are you able to confirm your availability for the retreat from April 2nd through the 9th?"

"Yeah, I'm free then."

The retreat coincided perfectly with her school's spring break; otherwise, she wouldn't have been able to go.

"The letter said all expenses were covered?" Lani asked quietly, turning away from Lucy.

"Yes, of course," Barbara said. "We will handle your transportation to and from the event. You'll stay at Dr. Fredricksen's estate for the duration of the trip, and all meals and any other accommodations you need will be provided there."

"Wow, thank you so much."

"Of course. Dr. Fredricksen is taking this grant very seriously and will spare no expense. Now, can I confirm your address so we can get started on arranging transportation on the 2nd?"

Lani spoke with Barbara for another thirty minutes before ending the call with an email confirmation of her flight to Hartford, Connecticut, and another one confirming a car would pick her up from her apartment next week.

"I assumed someone as rich as him would live in, like, L.A.," Lucy said after Lani relayed the information. "Or Hawaii."

"Maybe he has a bunch of houses," Lani said. "Or maybe he needs to stay on the east coast. A lot of the schools he speaks at are over there."

"Yeah, that's true. Are you going to tell your parents?"

The cloud that Lani had been floating on for the past hour disappeared, and she couldn't help but immediately roll her eyes. Calling their divorce 'messy' was an understatement, and since it was finalized last year, she hadn't been close to either of them. Lani had tried, she had really tried, to keep the peace, but then they had both told her that she had to pick one over the other to defend their side in court. When Lani refused, the phone calls from both became cold and distant, so eventually, she stopped calling.

Lucy was the one encouraging Lani to keep the relationship open even though Lani couldn't imagine why it'd be worth it at this point. To be fair, Lani hadn't told her roommate it was particularly crushing to be forced to choose between your adoptive parents and then punished when you couldn't, like you owed them something and couldn't deliver. Lani didn't think Lucy, who had grown up in a stable, loving home, would ever understand.

"They'll find out eventually," Lucy said. "It should come from you first."

Lani snorted.

"Honestly, I don't care."

"Look, I understand picking your battles," Lucy said. "But I think this is something that's only going to get worse if you don't bring it up first."

Lani sighed and shook her head.

"Yeah, you're right."

She pulled out her phone and sent each of her parents a quick text and a link to one of the news articles posted about the contest a few months ago so they didn't pester her with questions about its legitimacy.

"So, how are we celebrating?" Lucy asked. "Root beer floats at Uncle Bo's?"

Lani hesitated.

"I mean, I want to," she said. "But I have a paper due tonight and two quizzes to study for."

Lucy rolled her eyes and grabbed Lani's arm.

"Come on," she begged. "All you ever do is study. You ace everything anyway, so a couple of hours downtown won't hurt."

The only reason Lani did so well in school was because her grades granted her a full-ride scholarship, which was the only reason she was even at college at the moment. Her father's gambling problem and mother's alcoholism, both contributing heavily to their divorce, had also siphoned up the entirety of her parents' savings last year. Lani's parents had insisted she didn't get a job in high school so she could "enjoy her childhood," and Lani had instead spent her free time competing in sports and hanging out with friends. Which, sure, was great at the time. But her parents didn't drop the news of their debt until after she showed them her college acceptance letter to her dream school one day in March of her senior year, after which she was told they wouldn't be able to contribute anything towards her education like they had promised.

The college Lani had dreamt of attending had only offered a half-tuition scholarship, which wasn't enough for her to cover on her own, and the thought of accumulating that much debt so early in her life was terrifying. A government grant was also out of the question, as her parents earned a significant amount of money that left her out of the running for practically any support, even if they spent it all on themselves. Lani tried her best not to cry as she called the school to decline her attendance.

Fortunately, she had applied to several universities and was able to get a full-ride academic scholarship at a small religious school a few hours away. She got a job at the mall over the summer and saved up enough to cover living expenses for the first few months of college until she could find a job there. Lani's parents had been in such a brawl the morning she left that she didn't even hug them goodbye. They were so upset about it that they both left angry voicemails on her phone. She had deleted them immediately.

Lani was able to get a part-time job in the school cafeteria that barely covered rent, food, and the occasional drink with friends. Her scholarship stipulated that she had to maintain a perfect GPA with a full-time class schedule to continue to cover her entire tuition, which was proving more and more difficult as the semesters went on. For the past two and a half years, Lani's alarm went off at 5:00 in the morning to get her to work by 5:45, and she found herself unable to collapse into bed until well past midnight by the time she finished work, classes, and homework.

Lani took in a deep breath. She really could use a break.

"One hour," she said to Lucy. "That's it. Seriously."

Visibly ecstatic, Lucy grabbed her keys with a shake of her hips.

"Yeah, baby," she sang.

At the restaurant, Lucy and Lani laughed over ice cream and watched people stroll down the sidewalk outside.

"I'm getting us coffee," Lucy said after she finished her float.

Lani shook her head.

"I have too much to do today."

Lucy put her finger on Lani's mouth.

"Shhh," she said. "You just won a cool contest. We're celebrating. Chill out for a few minutes. Plus coffee will help."

Lani felt her phone vibrate as Lucy skipped over to the

counter. She pulled it out of her purse, and an icy wave passed over her body. It was him. Always a different number, always a similar message.

*You have one month. Don't forget, slut.*

As if she could forget. Hands shaking, Lani slid her phone back into her bag as Lucy came back to the table carrying two steaming cups of coffee. Lani tried her best to fake enthusiasm and downed the burning beverage as fast as she could, ready to go back to her apartment. She chatted with Lucy for a few more minutes so she wouldn't seem suspicious, then stood up from the table.

"I have so much to do," she said. "I gotta go, sorry. You can stay if you want."

Lucy, who had been eyeing a blonde-haired guy on the other side of the shop, smiled mischievously.

"Actually, I think I will stay for a few more minutes. I know one of the girls in that group," she nodded towards the boy. "Maybe I can get an introduction."

"Careful," Lani said, thinking of the university's strict dating policies. "Don't do anything you'll regret."

Lucy rolled her eyes.

"This school. Don't worry, I'll be a good girl."

Lani gave Lucy a hug and squeezed through the crowd until she was out on the street. She let out a sigh of relief and began the short walk home. The text was itching at her, like a bug crawling up her back. All she wanted to do was shower, go to bed, and forget about it for one night, but she had too much to do.

Lani spent the next five hours finishing a paper for her American history class, studying her statistics notes, and memorizing biology flashcards until she could barely keep her eyes open. She still wasn't confident about one of her two quizzes being held tomorrow, but she didn't feel like she was retaining information anymore. She looked at her phone. 11:43. Maybe she could get some more studying in at work if it wasn't too busy.

As she crawled into bed, Lani's mind went back to the texts from earlier. The familiar urge to throw up and cry at the same time swept over her, and she tried to push the thoughts out of her mind so she could fall asleep and escape everything for a few hours. The thought that had been hovering in the back of her mind all day crept to the forefront. *$100,000 would fix everything.* That thought was comforting enough to allow her to slowly drift off to sleep.

2

# Cameron

"Cameron, set the table."

Cameron didn't look up from the couch. His eyes were glued to the text message that had just popped up on his phone.

*10:00 behind Barry's. Banjo wants to talk.*

The text was from an unknown number, but Cameron understood. "Banjo" was Frank Cappelli's nickname. Al Capone used to play the banjo in Alcatraz, and Frank wore the nickname to both honor his idol and ridicule him for getting caught. Frank thought he was really clever, but Cameron thought the whole thing was stupid, even though he'd rather eat a dead rat than say that out loud in front of those guys.

Cameron hadn't talked to anyone from the group in weeks and had never met Frank in person. His roommate Joseph had set up the initial meeting with a couple of Frank's associates after Cameron found out about his connections. It took a few weeks of begging, but Cameron was desperate and Joseph finally agreed.

If Frank wanted to meet on a Sunday evening, it could only mean bad news. Sundays were for family, and he always threatened to cut anyone who contacted him on that day unless it was a life-or-death emergency. Cameron would never dream of hitting up any one of his guys today. So Frank wanting to meet him? Cameron felt his chest tighten.

"Cameron," he heard his mom call again. "Now!"

Cameron cussed under his breath, sent a quick affirmative reply, and got to his feet. He tried to push the meeting out of his head until after dinner. Frank's wrath was one thing; his mother's was another.

"Didn't hear you," Cameron said quietly as he entered the kitchen.

His mother gave a small huff without looking at him.

"Set the table so we can eat."

Cameron's mind wandered to his upcoming meeting again as he set plates at four spots around the dinner table. What could Frank want to talk about? He racked his brain for reasons and nearly dropped the last plate he was holding. Did it have something to do with the money? He had until the end of April to pay it back. He had time. But then again, Frank was known to bump deadlines at the last minute.

"Really?" Cameron's mother said as she walked toward the table carrying a hot pan of meatballs. "It looks like a three-year-old did this. Fix them."

"Why does it matter?" Cameron asked.

His mother glared at him and Cameron was taken aback. She didn't make eye contact very often anymore. It was almost enough to make up for the look of disdain she was throwing him, but she quickly moved her gaze over his shoulder.

"I am your mother," she said. "Why do you talk to me like that? Sit down. Paul! Greta! Table, now!"

Cameron gripped the back of his chair tightly. He hated

visiting his parent's house on Sundays. He only came back weekly from his apartment in Queens to check on his younger sister Greta and make sure she was being treated better than he was.

"Looks good," Cameron's father said as he entered the room and sat down. He gave his wife a brief nod and ignored Cameron.

Both of these actions sent a pang through Cameron's chest. Being treated like he was invisible wore on him, but the division between his parents hurt too. Two years ago, they were so affectionate towards each other that it grossed him out. Now, he was pretty sure the only reason they stayed together was because of Greta.

"Where's Greta?" Cameron's mom asked.

"Coming!" Greta squealed as she raced to her seat.

She sat down quickly and took a deep breath.

"Whew!" she exclaimed. "Sorry. Lily and Prince Derrick were having a party, and I barely got out."

Cameron smiled. Greta was only seven years old and had a vivid imagination. His parents had only planned on having two children initially, him and his younger brother Thomas. But Thomas died two years earlier in a hiking accident on a trip they had gone on together. That was when the house became cold and his parents started treating him like an unwanted guest. Last year, they decided they wanted another kid and six months ago, they adopted Greta.

"Thank you for changing your plans to accommodate ours," Cameron's mom said with exaggerated politeness. "Let's eat."

At least she tried to be upbeat around Greta. Cameron's mind wandered to his meeting again and he wished he could be alone. The minutes ticked by slowly, and as his mother was pulling dessert plates from the cabinet, he checked his watch. 8:30. It'd take him 45 minutes to take the train back to his place and then another 20 to meet up with the guys. He couldn't be late.

"I've got to go," Cameron said as he pushed himself away from the table.

"Did you not like the food?" his mother asked.

"It was good," Cameron said. "I have homework."

She sighed, and Cameron glanced at his dad. No eye contact.

"Fine. Are you coming next week?"

They asked him this every Sunday, but in a way that always made him feel like they were hoping he'd say no. Cameron glanced at Greta, who was cutting through the last meatball on her plate with intense concentration, and nodded. He stood up and walked to the couch to grab his wallet and keys. When he turned around, Greta was standing in front of him.

"Why do you have to leave?" she pouted.

Cameron knelt to her height and tucked a piece of hair behind her ear.

"I got a lot to do," he said. "But I'll be back soon, I promise."

"When is soon?"

"Next week. You think I'd ever miss a Sunday dinner?"

Greta threw her arms around Cameron, and he picked her up as she squealed with delight. He placed her gently on the ground, kissed her cheek, and headed out the door.

Cameron checked his phone a dozen times on the train ride back to his apartment, but nothing popped up. When he got back to his place, he found the front door unlocked and swore under his breath. Joseph had a habit of forgetting to lock the door when he was home. Cameron went to Joseph's room, but the bedroom door was wide open and the room was empty. So he had left the door unlocked while he was gone? Cameron huffed and went to his room to drop his things off. There was a small pile of mail sitting on his bed. He quickly shuffled through it.

Bill, bill, event flyer, and a letter from the Estate of Dr. Theodore Arnold Fredricksen. Cameron figured it must hold the results of the essay contest he entered, but he wasn't ready to open it yet. He had too much on his mind.

Cameron quickly changed his shirt, grabbed his things, and ran out the door. He was pushing it on time and couldn't be late. He rode the bus for two stops before getting off and walking another five blocks to Barry's, a small bar in a nice part of town. Cameron went around back to a green door near the dumpsters and knocked two times. A tall man in a black suit opened it and looked Cameron up and down.

"I'm here to see Frank," Cameron said.

His voice cracked a little, and he cleared his throat.

"Uh, I got a text that he wanted to see me."

The man looked over his shoulder and muttered something indiscernible to someone behind him. He stepped aside and gestured past himself.

"He's waiting for you in the back," he said.

Cameron stepped inside and tried to look more confident than he felt. He used to be someone who didn't feel nervous a lot, and he didn't realize how much he missed that feeling until Thomas died and it left him completely. Now he either felt nervous and jumpy or completely numb. He would have preferred the latter right now, but Thomas's death had also taught him how unpredictable his emotions could be.

Cameron walked through a small kitchen to a back room where three men were sitting at a table. Cameron recognized the one standing on the right as the guy who agreed to lend him the money the first time. The guy on the left was unfamiliar, and Cameron assumed the one in the middle was Frank. He was smoking a fat cigar and looked like he was in charge.

"Cameron," the man said. "Welcome. Have a seat."

He pointed to the empty chair at the table and Cameron sat down, hoping his shaking knees wouldn't give way. Dread was creeping up his spine.

"This is George, and you know Nicky," Frank said, gesturing to the men next to him.

Cameron nodded.

"You seem nervous," Frank said. "Something wrong?"

He smiled casually, like they were grabbing coffee together. Cameron shook his head.

"No. I just don't know why I'm here."

"Oh," Frank said, putting his hand on his chest. "Forgive me for the confusion. Kid, you wanna explain?"

The question was directed toward someone behind Cameron. Cameron turned around and froze when he saw Joseph tied to a chair. Blood was crusting over his battered nose and oozing from a cut on his lip. He locked eyes with Cameron, and Cameron's stomach twisted.

"I said, you wanna explain?" Frank called again.

Joseph, who was breathing heavily, shook his head.

"I'm—" he got out weakly. "I'm sorry, Cam. I didn't mean for this to happen. I tried to explain to them."

"You still look confused, so let me fill you in," Frank said to Cameron, who was able to pull his eyes away from his roommate at the comment. "A couple of days ago, my associate George here found some discrepancies in our finances. It wasn't a lot, but *nothing* goes unnoticed around here."

He emphasized the word.

"The signs pointed to one of you two."

He pointed at Cameron and Joseph with his cigar between his fingers.

"So we're here to figure it out, okay?"

Cameron couldn't breathe. He wasn't stealing any money, but that wouldn't matter if they suspected him.

"So I'll ask you," Frank said to Cameron. "Have you been stealing from me?"

Cameron was afraid he wouldn't be able to move, but he managed to shake his head.

"No," he said, wishing he sounded more firm. "No, I swear. I'd never do that."

"So tell me why this boy thinks you did," Frank said, nodding toward Joseph.

"I didn't say that," Joseph said back, his voice cracking. "You asked if I thought Cameron had been stealing, and I said I didn't know. But I didn't say he did it."

"What?" Cameron asked.

Anger bubbled up through some of the fear he was feeling.

"Why would you say that?"

"I'm sorry, man," Joseph said so sincerely that Cameron's anger dissipated. He sounded like he was about to cry. "I'm sorry, I just didn't know. I shouldn't have said it. I didn't mean it like that."

"Such a sweet moment between friends," Frank said. "Tell me why I should believe you."

It was directed toward Cameron.

"I'm not stupid," Cameron stumbled out. "I would never be dumb enough to steal from you guys, I swear. Plus, I wouldn't even know how to do that if I wanted to. Which I don't. Please, I swear I didn't do it."

"I dunno," Frank said. "You're both in college. Smart kids. Technology makes things like this easier and easier."

Before Cameron had a chance to react, the man Frank called George punched him in the stomach. He bent over and gasped for breath as pain seared through his ribs.

"Let me ask you again," Frank said. "Did you steal from me?"

"No," Cameron gasped, clutching his stomach. "No, I swear."

Frank stared at Cameron for a few moments.

"It's your lucky day," he said. "I believe you."

Cameron didn't say anything, but relief swept over him and the pain in his gut seemed to lessen.

"But I got two things to say," Frank added. "One. If I find out that it was you or I ever catch you skimming off my cash, that bastard over there is just a taste of what you'll look like. Two."

He tapped the end of his cigar over the floor.

"I'm moving the deadline up to pay back everything you've borrowed. You have until April 15th. If the money isn't in my hands by the end of the day, well..." he chuckled. "I have quite the imagination. I encourage you to dwell on that."

Cameron couldn't seem to draw his own breath, and it wasn't from his bruised ribs. He gave a small nod.

"Good," Frank said. "Get out."

For a second, Cameron hesitated and looked over at Joseph. He had his head leaned back and was breathing shallowly, but his eyes were closed.

*How can he close his eyes?* Cameron thought.

"You wanna take him?" Frank asked. "Go ahead. He's lucky I don't think he did it either. Get outta my face, both of you."

George walked over to Joseph and roughly untied the ropes pinning him to the chair. He grabbed Joseph's shirt collar and shoved him toward the door. Joseph grunted and fell to his knees. As he scrambled to get back up, Cameron grabbed his arm and hoisted him up, and they both hobbled out of the bar and back into the dark alleyway. They walked in silence, and it wasn't until they were on the deserted bus back to their apartment that Cameron finally spoke.

"What the hell, man," he said hoarsely. "What was that?"

Joseph, who had been clutching his stomach the entire time, shook his head.

"I don't know. I—I was at home, and they just burst inside, grabbed me, and said Frank wanted to talk. When I got there, they tied me up and started hitting me and yelling about how someone was stealing money from them. I said it wasn't me and they asked about you and," he looked sideways at Cameron, "all I said was 'I don't know,' man. That's all I said. Because I didn't know. After a while I guess they believed me, and they just sat around playing cards until you showed up."

"Do you really think I would steal money from those guys?" Cameron asked, furious at Joseph and once again deeply regretting his choices.

"No, but I didn't think you'd borrow money from them either."

Cameron sighed deeply and winced as the pain in his stomach flared up again.

"Yeah, that was the worst mistake of my life."

Joseph chuckled.

"At least you got things taken care of. Are you going to be able to pay them back in time?"

Cameron shook his head.

"I don't know.  I've been working extra shifts but the money's not adding up. And with him pushing up the deadline..."

"Dude, you have to pay them back. On time. Frank wasn't joking. I've seen what they can do."

"I'll figure it out."

"Seriously, tell your parents if you have to. You don't want to mess—"

"I said I'll figure it out."

Joseph took the hint and leaned on the seat's backrest and closed his eyes. Cameron took another look at him. Bruising had started around his eyes and nose, but the bleeding around his mouth had stopped. Cameron pushed the image of himself in that chair out of his mind.

They rode the rest of the way in silence and went to their rooms without speaking again. Cameron racked his brain for ways to make enough money by mid-April to pay Frank back, but no option would even come close. He got more and more angry at himself for being stupid enough to borrow in the first place. What was he going to do?

He began to change his clothes and noticed the pile of mail on his bed from earlier. He shuffled through it again and landed on the essay contest letter.  He quickly opened it, eager for something to take his mind off the previous hour.  He was surprised to find out he had been chosen as a winner, but didn't feel very excited about the retreat. He wasn't even sure if he'd go.  There were more important things to worry about.  As he skimmed the rest of the letter, his eyes froze on a single sentence. *At the end of the event, one attendee will be chosen to receive a $100,000 grant to help them pursue a full-time writing career.*

100 grand.  That would be more than enough to settle his debt to Frank and cover all his living expenses for the next year. He could get out of this.

It might be his only way.

# 3

# Allie

Allie stood over the sink staring at the three pregnancy tests she had taken in the last hour. Each one flashed a double red line. She had bought three tests because she heard that false positives were common, and she, as always, wanted to know the facts as soon as possible. After seeing the results of the first test, she had chugged several glasses of water so she could take tests two and three, and both had confirmed the answer she had been anxiously awaiting for the past week.

Allie took a deep breath and began pacing around the bathroom, setting the tests down next to a letter revealing that she had won a final spot in a prestigious essay contest she had entered a few months earlier. But this was more pressing. She was dreading what her boyfriend, Michael, would think, coming from such a conservative family. She had already decided what she wanted to do but wanted to talk to Michael before she scheduled an appointment at the clinic. Part of her assumed that he would agree with her decision. Michael had aspirations to run for political office one day, and she knew what a pregnancy outside of marriage would look like for him. What his family would think about it. She pictured his mother's ever-present smile turning into tightly pursed lips like it did when she passed two men holding hands along the street or learned of a family skipping church one Sunday to go camping.

Of course, she wasn't planning on telling Michael's parents about this at all, and she assumed Michael would feel the same way. His parents were some of the most old-fashioned people she had ever met, and she couldn't imagine the conversation ending well for either of them.

Michael was slightly less intense than his parents when it came to women's bodies, but he had picketed outside the local health clinic enough times to make his stance on abortion clear. Allie figured he would view this as an exception like all the other exceptions he had made throughout his life, but it still made her nervous. She didn't love Michael's views on abortion, but when she brought it up to him the first time, he told her that they didn't need to talk about political stuff and, well, they just didn't. It was a little ironic, considering his career goals, but it was what made their relationship work. Allie loved everything else about Michael—his intelligence, his charisma, and his kindness—so it seemed worth it to ignore a few of his beliefs, especially when they didn't affect her.

Until now, of course, which sent a heavy wave of guilt through her. She had always felt a little uneasy when her boyfriend talked about many of his political views, but she had also put up with them for years because she didn't want to lose him. All that stuff didn't feel relevant until now.

Maybe it was Michael's influence, but a tiny part of her wanted to let nature take its course. Having a baby fit into the future Allie had pictured with him for the last few years, albeit a little out of order. She and Michael were both going to graduate in a few months with bachelor's degrees, which would give them enough time to get settled into their new apartment in Philadelphia where Michael had been offered a job as a legislative assistant for a senator he had met the previous year. She could stay home and raise the baby while Michael worked. They could even get married, like they always talked about.

The timing was so perfect. Imagining the two of them laughing together on a couch, cuddling with a new baby, filled her with warmth.

Allie pulled out her phone and sent Michael a quick text.

*Do you know when you'll be off?*

Michael and Allie had agreed not to live together before getting married, so between their busy class and work schedules, they often only saw each other in the evenings.

Allie's phone lit up a few seconds later.

*Just clocking out. Meet me at my place in 20?*

*See you there,* Allie replied. *There's something I want to tell you :)*

*I hope you can tell me in bed,* he wrote back with a series of graphic emojis.

Michael was the one who had instigated sex for the first time last year. They had agreed to wait until marriage at his request, which Allie was fine with. Her mother had raised her in a conservative household as well but was fiercely independent—probably due to the fact that Allie's father had left them when she was three—and always encouraged Allie to make her own choices about her body.

When her mother died a few days after her 18th birthday, Allie still hadn't lost her virginity. Sure, she had been more preoccupied with her mom's cancer throughout high school than sleeping with a boy, but she also chalked it up to a lack of attractive guys in her small town. She had met Michael just one week into her first year at NYU while serving coffee to him at a cafe close to where he was attending Columbia. She quickly learned about his upbringing in Atlanta and his strong religious and political views, but he assured her it wouldn't be an issue as long as they were willing to be open-minded about each other.

She could tell at the time that Michael was more religiously toned down than his parents, who had moved to New York the previous year and ran a well-known church in the area. Michael had a firm stance on politics, and she didn't really know enough about any issues to have a strong opinion on anything. He was smart, ambitious, and passionate—all things Allie admired. Most of all, he treated her well. When Michael brought up sex, Allie was a little surprised and even turned him down the first time because she suspected he was drunk. But it happened again, and after a long conversation, they had agreed they were both ready.

Allie grabbed a change of clothes and a few of her things as she pulled up the taxi app on her phone. She didn't mind taking the train, but Michael insisted she take taxis everywhere for her safety. When she told him she couldn't afford it, he immediately created an account for her and loaded it every few weeks. His parents had a lot of money and allowed him to live a comfortable lifestyle, and he passed it on to her. She always felt a little guilty accepting his financial gifts, but he seemed to genuinely enjoy buying things for her. Her stomach lurched again as she thought about what she needed to tell him. She hated the idea of arguing with him, but she had to prepare herself for what might be their worst fight ever, depending on how he took the news.

She was just climbing into the car when Michael texted "*home,*" and she responded with "*on my way.*" A few minutes later, Allie's taxi driver dropped her off in front of Michael's apartment, a towering building lined with large glass windows. The doorman, Robert, held the door open for her as she walked by.

"Evening, Allie," he said cheerily. "How has your day been?"

"Really good, thanks Robert," she replied with a smile. "You?"

"Oh, just about the same as always," he said. "Been enjoying the lovely weather today."

"Well, I hope the sun sticks around," Allie called as the elevator opened. "Say hello to your family for me."

The elevator doors closed off the view of Robert waving to her, and Allie waited patiently until she got to the 7th floor. To her surprise, Michael was waiting right outside when they opened again.

"What are—" she said as he pulled her into a warm hug.

"Hey babe," he said into her hair.

Allie giggled and breathed in his cologne.

"How was the ride over?" he asked, breaking away from the hug but still keeping his arms around her shoulders.

"Great," she said. "Better than the train."

"Good." He kissed her forehead. "C'mon, let's go."

He pulled her bag from her arms with one hand and kept the other arm wrapped around her shoulders as he began walking down the hall.

"You're in a good mood," Allie said.

Michael shrugged.

"Had a good day at school. Dr. Callahan said he saw a great political future for me and said he wants to introduce me to a bunch of people at the convention in DC next week."

He rambled quickly, like he had been dying to get this news out all day.

"Wow!" Allie said. "That's great!"

"Yeah," he replied breathlessly. "It sounds like he has a lot of connections. It'll be a great place to get my name out."

Allie smiled at his face, slightly pink in the cheeks and eyes blazing like they always did when he talked politics.

"That's really awesome, babe," she said, squeezing his hand. "You'll kill it."

"So what did you want to tell me?" he asked as they reached his door.

The nerves came back and Allie hesitated. Was it the right time? Should she wait a while? No, she needed to tell him now. The sooner, the better. Probably.

"Um, let's get inside," she said.

Michael set Allie's things on the couch and pulled her in for a kiss before flopping down on the couch.

"Okay, I'm ready," he said. "What's up? Good news or bad news?"

Allie bit her lip.

"Uh, not necessarily good news," she said.

The smile on Michael's face faded a little.

"You okay?" he asked. "Does it have to do with work? Was that guy messing with you again?"

"No, no, it's not work. Um, I'm..."

She paused and took a deep breath.

"I'm pregnant."

Michael froze for so long that Allie felt like she was staring at a photograph. She was too afraid to say anything, so she stood frozen too. Finally, after what felt like an hour, Michael spoke.

"What?"

Allie nodded, still afraid to speak. Disappointment was rising in her chest.

"This isn't a joke, right?"

Allie shook her head.

"I took three tests this morning to make sure."

She waited for Michael to break into a smile, to hug her and tell her everything was going to be okay, but he was still on the couch, looking dumbfounded. He rubbed his eyes with his hands.

"What....how did..." he muttered. "How did this happen? I thought you were on birth control."

"I am. I was surprised, too. But they do say it's only 99.9% effective."

She let out a weak laugh that Michael didn't return. He took a deep breath and stared at her intently, his jaw slack.

"What are we going to do?" he asked.

Allie had a hard time reading the expression on his face. She sat down next to him and put her hand on his arm.

"Um, I mean, I know your beliefs and your parents' beliefs and everything about this, and I get that. But I think the best decision is to, you know, end it. With your career and everything, I know it would look really bad if people found out. But, um...if you wanted me, I mean us, to keep it, we could talk about that too."

His expression didn't change. She wasn't sure how much he was taking in.

"Allie, uh, what the hell?" he asked slowly.

Allie's heart dropped and she pulled her hand away.  She knew he would be upset, but the look in his eyes was something she had never seen before.  He seemed legitimately angry at her.

"What?"

"I can't, this can't—"

He got up from the couch and began pacing around the room.

"I'm running for office one day. As a Republican. A Christian Republican. You know that. Plus, my parents don't even know we've...I can't..."

He trailed off and gestured in the direction of Allie's stomach.

"I'm really sorry," she said shakily.  "I know this is a big deal. Would it be better to keep it? Maybe if we got married—"

"What? No. You don't get it," Michael cut her off.

His face scared Allie. He kept grabbing at the air like he was grabbing the shirt of an invisible person in front of him. He looked a little manic.

"This won't just impact my political career," he said, hitting the back of his hand into the other palm.  "I won't have one. A Republican preaching Christian values who knocked up his girlfriend in college? If I had some power I could talk my way out of it, but I'm a nobody. This is it for me."

Allie didn't say anything. She felt terrible. She should have been more careful.

"My parents still think I'm a virgin. They're going to hate me. This will ruin their reputation with the church if it gets out. Every time we visit...can you imagine walking into that place pregnant and unmarried? No, it can't, we can't..." he trailed off again and sat back down on the couch, as far away from Allie as possible.

They both sat in silence for several minutes.

"Um…" Allie finally said. "So…do you want me to…"

Allie didn't want to say it out loud. She was disappointed in herself for how she was acting, but she hated seeing Michael like this.

Michael put his hands on his knees for a minute before walking over to Allie's bag that he had left on a chair when they came in. He scooped everything up, moved to the front door, and opened it.

"I think you need to leave," he said, avoiding eye contact with her. "I need to figure out what to do."

The fear and guilt Allie had been feeling since she arrived was suddenly replaced with anger. He needed time to figure out what to do with *their* baby? Without her? They should be working this out together, and instead, he was kicking her out of his apartment. She opened her mouth to tell him this but, after thinking for a second, closed it again. Maybe some time alone would help. In a few hours, the shock would have passed, and he would be ready to move forward with whatever they decided to do together. She walked to the door and took her things.

"Love you," Michael muttered as he closed the door behind her.

"Love you too," she said quietly to the door, holding back tears.

As Allie walked down the hallway, she began to think about the other reason she didn't want to argue with Michael. He and his family had been so generous in accepting her into their family, and provided her with the financial support she now relied on to survive. She would graduate in a few months with a degree, but she hadn't exactly been taking her classes seriously because Michael always told her she'd never have to work once his career took off. He had actually encouraged her to become a stay-at-home girlfriend more than once, but she knew her mom would have wanted her to finish college. She was doing that, but barely.

Allie had no idea how she would be able to support herself without Michael, and for the first time since she met him, she was afraid he was going to leave.

# 4

# Kai

Kai sat in the waiting room and skimmed through his mathematical statistics textbook. He struggled with this topic under normal circumstances and could barely focus under the fluorescent lights and faint rubbery smell, so he wasn't taking anything in. After reading the same paragraph for the third time, he closed the book and slipped it into his backpack.

"You guys can see her now."

Kai looked up. His father was standing over him. There were deep circles under his eyes, and they looked pink and watery. Kai looked over to his two younger sisters quickly putting their phones away and getting up from their chairs.

"Come on," his sister Akiko said, tugging at his arm. "I wanna see mom."

Kai threw on a smile, grabbed his backpack, and followed his family down the hall. He watched his father turn into one of the many beige rooms in the hospital and sighed. He hated the smell here. Antiseptic and bleach and other chemicals, like they were trying to cleanse themselves of the toll this place took on families.

"Hi babies," Kai heard a weak voice say from inside the room.

He ducked inside and saw his mom, for the third time this year, surrounded by pillows and machines in her hospital bed. Akiko and his other sister Mia jumped on the bed and cuddled their mother from either side. Kai stood at the far end of the room and stared at the tubes coming out of his mom. Machines were monitoring her heartbeat, blood pressure, temperature, and a dozen other things Kai didn't understand. And they still couldn't figure out what was wrong with her.

"Kai, sweetheart, are you okay?" his mother asked.

Kai gave her a reassuring smile.

"Yeah. Just thinking. How do you feel?"

His mother sighed.

"Much better now, which is what usually happens."

"Do they know what's wrong?"

She shook her head.

"No. They're running more tests today, but..." She gave Kai's father a glance. "It doesn't look like they've found the cause."

"I'm going to talk to the doctor when he comes back," Kai's father said.

"I want to be there too," Kai said.

"We really need someone to watch the girls."

"They'll be okay for a few minutes in the waiting room. Please," Kai added. "I want to know what's going on."

"He's right," Kai's mother said. "The girls will be fine outside."

Kai's father nodded. He looked like he had aged ten years in the past three months. Kai's mother looked the same, but her change in demeanor had more to do with her body growing weaker without explanation. She had her first episode just after New Year's. On her way to the car, she suddenly passed out, nearly breaking her arm in the process. The doctors couldn't find a cause and said she seemed healthy otherwise, so they chalked it up to low blood sugar. The same thing happened a month later. Now, here they were again, with no explanation about her fainting spells, weight loss, and insomnia. And the hospital still charged them thousands of dollars for what? A "hope you feel better soon" wish?

"Mr. and Mrs. Nelson?"

Kai looked over to see his mother's doctor, a tall woman in a white lab coat, standing in the doorway.

"Yes," Kai's father responded.

"I'd like to discuss Mrs. Nelson's condition whenever you're ready."

"Sure. Girls, go grab some snacks from the vending machine and stay in the waiting room, okay?"

Kai's dad handed his sisters each a five-dollar bill. They hugged their mother and scurried out of the room. The doctor hesitated for a second while looking at Kai.

"What?" he asked.

She probably thought he shouldn't be there because he was one of the kids. The doctor just shook her head and looked down at her clipboard.

"Unfortunately, we're still unable to determine the cause of your symptoms," she said to Kai's mom. "We've ruled out any heart conditions, which is good news, as well as diabetes, Addison's disease, and hyperthyroidism. Like last time, there are still no signs of cancer, which is very good news. We'll run a few more tests today, but because we don't know what we're looking for, I'm doubtful we'll find any new information."

"That's it?" Kai asked.

"Kai," his mom whispered.

"I'm sorry," Kai quickly said. "I'm just..."

He sighed. He hated how angry he was at everyone in the hospitals, even though he knew they were all doing their best to care for his mom.

"It's alright," the doctor said kindly. "I understand how frustrating this is. We want to find out what's wrong as much as you do. I promise we'll let you know the second we find anything abnormal. The problem, Yumi, is that on paper, you seem perfectly healthy. Your cortisol levels are a little high due to the insomnia, but nothing that would concern me otherwise. I'm not saying—" she held up a hand to Kai, who had opened his mouth. "—that everything is fine because you are obviously sick. I'm just explaining why it's so difficult to determine what's wrong."

Kai closed his mouth.

"So, what do we do now?" Kai's dad asked.

"Well, I'd like to prescribe a new medication that may help with the insomnia and weight loss. And we'd like to run a few more tests."

Kai felt a pit in his stomach.

"Can I ask how..." Kai's father began to ask uncomfortably. "Do you have an estimate of what this will cost?"

"I'll have a nurse go over the details with you," the doctor said. "But I strongly recommend you take the medication and let us move forward with the tests."

Kai knew what that meant. *It's going to cripple you financially, but you have to pay for it because there's a tiny chance it might help, even though we aren't sure.*

There was never a hesitation in Kai's mind that they should

try a new treatment—of course anything that might help was worth a shot. He just often felt irked at how the doctors prescribed treatments so casually, unaware of how one scribbly signature could put someone thousands of dollars into debt. He glanced at his dad, who was rubbing his eyes with one hand.

"Okay, thank you," his dad said. "How much longer will she need to be here?"

"We have a few more tests to run and clear before she can go home. That will probably be in a couple of days."

Kai's dad nodded and thanked the doctor as she left.

"I'll get Akiko and Mia," Kai said.

Kai caught up with the doctor in the hallway.

"I'm sorry for being rude," he said.

She looked surprised but then chuckled.

"You weren't, believe me," she said. "I fully expect to be yelled at every time I deliver bad news. I truly am sorry that I can't give you anything else right now, but I promise we're doing everything we can to figure out what's wrong with your mom."

"I know," Kai said sincerely. "We all know that. It wasn't fair for me to be mad. Thank you again for all of your help."

Kai nodded at her and continued down the hallway to find his sisters. When he walked back into the hospital room with Akiko and Mia, he saw his dad sitting on the edge of the bed, whispering with his wife. They both stopped when their children walked in and flashed big smiles. Kai had seen that before.

"Dad," he whispered as his sisters jumped on the bed.

He jerked his head toward the door, and his dad followed him outside. As they stood facing each other, it struck Kai how much taller he was than his father. His dad seemed to have shrunk in the past few months, like the weight of everything that was going on was actually pulling him down.

"How are we going to pay for this?" Kai asked. "New medication and treatments are going to be really expensive."

"You don't need to worry about that," his dad said. "It's not your problem."

"It's our family," Kai said. "It is my problem. How can I help?"

Kai's dad smiled.

"I really appreciate that, but we're getting to a point where I don't think anything you can do will make much of a difference. We'll get the medication and...I don't know, maybe I can get a loan. Or sell the other car. I don't think she's going to be driving for a while."

"Come on, isn't there government assistance or something?" Kai asked.

Kai's dad chucked.

"There's a sweet spot in income levels where you make too little to afford emergencies like this but too much to qualify for very much support. It's the same reason you don't get much financial aid for school. We're right in that sweet spot."

"That's ridiculous."

"We'll figure it out."

"I'll talk to someone."

Kai turned around and wandered the white hallways until he found an administrative office. The person at the front desk there referred him to someone on the first floor, who referred him to someone on the second. He finally found himself in a small cubicle in front of a woman who looked like she wasn't getting paid nearly enough for her job.

"Let me pull up your family's file," she said after Kai

explained he was looking for information on financial aid.

"Thanks."

"Okay," she said. "I see you right here. The hospital does offer a limited amount of grants to help offset costs. You're free to apply, but I'm not sure if you'd qualify."

Kai thought back to his dad's comment.

"Because we make just too much money to be poor?"

The woman gave him a sympathetic smile.

"We treat a lot of patients here, many of whom make much less than your parents do. The grants usually go to those in the most financial need, and we have dozens of people on waiting lists for that money."

"What are we supposed to do?"

"I can give you some information about government financial assistance that may cover some of the costs. Hiring a medical bill advocate may also help, although we usually don't recommend that route until the debt is much bigger."

Kai rubbed his eyes.

"So basically, unless my dad wins the lottery, we're going to be in debt forever?" he said.

The nurse sighed.

"I'm sorry. I really am. I wish there was more we could do to help."

She seemed like she meant it, and Kai didn't want her to feel any worse than she probably already did.

"Thanks for your help," he said. "I know you can't control any of this. It's not you, it's just...everything else."

The woman looked slightly relieved.

"I'll reach out if I come across anything I think can help, okay?" she said.

"I really appreciate that," Kai said.

He shook her hand and navigated his way back to his family.

"Kai, there you are," his dad said as he walked into the room. "I'm going to take the girls home and get them ready for bed."

"Okay," Kai said. "I can stay here for a while."

"Go back to your apartment, sweetheart," Kai's mom said. "You look so tired. Get some rest."

"No, I can stay here with you. It's fine."

"Go home," she said, sounding more like her normal self.

Kai hesitated. He did have a lot of homework to do.

"Are you sure?" he asked. "I can stay. Seriously, it's easy to get stuff done here."

"I'll be fine," Kai's mom replied. "I'm tired anyway. I'd like to go to bed too."

Kai gave her a hug. She felt so much bonier these days.

"Alright," he said. "I'll come visit tomorrow after class."

On the drive to his apartment, Kai thought about getting a second job on campus. He had a few spare hours during the week between classes where he might be able to serve food in the cafeteria or clean classrooms. It wouldn't do much good, though. Even if he saved every penny, it'd take years to make a dent in his mom's bills. Plus, his grades were barely scraping by as it was. He doubted he could keep them up enough to maintain his scholarship if he had another job to worry about.

Kai let himself into his apartment and switched on the light. All three bedroom doors were open, which meant he was the only one home. He liked his roommates but was glad he had a moment to himself, grabbing the stack of mail on the kitchen counter and sinking into the couch. He turned on the TV and flipped through the stack of letters as game highlights blared in the background.

He landed on a fancy-looking envelope addressed to him and

quickly opened it. It was the result of the writing contest he had entered a few months ago. He was a finalist. Kai raised his eyebrows. He wasn't expecting that. He slowly read through the entire letter, and his eyes stopped on a number flashing at him toward the bottom. $100,000. Were they for real? He read the letter three times to make sure.

Kai set the paper down and stared at it. That would cover all of his mom's current hospital bills and leave some savings left over for the future. This was it. This was their way out. Kai wanted to text his dad and tell him the news, but he held himself back. The money was only for one person at the end of the retreat. He had no idea how many people would be there or how they would pick the winner. He knew he shouldn't get his hopes up.

He just had to focus and win.

# 5

## Lani

"Are you going to get that?"

Lani glanced at the phone vibrating on her desk and turned back to her laptop.

"Nope," she said.

Lucy checked the caller ID.

"Haven't your parents called like twenty times this week?"

Lani nodded, still looking at her computer.

"Do you think maybe you should talk to them? It might be important."

"The only reason they'd care this much is if they thought they could get something out of me. They probably heard about the prize money and want to make sure they're getting some if I win."

"Maybe they just want to ask you about it."

Lani sighed.

"I appreciate what you're doing Lucy, but stop. Please. You don't know them."

Lucy stuck out her bottom lip.

"I'm just trying to help."

Lani bit her cheek. She hadn't shared everything about her parents with Lucy, so she couldn't expect her to understand why Lani ignored them like this. Still, she felt like she had shared enough that her roommate should know when to leave it alone.

"I know," Lani said, sensing some real hurt from Lucy's extravagant pout. "I'm sorry. But it's not worth calling them back. They couldn't say or do anything that would change our relationship."

"Haven't they been apologizing a lot lately?"

Lani forced a laugh.

"Yeah, it's been really sincere. My mom obviously just wants to regain her social status with her friends, and my dad wants the prize money so he can bet on another horse or football player or whatever he does."

"People change."

"No, they don't. Sorry, but again, you don't know them. You can't do something like that to your only kid and expect it to be fixed a few years later."

Lucy frowned a little but didn't press the argument further. Lani was glad. Lucy, the 'give everyone a chance' type, never thought Lani's anger with her parents was justified. She was all about forgiveness, which Lani felt was a little unfair, considering Lucy had never been in a situation where she needed to forgive someone for something worse than accidentally bumping into her on the sidewalk. Lani knew she meant well, but that didn't make it less frustrating.

Lani checked her phone.

"I have to get to campus for my study group," she said.

Lucy nodded but didn't look up from her textbook.

"Want to go see a movie or something tomorrow?" Lani

asked. "My treat."

Lucy gave a small smile and rolled her eyes.

"Fine," she said.

"See you later."

Lani made the short walk from the library to the education building. As she waited for the elevator, she felt her phone buzz and pulled it from her pocket. Her heart sank when she saw the text.

*Thinking of you today. Can't keep you off my mind with these pics. Got the money yet?*

Lani suddenly felt like she was about to vomit. He had never talked about her like that. The idea that he was staring at the photos, doing...no. She wasn't going to think about that. She sent a quick text back.

*I'll get it soon.*

Her phone buzzed again a couple of seconds later.

*I'm starting to worry that you won't pay. Are you stalling so you can figure a way out of this?*

Lani fumbled with the touchscreen as she tried to reply quickly.

*No. It's a lot of money. I need time to get it. I'm not going to tell anyone.*

Thirty seconds went by.

*You're damn right you won't. If I hear about this from ANYONE I'll email everything to your school. Mommy and daddy wouldn't be able to keep you there even if they still had money.*

Lani could feel herself sweating. How did he know about her parents? He had never mentioned them before. What else did he know about her? Was it someone she knew? Why her? For the hundredth time since she received the first text threatening to release the photos, Lani's mind screamed at her to go to the police. But what good would it do? The person blackmailing her used a different phone each time, so she had no way to trace him. The police would have no leads, and if they couldn't catch him right away, he'd probably find out and send the pictures to all of her professors. Photos like that would get her kicked out of school immediately. She couldn't afford to transfer anywhere else without her scholarship, so she'd have to move back in with her mom or dad until she got back on her feet, which was not an option. She was over halfway done with her bachelor's degree. Even if she could afford to transfer somewhere else, her credits might not move over, and she could lose a year or more of the progress she had made to separate herself from her childhood.

Lani had weighed her options a dozen times already, and each time she came to the conclusion that paying this creep off and just moving on was the best thing to do. If, of course, she could find the money. She thought of the retreat again, and her heart rate picked up even more. For the first time in weeks, she had some hope. She sent another text.

*I'll get it to you. I just need a few more weeks. I have a plan.*

The elevator door opened to her floor, and Lani stepped off as a final message from her blackmailer came through.

*That's good to hear, baby girl. And so you don't get cold feet, here's a reminder of what I'll be releasing if you mess up:*

Under the text was a photo of herself in lingerie, holding a provocative pose in a lacy bra and panty set that barely covered anything. Lani quickly deleted the text and looked around, terrified that someone had seen it. Feeling nauseous, she looked at the picture again.

Considering their wild antics outside of the home, Lani's parents were incredibly strict when it came to her dating life in high school. These rules meant that she had only gone on a handful of double dates by the time she got to college and suddenly found herself thrown into a world she was wildly unfamiliar with. Her first boyfriend, Barrett, had asked for pictures of her a week after they started dating, assuring her that everyone did it when they really liked each other. Lani believed him, and over the next few months, she sent him a handful of sexy photos of herself, including the one on her screen.

Lani broke up with Barrett about six months later, and while he hadn't seemed happy about it, she hadn't heard from him since. That is, until a month ago, when an unknown number had texted her some of the photos with a threat to send them to her university if she didn't pay him $10,000 by the end of April. Lani had immediately assumed it was Barrett since he was the only person she had sent the pictures to. But after leaving several angry voicemails and finally getting a hold of him, he swore he wasn't behind the texts so fervently that Lani believed he might be telling the truth. At least, enough of the truth to convince her with the lie. Someone had access to pictures that she had sent to Barrett, so either he was her blackmailer, or her ex had shared nude photos of her with at least one other person.

"This is your fault, one way or another," she had practically screamed at him on the phone. "You disgusting pervert. I'm going to the police, and they'll track the photos—"

"I wouldn't do that," Barrett had cut her off.

"What?"

"Look, I don't want to sound like a dick, but my dad's a police captain, remember?"

"So?"

"So, it's probably not in your best interest to try to smear my name to them. I don't think you'll end up looking very good at the end of this."

"What's that supposed to mean?"

"I'm just looking out for you, Lani. Seriously, don't go to the police. The guy's probably bluffing anyway."

Lani had actually laughed.

"You're just looking out for me? What am I supposed to do then, huh?"

"I dunno, leave it alone. Just leave me out of it."

He had sounded a little panicked.

"Whatever, I'm going to the police. You'll have to explain to your dad why his good little church kid has naked pictures of his ex and why he shared them with his friends."

"Lani, seriously. Don't."

The panic was gone and replaced with anger.

"If my dad finds out, which he will," Barrett had gone on. "I guarantee that your name will be dragged through the mud, not mine. My dad isn't going to be embarrassed like that, and neither am I. I'm not going through this bullshit because you decided to be a slut and send me those pictures."

"You asked for them!"

"Actually, I never texted you about them, so there's no proof I asked for them, is there? Leave it alone, Lani. Seriously. Deal with it yourself and move one, but don't drag me into this."

He had hung up before Lani could use her full vocabulary of expletives on him, and instead, she had thrown her phone across the room before screaming into her pillow until she was hoarse. When her tears stopped, she had grabbed her phone again and was about to dial the number of her local police station, but her conversation with Barrett filled her with too much fear to tap the numbers. She knew her ex's dad wasn't a great guy—he had been involved in a number of scandals that had been swept under the rug, according to Barrett himself. Was it true that things would get a hundred times worse if she went to the police?

Lani had decided to hold off to see if Barrett was right about the guy bluffing about the whole thing. But a couple of days later, a text came from a new number warning her not to go to the police. The blackmailer threatened to release the photos as soon as they found out the cops were involved, which added another layer of fear to Lani's situation. After another text a week later, she knew this was serious and resigned to the fact that all she could do was get the money to pay him off so she could move on with her life.

Lani took a deep breath and shook out her hands. She needed to calm down and get ready for her study group. There was nothing she could do right now. She slapped a smile on her face and walked into the classroom to her right.

"Hey guys!" she said cheerfully to the five students sitting in a circle of desks.

They all waved and chanted greetings.

"Sorry I'm late," Lani said as she slipped into an empty chair. "My roommate got mad at me."

A girl named Ashley laughed.

"Again?" she asked. "What did you do this time, not tuck her in at night?"

Lani often vented to her study group about Lucy's tender feelings. She felt a little guilty about it, but figured it was better than taking her frustration out on Lucy herself.

"She wants me to reach out to my deadbeat parents so we can reconnect," Lani said, rolling her eyes. "I don't know how many times I have to tell her how awful they are until she believes me."

"Like, family is important, but toxic relationships are toxic relationships," a guy to Lani's left named Zion said. "You shouldn't feel like you have to forgive them just because they're your parents."

The rest of the group nodded in agreement. Lani vented to her group about her family a lot, too, although she had changed the story a bit. The version she shared with casual acquaintances involved her parents swindling money from her grandmother. Lani didn't like the idea of people knowing intimate details about her life, and this story left her parents in the same light in the end. She also found that telling the story as an outsider didn't hurt as much.

"They've both been texting me like crazy since I told them about this essay contest," Lani said. "They haven't tried to get in touch with me for like a year. The only reason they're doing it now is so they can guilt-trip me into giving them the prize money if I win."

"Oh yeah, that's coming up soon," a curly redhead named Delaney said. "Isn't it like next week?"

Lani nodded.

"I leave on Sunday."

"That's so cool," another guy named Sawyer said. "And isn't the prize like $100,000?"

Lani nodded, and everyone in the circle let out small "wows." Lani laughed.

"I mean, the chance that I win the whole thing is so low," she said modestly. "I don't know how many people I'll be competing with, and I'm sure everyone there is an amazing writer."

"What even is the competition?" Delaney asked. "How is he going to pick someone?"

"I don't know," Lani said. "They didn't give us a schedule or anything. It sounds like Dr. Fredricksen will just be watching people during the lectures and workshops and decide based on those."

"What are you going to do with the money if you win?" Ashley asked.

Everyone looked at her, and she put her hands up defensively.

"We're all wondering," she said. "I'd buy a car or something."

Lani glanced at her phone and shrugged her shoulders.

"I don't know," she said. "Maybe just pay for school. Uh, we should get started."

Lani tried to focus on her notes for the rest of the study group, but her mind kept wandering. What was the retreat going to be like? Was there a way she could get an advantage over the other writers? Maybe she could schmooze Theodore Fredricksen; professors loved to talk about their work and accomplishments. She felt like she was a good writer, but it was such a subjective field. What would he be looking for?

Lani's phone buzzed on her desk and everyone looked over.

"Sorry," she said.

Her mom was calling. Again. Lani declined the call and dismissed the five text messages from her parents she had received in the past hour. She sighed. Maybe she should just call them both and get it over with.

When the study group finished, Lani waved goodbye to her classmates and wandered the building until she found an empty corner to herself. She sat down on one of the unoccupied chairs in the hallway, took a deep breath, and dialed her mom's number.

"Lani," a sweet voice said after two rings.

"Hi, Mom."

"How are you?"

"Fine. So why have you been calling so much?"

Lani's mom huffed and her tone changed.

"We don't talk in ages and that's how you want to start our conversation?"

"Uh, do I need to remind you why we haven't talked in ages?" Lani asked, feeling anger rising in her. "Don't come at me with that."

"I'm not 'coming at you' with anything. I just don't think that's how a daughter should speak to her mother. I did raise you, after all."

Lani took a deep breath. This wasn't worth getting into a fight.

"So, why have you called so much?" Lani asked.

"Oh, no particular reason," her mom said, adopting her sweet tone once again. "I just wanted to see how you're doing."

"Fine."

There was a beat.

"Are you leaving soon for your seminar?"

Here it was.

"It's a writing retreat. And yeah, I leave in a few days."

Silence for a few moments, then—

"I saw something on the news about a financial prize?"

Lani had been right.

"Yeah, they pick one winner at the end of the week and give them some money specifically for their writing career. You're not allowed to use it any other way," Lani said.

She had prepared the lie in advance of this conversation.

"Well, it'd be hard to keep track of that," Lani's mother said with a chuckle. "I'm assuming they'd give you a check with the intention of it going toward your—"

"I don't know, Mom," Lani interrupted.

"Well, that would be more than enough for you to do… whatever it is you want to do with your life."

Lani thought of her blackmailer.

"I mean, it doesn't go very far when you have student loans and other expenses."

"If you know how to manage your money responsibly, a prize like that could go very far."

Was she kidding? Lani opened her mouth but shut it again. This conversation had happened before, and it never ended well. She didn't have to give anything to her parents, so there was no use giving her mom fodder to guilt her with later.

"It's a super competitive retreat, so I seriously doubt I'll win," Lani said.

Her mom laughed with the fake cackle Lani hated.

"Not with that attitude, darling!  I'm sure you're more talented than you think you are."

Lani felt a pang in her chest. That would mean much more coming from someone who meant it.

"I've got to go," Lani said. "Uh, class is starting soon."

"Goodbye, honey. I love you. I hope you know that."

Lani let out a sharp breath. Her mom hadn't said that in over a year.

"Bye," Lani said.

She hung up just before the tears started.  She threw her phone into her bag furiously. How dare her mom say that to her now. Did she even mean it? Lani still loved her parents, as much as she tried not to. Was her mom finally realizing her mistake? Was this her way of apologizing? Lani stopped herself. No. She wasn't going to try to justify their mistakes again.

Lani spent the next two hours doing homework before walking back to her apartment to change. She had a blind date tonight with someone Lucy knew from her job with the college admissions office. Well, "blind" meaning she had never met the guy but had already gone through all his social media accounts in advance. He was cute, sure, but it seemed like he had a lot of friends who were girls, which could be a red or green flag, depending on how you looked at it. Plus, he hadn't reached out to her at all since setting a meeting time yesterday, which made Lani pretty sure this was a pity date.

Lani threw on a pair of black jeans and her favorite leather jacket. She put on more makeup than usual and curled her hair so it bounced around her shoulders. When she stepped out of her room, she heard Lucy whistle.

"Ooh, you are looking *fine*," Lucy said. "Marcus is going to be all over you."

Lani rolled her eyes and smiled.

"Whatever. I'm probably his third date this week."

Lucy laughed.

"Considering how hard I had to work to give him the courage to ask you out, I don't think he's running around seducing women all day."

"Or he really didn't want to go out with me but finally caved from the pressure."

"Well, whatever, he's cute and you're hot, so have fun!"

Lani smiled reluctantly and was reaching for her purse when she heard a knock on the door. She opened it and was pleasantly surprised. Marcus was even more attractive in person.

"Lani?" he asked.

He seemed nervous. Lani smiled at him.

"Yep," she said as Lucy began to giggle behind them.

"Hi, Lucy," Marcus nodded to her.

"Have fun, you two," Lucy said.

"Okay, let's go," Lani said, quickly stepping outside and leaving Lucy's enthusiasm behind her.

"So you and Lucy work together?" Lani asked as they walked to Marcus' car.

"Yeah," Marcus said. "She's great."

There was a pause.

"Kind of forward sometimes."

Lani laughed.

"You think? She didn't ask me if I wanted to come on this date. She told me I was going whether I liked it or not."

"Is this okay, though?" Marcus asked, holding the door open for her, his cheeks suddenly pink. "I don't want you to feel like you have to be here."

"No, it's fine. I mean, I wanted to come."

"Okay, good," Marcus said. "I, uh...I was pretty nervous, to be honest."

*Nervous about what? If I'd be worth the trouble?*

"Yeah, dating sucks," Lani said.

Marcus drove them a few minutes away to an Italian restaurant Lani had never seen before. He held the door for her to walk through, and she immediately went to the hostess stand.

"Table for two, please," Lani said.

"I think I'm supposed to do that," Marcus said.

*Controlling,* Lani thought.

"And fall prey to traditional gender roles?" Lani said in mock disgust, testing him.

Marcus laughed.

"Alright, you do your thing."

Lani smiled. Those jokes didn't always fall well with guys at this school.

Five minutes later, they were sitting at a table near a window. The sun was just beginning to set and had cast a pink glow on the parking lot outside.

"So tell me about yourself, Marcus," Lani said.

"Well, I'm from Virginia. A little town outside of Richmond. I'm a senior, and I'm studying sociology."

*Probably trying to nab a wife before he graduates,* Lani thought.

"What do you want to do with sociology?" Lani asked.

"Right now, I'm really interested in counseling. Specifically for kids, maybe at a school. But I change my mind a lot. I'll figure it out in grad school."

"That's really cool."

"What about you?"

"I'm from here, actually. Just a few hours away. And I'm a junior, and I'm majoring in English. I want to be a teacher."

"What grade?"

"Something in high school. I like the idea of positively influencing teenagers."

*And helping them not rely so heavily on their parents.*

"That's awesome," Marcus said.

He seemed genuine. Almost too genuine. He didn't know anything about Lani. Why was he so interested in her? Maybe he had heard about the contest and wanted to get with her in case she won. She realized he was speaking and shook away her thoughts.

"—which is why I love the idea of helping kids, you know?" he was saying passionately. "Like, there are so many kids who don't have that parental support they need. It can really affect their lives."

"Yeah," Lani said. "It can ruin their lives."

She must have sounded particularly bitter because Marcus tilted his head and looked at her inquisitively.

"Oh, you just hear stories," Lani said quickly. "It seems like there are so many parents out there who take advantage of their kids and don't really care about them."

"I think most are doing the best they can," Marcus said. "But yeah, there definitely are a lot of kids who could use the support."

"Speaking of support," Lani said.

Time to get to the bottom of why he asked her out.

"I'm assuming Lucy told you I'm a finalist in a big writing contest."

Marcus looked surprised.

"Oh, yeah, she mentioned it. Um...why?"

"You heard about the prize money then?"

"I think I read about it in the news, yeah."

Lani leaned back in her chair, ready for his reaction.

"Well, there's like a 99% chance I'm not going to win. It's extremely competitive and there are like 20 finalists, and I doubt I'll come back with anything."

Marcus stared at her for a few seconds.

"Okay..." he said slowly. "Why are you bringing this up?"

Lani raised her eyebrows.

"That's why you asked me out, right?"

"What?"

"Come on, Marcus. A random blind date less than a week

before I leave and potentially bring home a lot of money? I'm not dumb."

"Are you..." Marcus shook his head slowly. "Are you accusing me of asking you out so I could get some of your prize money?"

"I'm not accusing you," Lani said. "I just want to know what your motive is."

She immediately regretted using that word.

"Motive?" Marcus said, his cheeks getting pink. "What the hell?"

"Okay, motive isn't the right word. But you know what I mean."

"I don't think I do. I asked Lucy to set us up because I thought you were pretty and Lucy always talked so much about how great you are. I wanted to do it months ago, but I was too nervous. Sorry if the timing didn't work for you."

The last line was dripping with bitterness, and something told Lani he was telling the truth. She felt her cheeks flush.

"Okay, well, sorry, but you can understand my point of view, right?" Lani asked. "I'm just being careful."

"Not really, Lani," Marcus said. "I get that we don't know each other, but do you really think so little of people that you would assume they're using you right off the bat?"

"I don't think little of you, I just..." Lani trailed off.

She didn't know how to finish that sentence.

"Let's just finish eating, and then you can go home and not worry about me taking advantage of you," Marcus said.

They sat in silence for the rest of the meal. Lani didn't have an appetite anymore, though. Marcus seemed genuinely upset that she accused him of the prize money thing. Maybe he really did just want to get to know her. By the time he finished his plate of pasta, Lani felt like she might vomit. She quickly pulled out her wallet to pay for her meal.

"No," he said. "I can cover it."

"It's okay," Lani said. "It's not really fair for you at this point."

"I like to pay on dates if that's okay with you. Besides, I wouldn't want you to think I was trying to take your money."

Lani let him pay and they left the restaurant. He opened her car door in the parking lot and again when they arrived at her apartment.

"You don't have to walk me to the door," Lani said.

"It's dark outside."

Lani hovered outside the door when they reached it.

"It was nice to meet you," he said before turning around.

"Marcus, I—" Lani blurted out. "Um, I'm sorry for that. I can't...I don't really know why I act like that."

"Not to go all 'counselor' on you, but it seems like you have some trust issues you need to work through."

Lani took a deep breath.

"I know. Could we maybe...talk about it over coffee some-time?"

Marcus shook his head.

"I'm sorry. I've been involved with people with those problems before, and I can't do it again. Let me know when you've worked through some of this stuff."

He walked around the corner and was gone.

Lani stood in the chilly March air for ten more minutes. What was her problem? Why did she do that? Of course he wasn't going after the imaginary money she probably wasn't going to win.

*I'm such an idiot,* she thought.

Lani figured Lucy was still awake, so she held back her tears until she made it safely to her room. With the lights off and her face pressed into her pillow, Lani cried herself to sleep.

# 6

# Cameron

Sunlight poured through Cameron's window right into his left eye. He blinked a few times to get used to the light and checked his phone. He missed his chemistry lab again. Whatever. He sat up and pulled on a pair of pants before heading into the kitchen. Joseph was sitting on their couch watching TV. Cameron walked past him and grabbed a bowl of cereal.

"Hey," Joseph said.

Cameron grunted.

"Hey man, do you think you'd be able to drive me to urgent care today?" Joseph asked. "My ribs are killing me, and it's kind of far to walk."

Cameron was one of the only people in their complex with a car. He knew this was important, but he didn't want to be near his roommate right now. He was still mad at him for suggesting to Frank that he might have been stealing money, and being around Joseph reminded Cameron of how mad he was at himself for getting tied up in this in the first place.

"Uh, I have a test in an hour," Cameron lied. "Sorry."

"Sometime later today?"

Cameron avoided looking at Joseph's bruised face.

"I'm going to be on campus all day. Sorry, man," Cameron said. "You can take a taxi, right?"

"Yeah, that's fine," Joseph said.

Cameron went back to his room, his appetite gone. He had to get out of his apartment. He put on a clean shirt and pulled together his books, ducking past Joseph and out the door without saying anything. It was a brisk morning, and he pulled his jacket up around his neck as he made the 20-minute walk to the campus cafeteria for a snack. Cameron strolled past the food stalls toward the convenience store in the back corner. He grabbed a bagel and brought it up to the counter. A pretty girl with curly black hair was at the register.

"Just this?" she asked.

Cameron nodded and paid for his breakfast.

"Do you want your receipt?" the girl asked.

"No, thanks," Cameron said before turning to leave.

"Well, I'm going to give it to you anyway," the girl said.

Cameron turned back to the counter and watched her scribble something on the receipt before handing it to him. He looked down at her phone number on the bottom, then back up at her. Her cheeks were bright pink.

"Give me a call if you ever need any more bagels," she said with a smile before quickly looking at the floor.

Cameron tucked the receipt into his pocket.

"Thanks," he said quietly, forcing a small smile before turning to leave.

He had other things on his mind.

Cameron munched on his bagel and slowly made his way to the English building. He had a creative writing class in fifteen minutes and always arrived early to grab a seat in the back.

He didn't really have anything else to do, so he figured he might as well go and get the participation credit. He settled into his seat and watched as the rest of his class started to file in. They were all a bunch of weirdos. Creative writing really brought out a strange crowd, but Cameron secretly kind of liked them, or at least liked being around them. There was something admirable about not being ashamed to be a dork around strangers. The class wasn't required, but Cameron was still figuring out his major and it filled an extracurricular credit.

"Good afternoon, my budding writers," his professor said as she strolled through the door.

Cameron watched as his teacher walked to her desk. She fit every stereotype you could imagine for a creative writing professor. Long flowy dresses, glasses on a beaded chain, and a voice that sounded like she was always about to burst into song.

"Good afternoon, professor!" a girl in the front row chirped.

Cameron couldn't remember her name, but this girl also fit every stereotype of the quintessential teacher's pet. Well, mostly that she was annoying, and Cameron could tell she couldn't stand him.

"Now, before we begin, I would like to offer congratulations," Cameron's professor said. "This morning, it was brought to my attention that someone in our very class was selected as a finalist in Dr. Theodore Arnold Fredricksen's highly publicized writing retreat. You should all be well aware of Dr. Fredricksen's work, as we have studied several of his books this semester."

A hush went over the classroom as everyone looked around, not sure who the teacher was talking about. Cameron sunk into his chair. What was she doing?

"Congratulations Cameron Falcone!"

She gave a dramatic gesture to the back of the room. All heads swung back and stared at Cameron. He saw mostly disbelief on everyone's faces, especially the girl who sat in the front. It was a small class, and it was no secret that Cameron didn't participate much. He shrugged his shoulders.

"Yep, it's me," he said.

"Cameron, I think we would all be interested in hearing about your application essay," his professor said. "Everyone here would benefit from hearing what you had to say that caught the attention of such a magnificent writer."

Cameron was pretty sure his teacher was in love with Theodore Fredricksen.

"It wasn't that big of a deal," he said.

"Please," she said in a voice that made it clear she wasn't asking.

Cameron cleared his throat.

"Okay, uh, I don't know who else applied here," he said, throwing a glance at the teacher's pet, who pursed her lips. "But there was only one essay question. You were asked to talk about a time that impacted your life. I, uh—I wrote about my brother."

Cameron suddenly felt a small lump in his throat. He didn't want to talk about this. He cleared his throat again.

"We went on a hiking trip a few years ago and we had a great time. It was hard but, you know, worth it. That's all I wrote about, no big deal."

He finished and crossed his arms. The lump in his throat wasn't going away, and he internally begged his professor to move on. Thankfully, she either read his mind or was disappointed in his answer because she changed the subject.

"Well, congratulations," she said. "And I'm sure I speak for everyone here when I say good luck next week."

Teacher's pet sent Cameron a glare that definitely wasn't wishing him good luck. He looked away and prayed that the lump in his throat would disappear. But as class dragged on, he realized this was going to be another one of those days. They happened every few months and made it impossible for Cameron to focus on anything. They were the reason he started gambling in the first place. The riskiness of the illegal activity was the only thing that could distract him from the memory of that day seared into his brain.

Cameron shook his head. No. He couldn't fall back into this. He tried to pay attention to what his professor was saying until class was over. Cameron darted toward the door as soon as they were dismissed but was stopped by a nervous-looking guy.

"Hey man, do you have a second?" the person asked.

"Not really," Cameron said.

"I just wanted to ask you a couple of questions about the contest," the guy said. "Theodore Fredricksen must have seen amazing potential in you. I was wondering if I could pick your brain a little bit."

"I have to go," Cameron said.

The lump was growing worse, and he needed to get out of there. The stranger stepped out of Cameron's way and Cameron rushed out of the room. He circled the building until he found a bathroom in a deserted hallway and ran inside. He went to the bathroom sink and quickly splashed cold water on his face.

*Get it together,* he told himself.

Cameron's phone buzzed and he pulled it out of his pocket.

*Hey man, can you pick up my shift today? I have a test tomorrow I'm definitely going to fail if I don't study.*

It was a coworker from the diner where Cameron worked. He had mentioned to everyone that he'd be glad to pick up extra shifts since he realized he wouldn't be able to pay Frank back with his gambling winnings. He left out the reason, of course, but he was everyone's go-to when they needed work covered.

*Sure. Be there in an hour.*

After a six-hour shift at Dolly's Cafe, Cameron dragged himself to his room. He pulled out a wad of dollar bills from his pocket and counted his tips for the day. $75. Not bad, but that didn't even scratch the surface of what he needed to save his skin. He thought of the essay contest again. He had already arranged his ride for next week, so now he just had to figure out how to win the whole thing. He reread his congratulatory letter three times to see if it gave any hints about what Theodore Fredricksen was looking for in a winner, but nothing jumped out to him. Maybe research was the way to go.

Cameron spent the next three hours reading everything he could find on the author online. He had heard the name before the contest but realized he barely knew anything about the guy. Apparently, he wrote a series of fantasy novels when he was in his 20s, became a millionaire, did a complete turnaround and switched to historical fiction in his 30s, started teaching at prestigious universities, retired as a reclusive billionaire when he was 60, and only recently came back to media attention when he announced he was holding a writing contest open to college students. Impressive, but nothing very helpful.

Cameron was getting ready for bed when he heard his apartment door open. He froze in his room, not wanting Joseph to know he was up and start a conversation.

"Thanks for the ride, man," Cameron heard Joseph say.

"No problem, I hope you're okay," another voice said. "I can't believe you got hurt this bad. I didn't even know you went biking yesterday, I would have come with you."

"Nah, it was a last-minute thing with a buddy of mine."

There was some rustling in the kitchen.

"Will you need another ride to your checkup next week?"

"Yeah, probably."

"Okay, I'll see what I can do, but I'm not sure I'll be able to get work off."

"Don't worry about it," Joseph said. "I can take the bus."

"Can't your roommate drive you?"

"Uh..." Cameron could tell Joseph was hesitating. "He's kind of busy."

"Too busy to drive his roommate with broken ribs to the hospital?"

"Bruised ribs," Joseph said, lowering his voice. "And yeah, I guess."

"Sorry he sucks."

"He's alright. Just has a lot on his plate right now."

Cameron frowned. Joseph was standing up for him. Cameron felt a pang of guilt for not taking him to the doctor.

*But,* he thought, *it was his fault I got beat up yesterday too.*

The voices became muffled and Cameron heard the front door close. He could also hear Joseph's footsteps heading toward the bathroom. Cameron stood still until he heard his roommate get in the shower and then finished getting ready for bed.

*Sorry he sucks.*

Cameron sighed. He had other things to focus on if he was

going to get the $100,000, pay Frank back, and avoid flunking out of school.

And if he won, he was going to buy Joseph a bike.

# 7

# Allie

Allie sat in the passenger seat of Michael's car and tried not to make a sound. They were heading to dinner at his parent's house to talk about…well, she didn't really know. After Michael had sent her home, she didn't hear from him for three days. Each day made her feel worse about the situation. Michael had never acted like this before, so she must have really messed up to make him this angry. By the time he finally called her, she was so desperate to see him again that she agreed to dinner with his family without asking any questions.

After a 45-minute ride in silence, Michael pulled into the driveway of a large Colonial-style home.  He parked just outside the three-car garage and turned off the engine. As Allie unbuckled herself, he walked to her side of the car and opened her door like he always did. It made Allie feel a little better.  But as he helped her out of the car and avoided her gaze, the pit in her stomach writhed again. He hadn't made eye contact with her during the entire ride, and she didn't know what that meant.

Allie and Michael walked to the front door and he rang the

doorbell.

"Michael, hello darling," Michael's mom said when she opened the door.

She was dressed in tan pants and a linen blouse. Her hair, immaculate as always, was in a tight French bun, and her wrists were draped with gold bangles. Allie was always intimidated by how put-together she looked.

"Hello, Nancy," Allie said politely.

"Allie," Nancy said with a smile.

Allie recognized the coldness immediately. Nancy pulled her in for a hug, but it was reserved even more than normal. Allie knew this was not going to be a pleasant visit.

"Come inside," Nancy said, moving to the side. "Dinner is almost ready."

Michael reached for Allie's hand and her heart skipped. But when she grasped it, her hand didn't sink into his like normal. It felt awkward, like it was their first date and they barely knew each other. Michael led Allie to the living room, where they sat down on the large white couch in front of the TV. Michael's father, Dale, was already there reading a newspaper. He set it down when they arrived.

Dale normally made Allie feel more comfortable in Michael's parents' home, but he wore the same cold smile as his wife. Had Michael already told them?

"Evening Allie," he said. "How are you?"

"Fine, thank you," Allie said. "And you? Have you taken the boat out lately?"

"Not yet. It's been a little cold."

Silence. Dale's boat was normally a trigger for an hour-long conversation about sailing. Allie shifted in her seat.

"How's school, Michael?" Dale asked.

"Fine," Michael said, not meeting his father's eyes.

During any other visit, Michael would have immediately brought up his retreat in DC next week and the encouraging words from his professor. His parents were over-the-moon proud of his political aspirations and seemed to genuinely love talking to him about them.

"Well, it might be more than fine if you were spending your free time more wisely," Nancy said, entering the room with a tray of hors d'oeuvres.

Allie felt Michael stiffen and her cheeks burned. So they did know.

"Nancy, they've just arrived," Dale said. "We can discuss this over dinner."

Nancy took a deep breath.

"I don't know why we should wait. What else are we going to talk about, Michael's dress choices? Please."

Allie looked at Michael, feeling wildly uncomfortable. But he continued to avoid her gaze and just stared at his shoes.

"Um, wait to do what?" Allie asked timidly.

Nancy and Dale looked at each other, and Dale gave a small shrug. Nancy must have taken that as a go-ahead because she turned back to the couple.

"Michael told us about your...condition."

Allie hesitated.

"You mean that I'm pregnant?" she asked.

All three family members seemed to stiffen at the word. Nancy closed her eyes.

"Yes, that you are pregnant—" she said it like it was a swear word. "—outside of marriage."

Allie waited for a chastisement about losing her purity, but another silence followed. It surprised her, and she realized

Michael's parents hadn't mentioned God or the Bible since they arrived. This was strange, since, as pastors, they normally didn't go five minutes without quoting scripture.

"I understand this was a huge mistake," Allie began. "I'm so sorry. We...we didn't make the right choices. I know that God is disappointed in us right now."

Allie didn't really believe that last part (she thought God was a cooler person than Michael's parents made him out to be), but she knew it was what Michael's parents were thinking. Again, to her surprise, Nancy and Dale didn't jump on the opportunity to talk about what God expected of her and Michael as a couple. Was it her imagination, or did they seem particularly uncomfortable when she mentioned God?

"Whatever the case," Nancy said stiffly. "A decision must be made."

Allie assumed they were going to request a quick wedding so the baby would be born after they were officially married. The topic of marriage had come up around Michael's parents before, and they always seemed supportive of the idea, even with Nancy occasionally throwing hints that Michael could do better. Still, if it meant they could remain together, Allie was fine having a baby a few years earlier than she had planned.

"Yes," she said quickly. "We could tell everyone we eloped a few months ago and hold the wedding whenever."

Allie felt Michael shift in his seat next to her. She looked at him expectantly, but he didn't say anything. He continued to look at his shoes with a blank look on his face. She frowned at him.

"Actually," Nancy said quietly. "I don't believe a wedding would be the best decision. People will find out what really happened. We can't risk that, for both Michael's and Dale's careers. I'm sure you understand."

Allie didn't.

"What do you mean? What else would we do?" she asked.

The room was silent. No one was looking at her. Nancy had moved her eyes to the ceiling, and Dale was looking out the window. Allie felt nervous and unsettled. They were all thinking about something that she didn't know about. Finally, Nancy cleared her throat.

"The three of us had a discussion, and we decided on what we feel is the best option," she said, looking past Allie's shoulder. "The only solution for all of us is to make this go away."

Allie understood immediately and was stunned.

"I know a place," Nancy said quietly, as if she didn't want the neighbors to hear. "We can take you. The clinic is very... discreet. It is quite a drive, but we can make all the necessary arrangements."

"You...want me to get an abortion?" Allie asked.

Everyone flinched at the word, but no one answered her. Allie's heart was pounding. She never imagined this option would be coming from Michael's family.

"I thought...I thought you didn't believe in that," Allie said. "The church—"

She looked over at Michael, and he finally met her eyes. His looked sad.

"Sometimes we are put in difficult situations," Nancy said. "And we have to make decisions based on the greater good."

"It's for the best, Allie," Michael finally said.

Allie stared at his face. He looked exhausted, like this conversation had taken a toll on him. Heat was rising in Allie's chest.

"Um," she said hesitantly. "What if I don't want to get one?"

Allie didn't realize Nancy's face could get colder until now. Even Dale looked away from the window and stared at her as if her comment caught him by surprise.

"We...we haven't made a decision," she said, glancing briefly at Michael. "I'm not sure what I want to do, but we have a few different options."

This conversation was making Allie want to raise a baby near these people less and less, but she didn't want to give in to their decision about her life this quickly. It felt so wrong for them to be encouraging this, considering their history. She wanted to see what would happen if she pushed back. She had never dared to stand up to Nancy or Dale, or even Michael, before, but the mix of feelings swirling in her stomach was giving her a newfound sense of courage.

Nancy made frantic eye contact with her son, and Allie looked over at Michael. He seemed taken aback and gently took Allie's hand.

"Babe, I know it's hard," he said. "But this is what needs to happen. My future career and my parents' careers will be over if it ever gets out that you and I had a baby together. Won't you do this for me?"

She stared into his eyes, and for a moment, she almost said yes. This man had done so much for her. She loved him. Wasn't he worth this? He didn't deserve to have his career ended because of her, and he had found a solution for both of them.

*No.*

A clear voice resonated through Allie's head. An emotion had been creeping up into her chest since the conversation started, and she was finally able to figure out what it was. Disgust. Michael's parents had protested outside of countless abortion clinics over the years, encouraged their congregations to vote against policies that would allow women to access medical services around the country, and repeatedly told people they would go to hell if they ever got one. Michael had made his fair share of comments about murdering babies himself, and here he was, suddenly okay with it because it finally affected him? For the first time in her life, Allie didn't feel like bowing down to Michael's parent's every wish. As difficult as it was, she tried to keep her cool. She still loved him and figured there had to be another option.

"Michael..." she said. "I don't know."

The sadness in Michael's eyes deepened, and Allie thought she saw a hint of anger, just like she was feeling. He looked over at his parents. Allie followed his gaze and saw Nancy staring furiously at her.

"Allie, I don't know if you understand the severity of the situation," she said. "If you want to be a part of this family, you can not have that child."

There it was.

"I'm sorry if you feel like this will affect your position in the church," Allie said. "But won't I go to hell if I get one? That's what you always say."

Nancy pursed her lips but didn't answer. That made Allie feel better than she had in days.

"I mean, are you really okay with your son being with someone who has murdered a baby?"

"I think you know how I feel about you being with my son," Nancy said quietly.

Allie felt her face get hot and grabbed Michael's hand.

"Michael and I will figure it out, whatever happens."

Allie felt Michael slip his hand out of hers. She whipped her head back and stared at him, but he had dropped his gaze again.

"Allie," he said quietly. "I don't know if we will."

Allie stared at the top of his head.

"What do you mean?" she asked, trying not to let her voice break.

"The way you're acting...I don't know if you and I can have a future."

Allie felt like she had been punched. He was doing this in front of his parents?

"The way I'm acting?" she said, doing her best to keep her voice steady. "You guys are going against everything you believe in. Do you not see how hypocritical that is?"

"Don't do this," Michael said angrily. "Don't make us the villains. You're the one who got pregnant."

Allie gasped.

"Considering you're the one who begged me to have sex in the first place, you know better than anyone that it takes two to tango."

Michael shot a glance at his parents, who were both turning red in the face. It gave Allie more courage.

"Am I supposed to forget everything you've said in church about abortion? Just throw that all away for appearances?"

Michael stood up.

"I've been working my entire life to become a politician," he said, his voice rising. "Years of work. And now there's an easy way to fix this, and I don't understand why you won't agree to it!"

Allie didn't know how to answer. The respect she had for Michael was fading by the second.

"Mom, Dad, can you give us a minute?" Michael asked his parents.

They got up quietly and left. Nancy gave her son's shoulder a squeeze on her way out of the room without looking at Allie.

"My career is extremely important to me," Michael said, staring at Allie intently. "You know that. You know how close I am. I can't throw it away."

"Are you kidding me?" Allie asked. "I've seen your parents tell people they're going to burn in hell for getting an abortion, and now you're all insisting I get one? What about throwing this baby away, huh?"

"What the hell, Allie? Don't talk like that," Michael said in an exasperated voice. "You've never been anti-abortion before. That's why I always change the subject when my parents bring it up. And now you actually need one, and you're refusing? What gives?"

"I've always told you that I believe in women controlling their own bodies," Allie said. "And it's the principle of the thing."

Michael took a deep breath.

"I can't have this in my life right now."

Allie waited for him to say more, but he just sat there and stared at her. His eyes looked a little watery, and it dawned on Allie that he was on the verge of tears. She had only seen him cry one other time, when his grandfather had passed away, and she didn't want to think about why this moment was making him feel just as sad.

"Well, what are we supposed to do?" Allie asked.

Michael shook his head.

"Not 'we.'"

It finally hit her.

"Are you...breaking up with me?" Allie asked slowly.

Michael didn't answer.

"So your career is more important to you than I am?"

Now her eyes were watery too.

"I'm sorry," he said.

He refused to look at her and instead put his face in his hands.

"But I gave you a choice," he said, his voice muffled. "I don't know if I'd ever forgive you if I lost everything."

Allie thought she might throw up. The shock, sadness, hurt, guilt, and anger were swirling in her stomach so fiercely that she felt like someone had grabbed onto her stomach and was shaking it vigorously. Her entire life for the past four years had revolved around Michael. She couldn't picture it, or her future, without him. But he wasn't the man she thought she had known, and she couldn't stomach the idea of being with him either if he was going to act like this. She didn't know if she'd ever forgive herself for that.

"Okay," Allie said, standing up.

She was afraid she was going to have a breakdown if she stayed any longer.

"If this is what you want, I'll go," she said.

A lump in her throat was forming.

"I'm sorry," Michael said.

He locked eyes and tried to pull her in for a hug. Allie let him hold her, but she didn't hug back. His arms didn't feel warm and comforting like they used to. This felt forced and stiff. She pulled away.

"Bye," she said.

She grabbed her purse and threw on her coat.

"Let me drive you home," Michael said.

Allie shook her head. He was letting her go. He wasn't changing his mind.

"I have a friend who lives nearby," she lied. "I can walk

there."

"Allie," Michael started.

"Don't," Allie choked, pointing a finger at him. "Don't say anything. This is your fault, not mine."

She turned her back to Michael and rushed out the front door in a haze as the tears started flowing down her cheeks. She walked through the wealthy neighborhood his parents lived in for 20 minutes until she called a taxi to pick her up. When she reached her apartment, Allie had barely locked the door when her legs gave out and she collapsed to the ground. She sobbed on the floor until her entire body ached and her throat hurt so badly that she forced herself to stand and get a drink of water. The movement gave her enough momentum to get in the shower before eventually falling asleep in bed.

The next morning, Allie called in sick to work and spent all day staring at the wall. As the initial shock of the breakup began to wear off, a new fear started to settle in. How was she supposed to support herself? Michael and his family had always been her fallback when things got tough financially, which happened a lot more than she liked to admit.

Allie's phone vibrated, and for a split second, she imagined it was Michael apologizing, telling her he was wrong to disregard his beliefs like that or that he had been wrong the entire time. She grabbed it but was disappointed to see it was just a calendar notification.

*Reminder: Flight to Connecticut in 5 days.*

She had forgotten the retreat was so close. Her heart rate increased as she remembered there was a $100,000 prize at stake given to one contestant at the end. That would keep her on her feet until she could get her life figured out. It might be the only way she'd get through this.

# 8

# Kai

"Hey, is anyone sitting here?"

Kai looked up from his textbook. A girl was standing in front of him.

"Sorry, I can't find a seat anywhere else."

The girl gestured to the crowded library room.

"Yeah, that's fine," Kai said.

He cleared away a stack of papers from the other side of the table.

"Thanks," the girl said as she sat down.

"No problem," Kai said, smiling at her before looking back at his textbook.

"World religions?" the girl asked.

Kai looked up. She was staring at the front of his textbook.

"Oh, yeah," he said. "Have you taken it?"

The girl shook her head.

"No, but I want to. It sounds really interesting."

Kai nodded. He didn't want to be rude, but he had a lot of reading to get through.

"I'm Amy," the girl said.

Kai held out a hand and she shook it.

"I'm Kai."

"Nice to meet you, Kai," she said with a bright smile.

Kai gave her a polite smile back and started reading again. He could feel the girl's eyes on him.

"Is that an extracurricular class?" Amy asked.

Kai could tell she wanted to talk and closed his textbook.

"Yeah, I've always been really interested in religion," Kai said. "Learning about different ones, I mean."

"That's so cool," Amy gushed.

Kai smiled again politely, then checked his phone.

"I actually have to head to work," he said. "But it was nice to meet you, Amy."

She looked slightly disappointed.

"Oh yeah, sure. Nice to meet you. Hopefully, I'll see you around."

"Yeah," Kai said as he grabbed his backpack and swung it over his shoulder. "Good luck with everything."

He left the library without looking back and decided to head to his apartment. He didn't need to be at work for another hour, but that was his go-to excuse when girls approached him. He didn't know how else to handle it without making them feel uncomfortable. It felt narcissistic to blurt out "I'm gay" any time a girl was nice to him, as if he assumed she was flirting. But it felt wrong to be too friendly just in case she was.

He opened the front door of his apartment 20 minutes later to the sound of excited yelling. Two of his roommates, Mateo and Dakota, were playing a video game on the TV.

"Kai!" Mateo yelled without looking away from the screen. "What's up?"

"Hey," Kai said. "Is this the new Madden?"

"Yeah, Jada got it for me for my birthday," Dakota said.

"Go Jada."

Dakota fist-pumped the air without looking away from the screen.

"She's the best," he said.

Dakota had told the apartment he was planning on proposing to his girlfriend, Jada, over spring break.

"She here?" Kai asked.

Dakota shook his head.

"She's at her parents'. It's her grandma's birthday this weekend. Then it's Cabo on Sunday night."

Dakota and Mateo high-fived, and Kai smiled. He couldn't understand how Dakota was ready to get married so young, but he and Jada had been dating since high school and seemed really happy. He grabbed an energy drink from the refrigerator and took a gulp.

"Well, good luck this week, man," Kai said. "In case I don't see you again before I leave tomorrow."

Mateo swore loudly and dropped his controller on the ground. Dakota whooped.

"And that is how it's done," he said.

He turned to Kai.

"Oh yeah, the writing thing."

"Kai's about to be $100,000 richer," Mateo said.

Kai laughed.

"Yeah, I don't know. It's so publicized. There's no way it's going to be easy to win."

"How's the guy going to pick? Have you each write a poem and he'll decide which is his favorite?" Mateo asked.

"No idea," Kai said. "I don't even know what I'm going to be doing there. All it said in the letter was 'writing workshops' and stuff like that."

"Dude, it's at his mansion, right?" Dakota asked. "It's probably one of those creepy old houses full of empty rooms. A hundred bucks you see a ghost before the end of the week."

Kai laughed again.

"Yeah, there's probably an old wardrobe that leads to a secret world, too. I'll make sure I do some exploring in my free time."

Kai's phone buzzed. It was his dad.

"I've got to take this," Kai said as he ducked into his room. "Hey Dad, what's up?"

"Hi," his dad said on the other line. "I know you like to be involved in mom's care, so I wanted to just give you a heads up on something."

Kai's heart started pounding.

"Is she okay? Is something wrong?"

"She's fine. But I was talking to the doctor today and he told me about this specialist in New York. Apparently, she's dealt with illnesses similar to your mom's and might be able to help."

"That's great," Kai said eagerly.

"It is good news. I'm still getting more information about her. I wanted to see if you'd feel comfortable with that if we could somehow make it work."

Kai immediately knew what his dad's tone at the end of that sentence meant.

"The doctor is a private specialist, isn't she?" Kai asked. "How much does she charge?"

Kai's father sighed.

"They only gave me a range. But even the lower end was—"

He paused.

"I don't know. It sounds promising, but don't get your hopes up just yet."

"Well, if it's that good of an opportunity, wouldn't it be worth more debt?" Kai asked. "I know that sounds really bad, but if it's a life or death matter, right?"

"This doctor only accepts certain financing plans," Kai's dad said.

He sounded like he always did when he was rubbing his temples.

"So like, you have to pay upfront?" Kai asked.

"I think you get a little leeway, but yeah. Not something we'd be able to sign off on right now. If we could cover all of our debt today, maybe, but..."

He trailed off. Kai clenched his fist and took some deep breaths.

"You okay?" his dad asked.

"It's just..." Kai said, trying to keep himself from yelling. "I can't believe we live in a world where mom has a chance and we might not be able to take it."

"I know. It's frustrating."

"It's more than frustrating, Dad," Kai said loudly. "It's ridiculous. Mom might die because we aren't rich. That's not fair."

Kai said the last line through gritted teeth.

"I know," his dad's gentle voice said from the other end. "I know it's not. Look, if it really comes down to...you know, the last resort, we'll find a way to make it work. Okay?"

Kai knew his dad was just trying to comfort him. What else could he do? Kai took a deep breath.

"Yeah, I know," he said. "I know. I'm just...annoyed. Uh, tell Akiko and Mia that I said hi. I'll text Mom."

"Alright. Have fun on your retreat."

"Thanks. Keep me updated on things."

"I will."

"Bye, Dad."

"Love you."

"Love you, too."

Kai hung up and flopped down on his bed. The idea that his mom couldn't get the care she needed because of money was infuriating. He couldn't even fathom the thought of her dying without exhausting every last effort to find out what was wrong. His mind wandered to the retreat prize money again. He had to win. He didn't care what it took.

After changing into khakis and a blue polo, Kai grabbed his keys and headed toward the door for work.

"Hey man, you okay?" Dakota asked from the living room. "We, uh, heard some shouting."

"I'm fine," Kai said.

"Do you want—"

"I'm fine, really," Kai said with a smile. "I have to go though. I'm going to be late for work."

Kai shut the door quickly. His roommates knew his mom was sick, but he didn't share details of the extent of her illness. People always seemed to look at kids of sick parents like they were frail too. He also didn't like talking about it in general. Kai got in his car and arrived at Pawsitively Perfect twenty minutes later. He barely remembered the drive, which was surprising in Seattle traffic.

"Hello, Kai," Jenny, the store owner, said.

"Hi, Jenny."

Kai had gotten the job at the pet store because Jenny was an old friend of his mom's.

"How is Yumi doing?" Jenny asked. "I sent some flowers to the hospital the other day, but I haven't been able to visit yet."

"She's okay," Kai said. "She said to thank you for the flowers."

Jenny waved her hand.

"It's the least I could do, really. That woman is something else. It's such a shame that...well, I just hope they can figure out what's going on."

"Yeah, me too."

"Can you start with the hamster cages? We're expecting some more later today and I want to give them a warm welcome."

Kai smiled. It was hard to find someone who loved rodents and birds more than Jenny.

"Sure thing."

For the next four hours, Kai cleaned pet cages, refilled food bowls, and restocked the shelves. It was a slow day and only a handful of people came into the small store. When his shift was over, he went to the back room to clock out and found Jenny at her desk. She had her face in her hands. Kai hesitated and gently knocked on the door, startling Jenny, who quickly looked up. Her eyes were a little red.

"Oh, Kai, I'm so sorry," she said, sniffing and quickly wiping her eyes. "I didn't see you there. Are you done for the day?"

"Yeah, I was just going to clock out. Sorry, I didn't mean to interrupt you."

Jenny waved her hands and got out of the chair, clearing the way for Kai to finish his shift on the computer. He sat down and couldn't help but notice a stack of bills that had been pushed to the side. Several had the words "OVERDUE" stamped on the envelopes in red. Kai turned away. He didn't want Jenny to think he was prying. When he was done, he waved goodbye and started to back out of the room. Then he stopped and turned around.

"Jenny, is everything okay?" Kai asked.

"Oh, I'm fine," she said. "Really. Just a little tired."

"Okay," Kai said. "Um, let me know if you need anything. I'm leaving for that writing thing tomorrow, so I'll be out all next week. But I'll be back first thing on Monday."

Jenny brightened up.

"Oh, yes, the writing retreat!" She said. "Have a wonderful time. You're such a gifted writer—your mother used to show me the things you wrote in elementary school. Well, you just had such a vivid imagination. Such fun stories, full of wonder and excitement. Anyway, I was so happy to hear you're pursuing that again."

"Yeah, maybe," Kai said. "I don't know if it's the career path I want but I figured I'd enter the contest anyway."

"You deserve it," Jenny said earnestly. "Really. You have a gift of seeing things that other people don't."

Kai felt his cheeks get hot.

"That's nice of you. I have to get going and pack. Good luck next week."

Kai waved goodbye and drove back to his apartment. As he packed his suitcase and got ready for bed, he thought about what Jenny had said. He had a gift of seeing things that other people didn't? He wasn't sure what she was talking about, but hey, maybe that would help him win.

# 9

# Lani

Lani stared out the window and watched dense trees whiz by. A town car had picked her up from the airport and was driving her to Dr. Fredricksen's home. The driver, Alice, was quiet, which Lani would normally find uncomfortable but appreciated today. Between thinking about her terrible date with Marcus and having a conversation with her dad that went about the same as the one with her mom, she didn't get a lot of sleep the previous night. Her dad had followed the same path: asked her how she was doing, tried to flatter her, then made her feel guilty about how hard his life was now. Then—oh, the money? He had forgotten about the money. But what was she thinking of doing with it? If she could only spare a few thousand dollars, he could finally get back on his feet and make things right between them. It had taken every ounce of Lani's willpower not to get into a shouting match before she lied about someone being at the door.

The only thing that could have made the night worse was—

Lani's phone buzzed.

*You've got to be kidding me*, she thought.

*Take some sexy pics for me on your trip,* the text on her phone said.

The nausea Lani had felt when she got the notification turned to fear. How did he know she was leaving today? She looked around frantically, for a moment thinking she might see her blackmailer in the car next to her. She shook her head a little and took a deep breath, trying to calm herself down. This contest was all over the news. If this person had photos of her, he could definitely match her name and pictures together based on what he saw on TV. Still, it was creepy.

The car slowed down and Lani looked out the window again. They had pulled up to a large iron fence surrounded by paparazzi.

"They want pictures of the contestants arriving," Alice said. "I can stop if you want or keep going."

"Oh, uh, I can wave," Lani said. "I'll just stay in the car though."

Alice nodded and rolled Lani's window down. She stuck her head out the window and smiled at the crowd of reporters with large television cameras. They all started yelling at her and asking questions she could barely understand. It was a little exhilarating.

"What are you thinking about?" one person asked.

"Have you spoken with Dr. Fredricksen yet?" a woman in a yellow dress called out.

"I'm excited," Lani said, trying to flash a bright smile. "I haven't met him yet, but I'm looking forward to it!"

"What will you do with the $100,000 if you win?" a man holding a microphone yelled.

Lani felt her face get hot. She pretended not to hear and quickly stuck her head back in the car and rolled up her window.

"I'm ready to go now," she said, trying to sound cheerful. "Don't want to get caught here."

Alice raised her eyebrows but didn't say anything. The car pulled through the gates and left the crowd of reporters clamoring for spots to film the car as it rolled down the driveway. Lani barely had time to think about why she wanted the money before she saw the house as they turned on a bend in the road. Her jaw dropped. It was the biggest house she had ever seen in her life. Actually, it wasn't a house—it would definitely be classified as a mansion. The building looked like it was made entirely out of stone, with columns around the front and large spirals on each side. As the car curved around the driveway, Lani caught a glimpse of the back of the house and saw that it stretched back even further. It must have had dozens of rooms.

"Wow," Lani whispered.

"It's beautiful, isn't it?" Alice said.

"Have you been here before?" Lani asked.

"I've brought a few guests to and from the airport. It always amazes me."

The car stopped right in front of the house. Lani got out and waited for Alice to grab her bags before handing her a $20 bill.

"Oh no, you don't need to tip me," Alice said, shaking her head. "This is all complimentary."

"You've been great," Lani said. "Seriously, please."

Alice smiled and shook Lani's hand.

"I appreciate it. Do you want me to help you with your things? I believe they're waiting for you just inside."

"I'll be fine. Thanks again."

"Have fun," Alice said before getting in the car and driving away.

Lani took one last look at the front of the mansion before grabbing her suitcase and pulling it up the steps. When she reached the massive front door, she grabbed one of the lion head door knockers and hit it against the door twice. She waited a few seconds and was reaching for the handle again when the door opened. An older woman wearing a black skirt answered the door.

"Ah, Lani, is it?" the woman asked.

"Yes, ma'am."

The woman smiled. She had a stern-looking face but kind eyes.

"Welcome! Please, come in. Let me take your bag."

"Oh, it's okay," Lani said. "I've got it."

She pulled her suitcase inside and her jaw dropped again. She had just stepped into the largest home entryway she had ever seen. While the outside of the house was made of stone, the interior seemed to be completely made of deep brown mahogany. Hallways led to her right and left, and in front of her was a large spiral staircase that went higher than she could see. Two chandeliers hung from the ceiling and illuminated the room with a soft glow. Although there had been a brisk breeze outside, the house felt warm and cozy. Lani didn't even want to think about how much it cost them to heat it that well.

"You can leave your suitcase at the bottom of the stairs, and we'll have it taken to your room," the woman said.

Lani nodded and rolled her suitcase to the bottom of the staircase. She looked up briefly and saw that it led to two additional stories.

"My name is Barbara," the woman announced. "Please let me know if you need anything during your time here."

"Nice to meet you," Lani said, holding out a hand. "I'm

Lani."

Barbara seemed impressed and returned Lani's handshake with a firm one of her own.

"Please follow me to the living room," Barbara said. "You can meet the guests who have already arrived."

Lani followed Barbara to the left of the entryway and down a long corridor. It was lined with beautiful paintings hanging from the walls. Lani paused at one that caught her eye.

"That looks like..." she said.

"Norman Rockwell," Barbara finished, her voice full of pride. "Yes, Dr. Fredricksen is quite a fan of his. One of Rockwell's lesser-known paintings, of course, but an original nonetheless."

"Wow."

"This way, please."

Barbara seemed like a no-nonsense type of person, Lani thought. Not unkind by any means, at least so far, but probably not to be messed with. When they reached the end of the hallway, Barbara turned to the right and entered through an archway. It put them into another large room, this one full of plush couches and chairs. At the far end was a beautiful stone fireplace with an abstract-looking painting above it. In two of the chairs near the fireplace were two people. One was a beautiful girl with long blonde hair and blue eyes. She seemed uncomfortable, Lani thought. Or maybe she was preoccupied with something else, the way she was chewing on her thumbnail and looking around the room repeatedly. In another chair was a guy with dark curly hair and a splattering of freckles on his face. He was wearing black jeans and a black jacket, looking at his phone with an expression on his face that looked like a scowl. Lani frowned herself. He gave off the vibe that he thought he was better than everyone else.

Barbara led Lani to the guests.

"Lani, this is Allie and Cameron," she said, pointing at each respectively. "We are still waiting on one more student. He had a longer journey to get here, I believe. He should be arriving soon, and then we can get started."

Barbara left the room. Lani raised her eyebrows and turned to Allie and Cameron.

"Only one more person?" she asked. "There are only four contestants?"

Allie and Cameron both looked surprised too. Allie looked down and began fidgeting with her hands while Cameron's scowl softened ever so slightly.

"Nice to meet you two," Lani said brightly. "Where are you going to school?"

Allie glanced at Cameron, and when he didn't say anything, she replied.

"I'm going to NYU," she said. "I'm graduating in June."

She had a soft voice that sounded almost sad.

"Very cool," Lani said enthusiastically. "I've never been to New York, but I'd love to go someday. We'll have to meet up and you can show me around."

Allie gave a small laugh.

"Yeah, sure," she said.

Lani turned to Cameron.

"And you, Cameron?"

He looked over, the expression on his face unchanged. Lani tried not to roll her eyes at him. She couldn't stand people who were full of themselves.

"I'm at Queens College," he said.

"We're not far from each other then," Allie said with the

first real smile Lani had seen on her face so far.

Cameron shrugged.

"Yeah."

"Where are you going to school?" Allie asked Lani.

"Gray College. It's a tiny school in Texas. No one's ever heard of it."

"That's interesting," Allie said. "Why did you choose to go there?"

Lani instantly felt the resentment toward her parents rise in her chest.

"Uh, it just kind of worked out that way," she said. "What about you? Why NYU?"

"I'm from New York," she said. "My mom and I moved there when I was fifteen, and she wanted me to go to school there too, if I could get a scholarship to pay for it. We used to live in a small town in Georgia, and my mom worked really hard so we could move to the city. She always called it the place of limitless opportunity."

She said the last part with a tone that indicated she hadn't quite found the said opportunity.

"Well, I'm sure your mom was proud of you when you got in," Lani said.

"Uh," Allie hesitated, glancing at the floor. "She, um, died a few weeks before I got the acceptance letter. So she never actually knew."

Lani felt her face burn and covered her mouth with her hands.

"Oh my gosh, I'm so sorry," she stammered. "I shouldn't have said anything."

Allie waved a hand politely.

"It's okay, really. How would you have known? And it was a

long time ago."

Lani thought Allie looked sadder than she was letting on, so she moved back to Cameron. He was still slouched in his chair and looking away from them.

"What about you?" she asked. "What made you choose Queens College?"

For a second, Lani thought Cameron was going to ignore her, but then he turned around and faced both of the girls.

"My family lives close by," he said.

Lani was a little surprised. He didn't seem like someone who was super chummy with his parents.

"How many siblings do you have?" Lani asked.

Cameron's hand twitched slightly. He held eye contact with Lani for another second before looking at another part of the room.

"One."

Lani frowned.

"Okay," she said, putting her hands up. "Just trying to break the ice."

She looked over at Allie and gave her a "Can you believe this guy?" look. Allie smiled and shrugged, but Cameron didn't seem to notice. Asking about his family didn't seem like an intruding question, Lani thought. She looked around the room and her eyes fell on the painting above the fireplace she had noticed when she first walked in. She walked closer and studied it. It seemed to be a large cloud full of smaller images and symbols. She recognized an owl, a bird, and a couple of snakes, but there were some other symbols she didn't understand. One looked like an upside-down pyramid made from smaller triangles and another looked like an egg-shaped guitar.

"Hmm," she murmured.

"What is it?" Allie asked, walking over to meet her.

"Do you know what this painting means? It all seems so... random. At least compared to the other art I saw on the way in."

Allie studied the painting for a few minutes.

"I think these are symbols of wisdom," she said finally.

She pointed to the pyramid shape.

"That's one of the symbols of Saraswati," she said. "She's known as the Goddess of Knowledge in Hinduism. And then there's the lotus flower, the serpent, and the owl. They all represent knowledge or wisdom in different cultures."

"Wow," Lani said, turning to Allie. "Look at you."

Allie blushed.

"I don't recognize all of them though," she said, looking back at the painting. "Like this bird...it looks familiar, but I'm not sure what it's referring to."

She turned over her shoulder.

"Do you know what this is, Cameron?"

"It's the ibis bird," Cameron said without looking up from his phone.

Lani stared at him.

"How did you know that?"

Cameron looked up.

"I was looking at it earlier," he said flatly. "It's from Egyptian mythology. The ibis was associated with Toth, the god of wisdom, and other stuff."

"Okay then," Lani said, trying not to be too impressed with Cameron. "A painting of all the symbols of knowledge and wisdom. Interesting."

"It must be important to Dr. Fredricksen," Allie said.

"Well, he is one of the most respected scholars in the

country," Lani said. "It makes sense, I guess."

Lani heard footsteps behind her and turned around. Barbara was walking toward them with someone else.

"Ladies and gentlemen, this is Kai," Barbara said.

Kai gave a quick nod to everyone, and Lani had to catch her breath when he briefly looked at her. He towered over Barbara and had a toned and muscular frame, emphasized by his fitted t-shirt. His jet-black hair fell into his eyes and further defined his razor-sharp jawline. He wasn't exactly smiling, but he wasn't wearing a scowl like Cameron—Lani thought he looked more like he was concentrating hard on a lot of things at once. Her heart started to beat quickly and she prayed no one could tell she was suddenly sweating.

"Kai, this is Cameron, Allie, and Lani," Barbara said.

Lani flashed a smile when Kai looked at her, and he gave her one back. Her heart skipped.

"Kai was the last contestant we were waiting on," Barbara announced. "So this marks the official beginning of your retreat. I will go and alert Dr. Fredricksen, who will greet you in a few minutes. In the meantime, he has asked that no phones be used for the rest of the week. A last-minute decision, which I do apologize for, but he has insisted. We will keep your phones charged and alert you of any important messages or pending voicemails. Before I get back with Dr. Fredricksen, I'd encourage you to let your friends and family know about this rule so they don't panic if they can't get in touch."

Barbara left the room. Lani looked at the other contestants, who seemed just as surprised as her.

"No phones?" Allie said. "What if we're expecting..."

She trailed off and looked a little embarrassed, although Lani didn't understand why. Besides being bored, Lani wasn't worried about leaving her phone for a week. It might actually be nice, she thought. No texts from her parents to worry about. None from him. A thought popped into her head, and she quickly sent a text to the most recent number he had used.

*I'm at a retreat this week and they're taking our phones away. If I don't answer, that's why. Still getting the money.*

She didn't want her blackmailer to think she was trying to run away and leaking the photos anyway. Lani also sent a text to Lucy just in case her roommate tried to get in touch with her. Then she slipped her phone back into her pocket and waited until the rest of the group was done messaging their friends and family. Trying not to seem obvious, she stole glances at the other contestants. Cameron's face was scrunched up in a frown as he typed furiously on his phone. Allie had one hand on her stomach and seemed uncomfortable, but was still typing with her free hand. Kai put his phone down and looked up to meet Lani's eyes just as she glanced over at him. She felt herself blush but tried to recover with a smile.

"I'm Lani," she said, holding out a hand. "I know Barbara said that already, but, um, hi."

Why was she so nervous? Kai returned her shake firmly and smiled at her.

Oh, yeah.

"Nice to meet you," he said.

He had a deep voice.

"So we were all talking earlier about school," Lani said. "Where do you go?"

"The University of Washington. In Seattle."

"Oh, all the way on the west side of the country," Lani said. "Cool."

Cool? Why was she being so awkward?

Kai smiled politely.

"Yeah, it's a great place."

"What are you studying?"

"Business," Kai said. "Probably applying for law school next year. What about you?"

"English," Lani said. "I guess I assumed everyone here would be heading down a writing path of some kind. I mean, I want to be a teacher, not a writer, but still."

Kai shrugged.

"I might switch career directions. My mom really wants me to go into something with security, so she always pushed me to be a doctor or a lawyer. Being a lawyer sounded better. But I don't know."

Lani wanted to continue talking to Kai for the rest of the evening, but she couldn't be that obvious. She turned away from his dark brown eyes and looked at Allie.

"What are you studying, Allie?" Lani asked.

"Music," Allie said. "I think I want to teach too."

"So cool!" Lani said. "We should definitely keep in touch after this and help each other through our student teaching."

Lani held out a hand and Allie gave her a high-five while giggling.

"And you, Cameron?" Lani asked, not wanting to intentionally leave him out.

"Haven't decided," Cameron said.

"So what type of stuff do you guys think—"

Lani was interrupted when Barbara walked into the room, followed by a tall man. He was wearing a dark brown suit and a maroon tie, with silver glasses and several matching silver rings. Just above a long white beard that seemed a little wild, but not completely untamed, was a wide smile.

"Welcome, contest winners," he said. "I am Dr. Fredrick-sen."

# 10

# Cameron

Cameron sat up in his chair. Dr. Fredricksen looked like he'd come straight out of a television show. Everything from his suit to his beard screamed "eccentric billionaire," but, to be fair, that was what he was known for. The retreat, and the $100,000, suddenly felt very real.

"I am so delighted to meet the four of you," Dr. Fredricksen said. "I received thousands of contest entries, but there was something special about each of your essays."

The professor moved toward Kai.

"Kai," he said, shaking Kai's hand.

"Allie. Lani." He did the same to the two girls.

"Cameron."

Cameron returned the handshake of Dr. Fredricksen. He had bright blue eyes that Cameron hadn't noticed right away. They almost looked fake. Did this guy wear colored contacts?

"Now, I know you're all tired and looking forward to dinner and a good night's sleep," Dr. Fredricksen said. "But first, we must attend to some business."

He didn't have a British accent, but he spoke like he did.

Cameron thought it seemed pretentious.

"As mentioned, Barbara will be taking your phones for the week," the professor said.

He gestured at Barbara and she held out a small basket. Cameron stepped forward and placed his phone inside. He had sent his mom a text just in case, but he doubted she'd care. He also told Joseph about the situation so there wasn't a misunderstanding if Frank or one of his guys wanted to talk early.

"Thank you," Dr. Fredricksen said when Barbara was done. "Now, a few housekeeping items. Breakfast is held every morning at 8:00. Schedules will change daily and you will find an updated itinerary in your room every evening. You are free to look around my home in your free time. However—"

His voice became ominous.

"I must warn you not to enter the west wing tower if you wish to survive the week."

Cameron side-eyed the rest of the group. They all looked nervous, especially the black-haired girl, Lani, who Cameron could tell didn't like him. After a few seconds of silence, Dr. Fredricksen broke out laughing.

"I'm only kidding. Bit of humor for you."

Everyone except Cameron laughed nervously. Something about this guy felt weird.

"My home is yours. On a serious note, please do not attempt to break into any locked rooms, as these are likely bedroom quarters of my staff. I doubt that will be a friendly visit for either party. While you're here, I would also like you to spend a generous amount of time thinking about *why* you are here. What are your goals as a writer? Do you aspire to wealth and fame, or do you want to share your talents and knowledge with the world?"

Dr. Fredricksen made eye contact with each of the students and hovered for a few seconds on Cameron. Cameron's neck prickled. He looked away but he could still feel the professor looking at him.

"This will be a topic we cover in our one-on-one sessions later in the week. Now, you must all be very hungry. Barbara will show you to your rooms where you can freshen up, and dinner will be served in the banquet hall just through these doors," he pointed to his left, "in twenty minutes. I won't be attending, but I can promise you will be well taken care of. Good night, and I will see you bright and early tomorrow."

"Goodbye," Lani said. "It was so nice to meet you! We're all looking forward to the week."

She flashed a brilliant smile at the professor. She was pretty, Cameron thought, but a little too...bubbly.

Dr. Fredricksen left the room and Barbara re-entered a moment later.

"Follow me," she said. "I'll show you to your rooms."

They exited the living room and went back to the entryway. Barbara led them up the winding staircase to the third floor.

"The nicest guest rooms are on the top floors," she huffed when they reached the top. "I'm not sure why."

After catching her breath, Barbara led them down a long hallway and turned to a door on the right.

"Lani," she said. "Here is your key."

She held out a small brass key that Lani took. Lani turned and gave the group a small wave before disappearing into her room.

They walked a little further down the hall.

"Allie."

Barbara gave Allie a similar-looking key, and she disappeared just like Lani. Cameron was left walking next to Kai for a longer period of time than elapsed between the girls' rooms. They probably wanted to keep girls and guys separate, as if that would make a difference for any college students who were remotely interested in each other. Cameron gave Kai a quick glance. He was taller than Cameron by quite a bit, and wore a stone-faced expression that made him look tough.

"Kai," Barbara said, stopping in front of a door. "Your room."

Kai took the key from Barbara and didn't look back as he went into his bedroom. A few seconds later, Cameron was standing in front of a tall wooden door that looked like all the others he had passed. Barbara held out the final key.

"Remember, dinner is in fifteen minutes," she said before turning around and walking back in the direction they came from.

"Thanks," Cameron said quietly.

He turned the key in the old lock and opened his door, and his jaw went a little slack. The room was massive. It must have been the size of his entire apartment. A large canopy bed was positioned at the far end next to a massive window. Arranged inside was also a desk, two comfortable-looking chairs by a coffee table, and a long dresser lining the wall. He saw another door on the right side and assumed it led to the bathroom. His suitcase was sitting just inside.

"Wow," Cameron breathed.

He walked over to the window and looked outside. He had a view of a sprawling garden surrounded by a tall stone wall. There was a large fountain in the middle and stone walkways in various patterns around the garden. He could see what looked like a gazebo all the way at the far end. The garden was clearly kept well, but he didn't see anyone outside working on it.

Cameron moved into the bathroom.  Like the rest of the house, it was the largest one he had ever seen. There was both a shower and a white bathtub with gold claw feet holding it up. He checked his reflection in the mirror above the sink and quickly combed his hair back with his fingers before turning away.  He and Thomas were often asked if they were twins because they looked so similar, and he didn't like the reminder.

Cameron checked his watch. Dinner would be starting soon and he needed to give a good impression if he was going to win the prize, even if Dr. Fredricksen wasn't going to be there. They could be watching all of them on hidden cameras for all he knew. Cameron left his jacket on the bed—the house was plenty warm—and headed back to the hallway.

He didn't run into anyone on his way to the dining room and realized why when he got there as the other three contestants looked up at him entering the room. The dining room was smaller than Cameron expected it would be but still bigger than any other one he had ever seen. A large window past the table overlooked the garden he could see from his room. There were only four chairs set up along a long table that could easily fit ten people. Cameron grabbed the last empty seat next to Allie. She smiled at him when he sat down. He gave a small nod back.

"Aren't our rooms beautiful?"  Lani asked as soon as Cameron sat down.

The question seemed to be addressed to him.

"Uh, yeah," he said. "They're pretty nice."

"We were just talking about them. Does yours look over a big garden too?"

"Yep."

"I hope we get some free time to look around," Allie said.

Lani opened her mouth to say something but was cut off by four men dressed in tuxedos strolling into the dining room with silver platters in their hands. They each placed one in front of the contestants and silently left the room. Cameron looked around at the group, waiting for someone to do something. Kai looked at the door where the servers had disappeared.

"I guess we can eat?" Kai said. "That was kind of weird."

Cameron took the lid off his platter and was surprised to see a steaming bowl of minestrone soup. A large chunk of toasted bread sat next to the bowl, slathered with slightly melted butter. His mouth immediately began to water—this had been his favorite dinner as a kid. His mom used to make it for him and Thomas in the winter after a long day at school or playing outside on the weekend. As good as it smelled, Cameron's heart began to pound unpleasantly. He hadn't eaten it in at least two years.

Cameron heard a small gasp and looked up. Lani was staring at her plate with a large smile on her face. She looked up at the rest of the group and, seeing they were all looking at her, blushed.

"Sorry," she said. "It's just, this is Kalua pig. My parents got this for me all the time as a kid because it's Hawaiian. It's my favorite."

She paused for a second, and Cameron thought he saw her frown before she continued speaking with her smile back on her face.

"I was adopted when I was a baby," she explained to the table. "My parents really tried, when I was younger at least, to help me connect to my roots. This was one of the only dishes they could find in our city, so I think I had it like once a week."

She paused and looked a little embarrassed.

"Sorry, I'm just really excited to eat it," she giggled. "I haven't had it in forever."

Lani looked around at everyone's plates.

"We all have something different," she said.

Cameron looked around too and saw that Lani was right. Kai's plate was filled with what looked like a fried piece of meat on a pile of rice covered in a dark sauce. Allie was looking at a large bowl of thick soup.

"What is that, Kai?" Lani asked.

"*Katsukarē*," Kai said. "It's fried pork with rice and curry. My dad makes this all the time."

"And you, Allie?" Lani asked.

"It's clam chowder," Allie said with a smile. "I don't have a great backstory or anything. I just really like it, so my mom used to make it for me a lot when I was younger."

"Interesting," Lani said. "That must have been what the question was for."

Cameron frowned for a second but then remembered what she was talking about. The essay contest they entered had a questionnaire attached with questions about their interests, allergies, and other things. Cameron thought some of them made sense and others didn't, but he had filled his out honestly. One of the questions had been a food they enjoyed when they were young. But...

Cameron stared at his soup. This was too perfect. All he had written down was "minestrone soup." Not his mom's recipe with pancetta, parsnips, and leeks. And he hadn't said anything about topping his bread with so much butter that his mom would take the pat away.

He took a bite. And a mix of pleasure and uneasiness filled his body again. It tasted exactly like his mom's, so much so that he could almost feel his old dining room chair under his legs. He swallowed and stared at the bowl, nervous to take another bite. Did they reach out to his mom for the recipe? Did she care enough to give it to them?

Cameron looked around at the rest of the table. They were eating their food eagerly.

"I can't believe how good it is," Lani said. "This tastes exactly like the stuff at the restaurant near our house."

"Yeah," Allie said. "Me too. It's almost..."

She trailed off, and Cameron could tell she was thinking the same thing.

*It's almost too similar.*

"My mom tweaked the recipe she followed," Allie said. "She added some spices and things. I've never tasted anything quite like it except for this."

She looked down at her bowl with a puzzled expression on her face.

"That's weird," Kai said, putting his chopsticks down. "Now that you mention it. Katsu is pretty standard but this curry is...yeah. Exactly like my dad makes it."

Everyone turned and looked at Cameron.

"It's minestrone," he said. "Tastes like my mom's."

"It's a little strange, isn't it?" Allie asked. "How would they know how to make these recipes?"

"Come on guys," Lani said. "I mean, it's food. Maybe the chef got lucky. Maybe they reached out to our friends or family or something. But..."

Her tone seemed to change at the end of the sentence. She

bit her lip.

"But that would be weird," she muttered, almost to herself. She shook her head and smiled at everyone.

"I think it's fine. Let's not worry about it and just enjoy the food. We're probably all tired."

Maybe she was right, Cameron thought. He was really tired. He found himself actually looking forward to a week without school or the panic attack he had every time a text popped up on his phone.

Cameron finished his soup and waited at the table until everyone was done with their dinner. They all walked upstairs together, and Lani and Allie waved goodbye as they entered their rooms.  Kai paused outside of his door as they were passing it.

"I feel it too," he said.

"What?" Cameron asked.

"That something's off here. Not just with the food, but…"
He sighed.

"I don't know. I can't explain it. Something about this whole place feels a little weird. Dr. Fredricksen seems like an odd guy. I could tell he freaked you out."

Cameron didn't respond.

"But maybe we are just tired," Kai said.

Cameron nodded.

"Yeah."

"See you tomorrow," Kai said before heading into his room.

Cameron quickly walked down the hall and locked his bedroom door. He got ready for bed and collapsed into the soft mattress, trying not to think about Dr.  Fredricksen or the weirdly intimate dinner. He set the alarm clock next to his bed to 7:30 and fell asleep before he could spend time thinking about anything else.

# 11

## Allie

Allie woke to the old-fashioned alarm clock blaring next to her. She rolled over and hit the top button three times before it turned off, then sat up in bed and rubbed her eyes. Sunlight was pouring through the small crack in her curtains and illuminated the room with a soft glow. Allie got out of bed and threw open the curtains, squinting as the full blast of sun hit her. It was a trick her mom had taught her as a teenager, and it always worked. After standing in the light for a few minutes, Allie felt wide awake and went into the bathroom to shower.

Just before stepping into the hot water, she leaned over and wrapped her arms around her stomach as cramps shot through her lower body. She had been experiencing them in waves since her abortion three days ago. Her doctor said it was normal, and because Allie had always been prone to horrible cramps during her period, it seemed like she simply had the unfortunate luck of experiencing a difficult recovery.

The cramps went away in a few minutes, which Allie was thankful for, but it made her nervous. She didn't want to tell anyone here about her abortion, but she was sure people would ask questions if she had another wave of pain in front of them and couldn't hide how uncomfortable they were. This made her think about Michael again, for the hundredth time since she had arrived at the professor's home, and tears filled her eyes. Her respect for him had all but vanished during their last conversation, but her love didn't, no matter how much she wished it had. Allie hopped in the shower and let hot water pour over her face until the stinging in her eyes went away.

When she was done showering, Allie realized she only had 20 minutes before breakfast and quickly got dressed and did her makeup. She was putting on her earrings when she heard a knock on her door. She opened it and saw Lani standing outside, dressed in a cute blue skirt and matching top.

"Hi," Lani said brightly. "I was wondering if you wanted to walk to breakfast together."

"Oh," Allie said. "Yeah, I'm almost ready. Come in."

Allie stepped back and let Lani into the room.

"Oh, yours is a little different than mine," Lani said. "My bed is over there."

She pointed to an empty corner of Allie's room.

"Oh," Allie said, still trying to shake Michael's face out of her mind.

"You okay?" Lani asked.

Allie turned around and saw Lani looking at her genuinely. She seemed to be very observant.

"You just seem more tired than yesterday," Lani said. "Sorry, I don't mean to assume anything."

"No, you're fine," Allie said. "I don't feel great this morning. I, uh, didn't sleep very well."

"Me neither," Lani said, shaking her head. "I had a dream

about winning the money and I woke up really nervous. I can't really remember it though."

Lani rattled off the last sentence quickly, like mentioning her dream made her flustered. Allie also had a dream about winning last night. But in her dream, Michael had called to apologize and tell her he had been wrong and that she should do whatever she wanted, regardless of how it made him look. So they had saved the money and decided together how they should use it. In her dream, she also used some of it to hire someone to help her locate her father, something she had thought about a lot since her mom had died. But...it didn't make sense to even think about it.

"Yeah, it would be great to win," Allie said.

It would be more than great. It might be necessary.

"Yeah," Lani said.

Lani suddenly looked five years older to Allie, like some heavy weight had been etched into her face. Allie's hand twitched as she felt an urge to hug her, but she didn't want to intrude in her space.

"You ready?" Allie asked. "They'll be waiting for us."

Lani seemed to come out of a daze and flashed a bright smile.

"Yeah, let's go!"

Allie followed Lani, who walked quickly, down the long spiral staircase. They reached the dining room and Allie noticed that her prediction was right—Kai and Cameron were both sitting at the table already. They looked bored, like they had been there for a while.

"Sorry," Lani said. "We were talking."

"No worries," Kai said with a smile.

Allie shot a glance at Lani, who, as Allie suspected, was pink in the cheeks. She had noticed that Lani couldn't keep her eyes off of Kai last night. And she didn't blame her—he was very attractive. This immediately made Allie think of Michael, so she looked away from Lani and Kai and looked over at Cameron. Not to her surprise either, he seemed to keep shooting glances at Lani while looking annoyed. They didn't hit it off well last night, but she didn't blame Lani for that one either—Cameron seemed to be grumpy all the time.

The girls sat down, and almost immediately, the same people who had served them dinner the previous night came forward carrying more silver platters. Or were they the same people? At second glance, Allie thought, these servers looked completely different. Did Dr. Fredricksen hire new servers for every meal?

"Thank you," Allie said when her tray was placed in front of her.

"I'm so sorry," a waiter was saying to Cameron. "The tray slipped and I must have bumped you when I reached to catch it. It won't happen again."

"It's fine," Cameron said, not making eye contact with the waiter. "Don't worry about it."

Interesting, Allie thought. She would have pegged him as someone who'd get upset when they were bumped into. But he didn't really have any kind of expression on his face or in his eyes, which struck Allie as quite odd. Just then, Cameron looked up and made eye contact with her. She blushed and quickly looked down at her plate. She half expected to see a Greek yogurt parfait, one of her favorite morning meals, but found an American breakfast instead. Bacon, eggs, toast, and some fruit. Looking around the table, she realized everyone was being served the same thing as her. The special dinner must have been a one-time thing.

The four students ate in silence for most of the meal, including Lani. Were they all as nervous as Allie was about their first lecture? Did they all feel the same pressure to win the money but didn't know how to do it?

When they had finished breakfast, the group was led to the other side of the house into a large, open room. A long table was facing a wall that was covered with a projection screen. Allie sat down in the chair on the far end. Lani sat next to her.

"Here we go," she said with a nervous smile.

They waited in silence for a few minutes until—

"Welcome, my students."

Allie turned and looked at the door they had just entered. Dr. Fredricksen was standing in the door frame with one hand on the wall. It seemed a little over dramatic, but she didn't dare laugh. He was borderline creepy and she didn't want to create any bad feelings between them, especially since it would be up to him to pick the winner in the end.

"You are here because you want to be writers," Dr. Fredricksen said.

He strolled across the room and stopped in front of the projection screen.

"What does that mean?" he asked.

Lani raised her hand and he nodded at her.

"Well, I want to be a writer to help people," she said. "Like, help them learn to share their stories."

The professor nodded.

"Good. What else? You."

He pointed at Kai.

"In your application essay, you wrote a deeply moving anecdote about your mother."

Kai looked slightly uncomfortable but nodded.

"Why did you write that?"

"Um," Kai answered. "I thought it would resonate with you. Or anyone who read it, I guess."

"Resonate," Dr. Fredricksen said. "Yes, excellent choice of words. And you?"

He pointed to Cameron.

"Another story about a family member."

Cameron looked even more uncomfortable than Kai, so much so that Allie felt sorry for him.

"Why that story?" the professor asked.

Cameron cleared his throat before speaking.

"Same reason," he said quietly.

Was Allie imagining things, or was Cameron's voice breaking? He seemed to be having a hard time getting his words out. She wondered who he had written about.

"And you," Dr. Fredricksen said. "Allie."

Allie jumped slightly, pulling her attention away from Cameron.

"You wrote about your mother, like Kai. Why?"

"Oh," Allie said. "I wanted to share her experience. Like how hard it was for her and us, I guess, to go through that. I think a lot of people don't understand what it's like. Cancer," she said briefly to the rest of the room.

Allie felt pinpricks in the corners of her eyes and was annoyed at herself. How long was it going to be until she could mention her mother without crying? She felt a gentle hand on her arm. It was Lani.

"Yes!" Dr. Fredricksen cried out.

Allie jumped again and Lani pulled her hand away.

"So, what is the connection between all of your stories?" he asked eagerly.

"They're all about family?" Lani guessed.

"True," the professor said. "This is true, and very interesting. But that is not what I'm looking for."

The room was silent for a few minutes.

"Knowledge!" he finally said. "Each of you was inspired to write about a personal experience, yes, but one that brought knowledge to the reader. From Lani, I learned about the true meaning of service, from Kai, I learned how illness and sorrow force you to grow up, from Cameron, I learned about a brother's love, and from Allie, I learned about end-of-life wisdom and grief. I picked your essays because they taught me something I didn't know. Which, I have to say, is a rare feat."

He stared at the students for a few moments. Allie wasn't sure what his point was. Suddenly, he turned around and pointed at the screen behind him, and a painting of what looked like ancient Greece flashed onto the screen.

"Knowledge," he said. "The most desirable thing that ever has and ever will exist. The ancient Greeks were some of the first to realize the potential that extensive wisdom had, personifying it with the goddesses Metis and Athena. Every luxury we have ever been afforded, from fire to the modern-day vaccine, has been created because someone sought for knowledge."

He turned back to the group, and Allie was surprised to see that his expression had changed. Where before his face had been full of excitement and passion, it now looked dark and a little morbid. Allie glanced at Cameron, whose brow was furrowed more than ever. He must have noticed it too. The professor was still talking but it didn't seem like he was speaking to them anymore.

"Knowledge is too great a power to entrust to anyone," he said quietly. "It is only safe in certain hands. It cannot be kept in those hands forever, of course, but to a select few…"

He trailed off and looked up, making eye contact with Allie. She took in a sharp breath. Was she imagining things, or did his eyes have a slightly manic look to them? But as quickly as the expression registered in Allie's brain, it was gone. The professor turned away from Allie and smiled at the rest of the group, back to his cheery and slightly odd self.

"Anyway," he said, as if nothing strange had happened. "A writer's ultimate goal is to bring knowledge to the world. This may be through true stories or fictional ones, but your desire is to add something new to what we already have. Our first lesson today is to help you explore the knowledge you possess and how you can share it."

He stared at them in silence for an uncomfortably long period of time.

"What do you want us to do?" Lani finally asked.

"I want you all to write me a story," Dr. Fredricksen said. "A fictional one. It can be short, but detailed. Your prompt is this: a young boy has just been told a secret by someone close to him. Something that he promised not to share with anyone else. How does he cope? Does he choose to share the secret preemptively? How does this task affect him? Any questions?"

Allie raised her hand timidly.

"My dear, the quiet one," Dr. Fredricksen said. "What is it?"

"What is the secret?" Allie asked. "I'm a little confused. Is it a good thing or a bad thing that he learned?"

Dr. Fredricksen smiled.

"That is the question, isn't it?" he asked, raising his eyebrows.

Allie looked over at Lani, who was staring at Dr. Fredricksen with her mouth half-open. That made Allie slightly more optimistic about how she was feeling.

"Now," Dr. Fredricksen said. "I have business to attend to. You are free to use this room to write or find somewhere in my home. You will be sharing your stories with me and the rest of the group tomorrow morning after breakfast. There will be no more lectures today. Please, enjoy yourselves. I also encourage you to visit my library and lose yourselves in the many stories there. The best way to become a better writer is to read, after all."

He darted out of the room and everyone sat in silence for a few minutes.

"That was...weird," Lani said. "And short."

"Maybe he's just easing us into things," Kai said.

"We're not here for very long," Lani said. "Shouldn't we—I mean, I'd like to talk to him more."

Lani looked a little flustered, and Allie could tell she was thinking about the prize. They probably all were. She needed the money too, and she was also disappointed that she had barely spoken on the first day. There was no way Dr. Fredricksen would pick her as a winner if she never talked to him and only asked stupid questions.

"Well, do you guys want to go to the library together?" Lani asked. "We could work on our stories there. Cameron?"

Allie turned to Cameron, who was back to looking bored. He stood up and shook his head.

"I'm good."

He left the room and Kai stood up. His gaze lingered for a few moments on Cameron, who was slowly making his way out of the room.

"I'm going to chill for a minute," he said. "I didn't sleep

great last night and could use a nap. But we can get together later to work on some stuff if you want."

He left too. Allie looked at Lani, who was staring at Kai with a disappointed look on her face.

"You okay?" she asked.

Lani quickly looked away from Kai.

"Oh yeah," she said, her cheeks getting pink.

Allie waited until Kai was well out of earshot.

"He is really cute."

Lani laughed and covered her face with her hands.

"He's so hot," she groaned. "I'm acting so stupid around him, but I can't help it."

Allie laughed too.

"You're not acting stupid. He actually seems like a nice person, so I don't think he'd notice even if you were."

Allie paused.

"Cameron would be too, if he wasn't so moody all the time."

"I know," Lani exclaimed. "What is his problem? I'm trying to include him, but it's like he doesn't even want to be here. It is unfortunate because, yeah, he is kind of hot, but like, not attractive at all when he acts like that, you know?"

For the second time that day, Allie thought of Michael and nodded.

"I wouldn't mind exploring the house a little bit," Lani said. "Wanna come with me?"

Before Allie could nod her head, another wave of cramps hit her and she groaned.

"Are you okay?" Lani asked, her voice sounding panicky. "Do I need to call someone?"

Allie pulled her head up and shook it back and forth.

"No, I'm—"

Her cramps hit again and she grimaced.

"I'm fine," she said. "Sorry."

"Sorry? What are you apologizing for? Seriously, are you okay?"

Allie took a deep breath. She waited for another wave of cramps, but they seemed to have died down to prickly discomfort. She looked up at Lani's concerned face.

"I'm..." she started.

As Allie thought of a way to explain her cramps, she realized she kind of wanted to tell Lani about her abortion. She hadn't told anyone else since it happened, and it would be nice if someone knew besides her and her doctor.

"I had an abortion a few days ago," Allie said, not meeting Lani's gaze. "I've been getting bad cramps ever since. My doctor said it's fine and they should go away soon, but the bad ones are pretty bad."

"Oh," Lani said. "I'm...I mean, do you...is there anything I can do?"

Allie finally looked at Lani, who seemed uncomfortable but not angry or judgmental.

"Thank you, but not really," she said. "I have pain medication that works pretty well; it's just these big cramps that catch me off guard."

They sat in silence for a few minutes, and Allie could feel the tension. She almost regretted telling Lani and opened her mouth to explain why she did it, but Lani beat her.

"I'm sorry," Lani said. "I grew up in a really conservative family and go to a religious school, so I've never really talked about abortions before. Openly, I mean. I think women should have control of their bodies, of course, but I'm just...sorry, I don't mean to be weird about it. I know that was a hard decision, and I totally support you."

"That's okay," Allie said. "At least you're not telling me how evil I am."

Lani grimaced.

"Has someone done that?"

Allie felt her eyes fill with tears immediately. She took a deep breath and told Lani all about Michael and his parents and everything that had happened in the past few weeks.

"Allie," Lani said when she was finished. "I'm so sorry. They sound like the worst people. You didn't deserve that."

Allie bit her cheek.

"Yeah, well, now we're done, so..."

Lani pulled Allie in for a hug and didn't say anything else. Allie hugged her back and felt a little bit of sadness fade away. She liked Lani.

# 12


## Kai


Kai fell onto his bed and closed his eyes. He hadn't slept well the night before and could use a nap. But after lying completely still for 20 minutes, he realized sleep wasn't going to happen. He sighed and rubbed his eyes, unable to shake the unsettling feeling that had been crawling through his body since he first walked through the front door yesterday. Something about this place felt intense. Not wrong, necessarily, but...heavy. The oddly specific dinners last night and Dr. Fredricksen's seminar today made things feel even stranger. Kai wasn't sure if anyone else had noticed, but there had been a moment when the professor was talking that his tone changed from passionate to almost angry.

Kai shook his head. Maybe he was overthinking things. He knew he was tired and stressed, and instinctively reached for his phone to ask his dad how his mom was doing. After a brief moment of panic at the feeling of his empty pocket, he remembered that it had been taken away. Kai hated being cut off from his family like this, even if they did promise to notify anyone of an emergency. It was hard enough coaxing information out of his parents under normal circumstances, as if he wasn't an adult who had a right to be updated on the health of his own mother. He loved his parents, but for as long as he could remember, they had expected him to act like an adult, until his mom got sick and suddenly he was a little kid not mature enough to handle tough conversations.

Kai didn't want to sit and think about his mom if he couldn't do anything, so he got out of bed and stretched to wake himself up. He thought about working on the short story assignment, but knew he wouldn't be able to focus. He wrote best late at night anyway. He decided to explore the house like Cameron had said he was going to do, although he wasn't sure he wanted to run into the dude. Kai could tell something was going on in Cameron's life that was making him so pissed, but he didn't know if he wanted to help him fix it or avoid him completely.

Kai stepped out of his bedroom and decided to head to the right down the hallway. He passed another door and then came to a T, where he took another right. This hallway was narrow and looked like it had no doors at all. It was lined with a red rug that stretched all the way to the far end before it stopped in front of what looked like a table with someone's bust on it. Kai began walking down the hallway and felt the hairs on his neck stand up. He shivered and shook out his arms. When he reached the bust, he stared at it for a few seconds before turning away. It didn't look like it was anyone famous—probably Dr. Fredricksen's great-great-grandfather or something.

He turned left and wandered the maze of creaky hallways for another ten minutes or so. When he reached the third dead end of his journey, he started to turn around and head back to his room when he noticed a door on the left wall. It had looked like it was part of the large mural that stretched along the entire hallway when he first glanced at it, but he now noticed that it was slightly ajar and sticking out a few centimeters from the wall. He paused for a second, immediately getting a feeling that he shouldn't be there. But his curiosity got the better of him, and Kai slowly grabbed the small doorknob and pushed the door open.

After his eyes adjusted to the dark, Kai realized the door opened to a small library. He stepped inside and was filled with a sensation that told him this room was important. He looked around for a light switch and finally found one, flicking it on to ignite a weak bulb on the ceiling that illuminated the room. Every inch of wall space was covered in rows and rows of books except for a small space that held another door at the far end of the room. In the middle of the library stood a round table with several piles of large books scattered across it. Kai stepped closer to the table and realized that one of the open books was a journal. A pen sat on an open page that was half-covered in scribbles. Kai squinted but couldn't make out any of the words. It looked like a foreign language, but he couldn't tell what it was.

Kai looked around the room again, and his eyes landed on the door on the far end. He walked over to it and turned the knob, but felt resistance. He found himself trying again and again, filled with a deep disappointment that he couldn't get to the other side. Suddenly, as he was still trying to turn the doorknob, an image of his mom getting out of her hospital bed and hugging him popped into his head. He saw his entire family walking out of the hospital and his mom striding down the sidewalk to their house without the help of a wheelchair or walker. Kai felt a burst of hope and joy, a sensation he hadn't felt since his mom first collapsed. He could even smell the specific incense she loved to burn at home. Then, as quickly as the sensations came, they left him, like someone had snatched them out of thin air.

Kai stood frozen by the closed door, desperately trying to recreate what had just happened. The familiar ache of disappointment and worry felt so much worse after losing it for a moment. But the vision didn't come back, and Kai eventually gave up grasping at the feeling, sliding down the wall to the floor.

What was that? Sure, he had imagined his mom getting better before, pretty much every day since she got sick, but this had felt so much more tangible than his previous daydreams. As he puzzled, a new thought began to nag at the back of Kai's mind—a feeling that his mom's cure was within reach. He looked around the room, believing for a moment that a book containing some herbal remedy would open up in front of him. He stopped himself. What was he doing? Where were these thoughts coming from? Kai strained at the questions until his head started hurting.

A loud creak broke Kai's focus. He looked up and saw Cameron standing just inside the room. Kai stood back up.

"Oh," Cameron said. "Hey."

"Hey," Kai responded.

"What were you doing on the floor?"

"Uh," Kai said. "Looking through some of these books."

He gestured to the bookshelf closest to him. Cameron looked at him blankly but didn't press it.

"I was just exploring the place," Cameron said.

He looked around.

"Cool room," he said.

"Yeah."

"What's this?"

Cameron had moved over to the journal Kai found earlier.

"I don't know," Kai said. "It looks like a journal, but I don't know what language that is."

"Yeah, me neither," Cameron said. "Do you think it belongs to Dr. Fredricksen? It looks like someone wrote in it recently."

"Maybe."

Cameron suddenly shivered.

"You good?" Kai asked.

"What?" he answered. "Yeah, I'm fine."

Kai wondered if Cameron felt like he shouldn't be there either.

"Where does that lead?" Cameron asked, gesturing to the door behind Kai.

Kai shrugged.

"I don't know, it's locked."

Cameron walked over to the door and Kai stepped aside to let him pass. Cameron wiggled the handle and then shook it forcefully, but it didn't budge. He knelt down and peered through the keyhole.

"We could probably pick this if—"

Cameron suddenly whipped around and stared past Kai. His eyes were bulging and his face had gone completely white. Cameron's eyes darted around the room for a few moments and Kai could hear him breathing heavily. Kai quickly looked around the room too, expecting to see someone else behind them, but they were alone.

"Dude, are you okay?" Kai asked, taking a step toward Cameron.

Cameron blinked a couple of times, glanced around the room again, and looked at Kai. The color was starting to come back to his face.

"Yeah," Cameron muttered. "I just...yeah."

He sounded...well, Kai wasn't sure. Angry? Disappointed? Kai had a feeling that Cameron had some strange thoughts like he had about his mother, but he didn't say anything. That was a step too weird for him to process.

"How did you find this room anyway?" Kai asked, feeling like Cameron could use a change of subject. "I wandered forever and just kind of stumbled on it. Seems weird that we would both find it at about the same time."

Cameron paused, his breathing slowing down, and frowned.

"I don't really know," he said. "I was just walking around too and, like, felt like I should go this way."

"Hm."

"What?"

Kai didn't know how much he wanted to talk to Cameron about this. But Cameron was staring at him curiously, and for a second, Kai felt like maybe he wasn't such a bad guy. Whatever he had just seen seemed to really shake him up and had apparently shed some of his jerk exterior in the process.

"Does this place seem kind of weird to you? You know, like what I said yesterday?" Kai asked. "I don't know, the vibes are weird to me."

To Kai's surprise, Cameron nodded.

"Yeah," he said. "The whole place feels creepy. And Dr. Fredricksen. I don't know if you noticed, but during the lecture, there was a second where he looked really angry, then changed back to normal right away. It was super weird."

Kai nodded.

"Yeah, he really freaked me out. Glad I'm not the only one who saw."

The two stood in silence for a few moments.  Cameron cleared his throat and began walking around the room.

"Man, this guy is really obsessed with learning," Cameron said. "Look at this. *Encyclopedia of Medicinal Plants*, *Essays in Modern Jewish History*, *Pathophysiology Guide*. There's a book here for literally everything. Oh, ancient Egypt."

Cameron pulled a large gold-bound book from the shelf and opened it. As he flipped through the pages, he pulled up his shirt sleeves and Kai noticed he had a large scar on his right forearm. It looked like two uneven white lines that stretched from the side of his hand up about halfway to his elbow.

Cameron glanced up and met eyes with Kai, then followed Kai's gaze to his arm. Cameron quickly shook his shirt sleeves down and closed the book.

"It's probably going to be lunchtime soon," Cameron said, now avoiding Kai's eyes.

"Yeah," Kai said.

Kai exited the room with Cameron beside him.

"This house is insane," Kai said as they zig-zagged through the hallways, trying to find their way back to their rooms.

Cameron nodded.

"It's bigger than my apartment complex," he said. "Must suck to heat though."

Kai laughed.

"Yeah," he said. "You'd think it'd be freezing, but it's—oh, excuse us."

Right as Kai and Cameron had turned a corner, Dr. Fredricksen had appeared, and the three had almost collided.

"Gentlemen," Dr. Fredricksen said. "Excuse me, I was just—

"

The professor looked at both Kai and Cameron, then past their shoulders down the hall they had come from. Kai noticed he was a little out of breath.

"Just on my way to a meeting," Dr. Fredricksen finished. "And you? Working on your stories or exploring my home a bit?"

He stared at them intently.

"We were just looking around," said Kai. "I hope that's okay?"

The professor's expression was making him feel uncomfortable. His eyes kept darting nervously between Kai and Cameron and the hallway behind them. Kai noticed Cameron glance behind them as well.

"Is there a problem?" Cameron asked.

Dr. Fredricksen seemed to snap out of whatever anxious funk he was in.

"Of course not, gentlemen," he said quickly. "I do hope you're being careful, that's all. You can get lost in this house if you aren't."

"Yeah, it's huge," Kai said. "Thanks for the warning."

The professor nodded and moved past them.

"I'll see you two tomorrow morning after breakfast," he said over his shoulder. "I look forward to your stories."

Kai and Cameron watched Dr. Fredricksen walk briskly down the hall until he disappeared around the next corner.

"Dude, that guy is so weird," Cameron said, not trying to be quiet.

"Hey," Kai hushed him. "He might be able to hear you."

"You don't think he's a freak?"

Kai grabbed Cameron's arm and walked him down the hall

until they rounded the next corner.

"Dude, you've got to be more careful about what you say," Kai said. "Do you, like, not care about other people at all?"

Cameron looked angry and opened his mouth, but seemed to hold back whatever he was going to say. Then he took a deep breath and lowered his gaze from Kai's, pulling his arm away.

"Yeah," he muttered. "I know."

Kai raised an eyebrow. He didn't understand this guy.

"You also need to be careful if you want a chance at winning this thing," Kai said, his annoyance at Cameron fading.

It was Cameron's turn to raise an eyebrow.

"Why are you telling me that?" he asked. "Don't you want to win?"

"Yeah, but fairly. Not because some jerk insulted the sponsor."

Cameron looked like he had a retort again, but he kept his mouth closed.

"Whatever," he finally said. "He just gives me the creeps."

"Yeah," Kai agreed. "Same. But...I don't know, just don't say it out loud."

Cameron nodded, the stone-faced expression back.

"It's probably time for lunch."

The two wandered the hallways of the mansion until they reached Kai's room.

"I need to grab something," Kai said. "I'll see you down-stairs."

Cameron nodded and continued down the hall. Kai stepped into his room and closed the door. He didn't really need to get anything, but he wanted a minute to himself to think about what had just happened. He looked down at his hands. They had been shaking since he saw the vision of his mom out of the hospital, and they still felt a little weak. Not only could he see his family when it happened, but he could feel the joy and relief that they all felt at the news of his mom getting better. He could feel what it would be like to know that she was going to be okay. That they were all going to be okay, hospital bills and all. If someone had asked him to explain what he saw and felt, he wouldn't have known how to, only that it was disturbingly and tauntingly real. And now that it was gone, Kai felt like it had been ripped away from him in real life.

Kai shook his arms to try to snap himself out of the feeling. It was probably the stress of the retreat that had him on edge and was making him see things. He had been thinking about his family all day, especially since they couldn't communicate. He needed to focus. Winning the money at the end of this retreat was the only real way that vision could come true. Kai thought back to what he had said to Cameron about winning fairly. He knew that was the situation he would feel best about in the end, but maybe it wouldn't be so bad for some of his competition to be weeded out.

# 13


# Lani


"Do you want to go to lunch?" Lani asked.

Lani was sitting on her bed and Allie was on the windowsill staring outside. Allie stretched her arms over her head and nodded.

"It'd be good to walk around," she said with a yawn. "I think I dozed off for a second."

"Yeah, you said you didn't sleep well, right?"

Allie nodded. Lani hadn't gotten much sleep either. She had dreamed about a shadowy man following her, and no matter where she turned or how fast she ran, the man stayed on her tail. Toward the end of her dream, Lani noticed the man's face getting less blurry. But just before she could make out who he was, she had woken up in a cold sweat.

"I think everyone's a little nervous," Allie said. "There's a lot riding on this retreat."

Lani thought she could hear a change in Allie's tone, and she wondered if Allie needed the money as badly as she did.

"Yeah, well, I'm hungry," Lani said as she threw her notebook to the side. "How far did you get with your story?"

"Not very far," said Allie. "And I don't think it's very good."

"I'm sure it's great," Lani said encouragingly. "We can give each other pointers after lunch."

Lani put on her shoes and walked downstairs with Allie. They were the first two in the dining room and sat down at the large table.

"So," Lani said, wanting to break the silence. "You said you moved to New York when you were fifteen? That wasn't that long ago."

"Yeah," Allie said. "It was a big adjustment."

"Do you like it there, or are there things you miss about Georgia? Probably both, I would guess."

Allie smiled and nodded.

"You're right, a little of both. We lived pretty well in Georgia because money goes further there. That was the only way my mom could afford to move us to New York in the first place. Sorry, I'm not trying to brag about having money or anything, because we really didn't," she said, her cheeks flushing.

"No, you're fine," Lani insisted. "Go on."

"Well," Allie said, tucking her hair behind her ears. "It was hard moving at that age. I had a lot of friends that I didn't know if I'd ever see again. But my mom had been saving forever, and once she decided she wanted to move, that was kind of it."

Allie paused for a long time, and Lani felt like she shouldn't interrupt.

"Anyway," Allie went on. "My mom and I moved to New York and she started working, but the company went under a few months later and she lost her job. She got another job that didn't pay as well, but we were able to make ends meet for a while. Then she..."

Allie paused again and looked like she was about to cry. Lani put her hand on Allie's arm.

"You don't have to talk about it if you don't want to," Lani said.

Allie smiled gratefully.

"It's okay," she said.

Lani could hear her voice crack a little.

"I actually don't talk about it much," Allie said. "So it's okay. It's good."

Allie took a deep breath.

"Um, she was diagnosed with cancer when I was sixteen. Chemo worked for a while and it looked like she was going to be okay, but the cancer came back all of a sudden. She died a few weeks after I turned eighteen. I was halfway through high school."

"I'm so sorry, Allie," Lani said.

"Thank you," Allie said quietly. "It was awful. There was all this legal stuff I had to deal with because I was still in school but technically an adult, and it was just super overwhelming. My mom had saved a little bit of money and I got a job as soon as I could and started college that fall."

Lani stared at Allie, who was playing with a strand of her hair and gazing off in another direction. She seemed so poised and calm all the time. Not only had she gone through all of that as a teenager, but her boyfriend had just pressured her to get an abortion for his political career too?

"How did you move on?" Lani asked slowly.

"I had to," Allie said. "I didn't really have a choice."

"Yeah, I get that," Lani said without thinking.

"Really?" Allie asked.

Lani hesitated. Allie's face was kind and curious. Lani was tempted to share everything—her parent's gambling and alcohol issues, how she had to turn down her dream school and struggle her way through college, and what her blackmailer had been threatening her with. But...she still didn't really know Allie. And, as Lani had just learned, Allie needed to win this competition as much as she did. Oversharing would probably end up hurting her later on.

"Uh, I just had to get a job in high school," Lani quickly lied. "My parents didn't make a lot of money, so I had to help out as much as I could. It sucks to have to deal with that when you're still a teenager."

Allie smiled sympathetically.

"I'm sorry about that. It's really sad that so many kids have to hold the responsibilities of adults. We should be able to enjoy our childhoods."

Lani felt a little sick. Allie really seemed like she cared. Fortunately for Lani, Kai walked into the dining room at that moment and she was able to shift the conversation.

"Hey!" she said brightly.

Kai smiled and gave Lani a slight nod.

"Hey," he said back while checking his watch. "Lunch hasn't started yet?"

"Nope. They must be running a little late."

Kai looked around.

"Is Cameron not here?"

"Am now."

Kai turned around and Lani looked past his shoulder to see Cameron standing in the doorway.

"I thought you would have beat me," Kai said.

"I stopped by my room too."

The two guys shared a look that made Lani suspect something had happened.

"We're you guys working on the assignment together?" she asked.

Kai looked at Cameron, but he was already moving to his seat at the table.

"No, I was exploring the house and ran into Cameron," Kai said.

"Ooh, any cool libraries or secret entrances we should know about?" Lani asked eagerly.

Lani noticed Kai glance at Cameron again, but Cameron was picking at the tablecloth.

"Um..." Kai hesitated. "Yeah, we actually did find an interesting room. That's where we ran into each other."

Lani looked back and forth between the two guys.

"You're acting weird. Did something happen? Did you kiss?" Lani asked jokingly, trying to lighten the mood.

Kai laughed but Cameron frowned.

"No," he said. "It was just a creepy room."

"I was just kidding," Lani said quickly. "What do you mean it was creepy?"

"It's hard to explain," Kai said. "You know how sometimes you feel like someone's watching you when there isn't anyone there? That's what it felt like to be in the room. And I..." he paused. "Uh, I just felt weird being there."

Lani suspected he wasn't sharing everything.

"Oh," she said. "Where was it? I want to check it out."

"Uh," Kai hesitated again.

He paused for a second before apparently deciding to divulge his secret.

"It's on the same floor as our rooms. You have to wind through a lot of hallways to get there though. I'm not even sure I'd find it again."

Lani nodded. The way Kai was talking about this room and avoiding eye contact made her want to find it even more. Before she could get any more information out of Kai, four people walked into the room carrying plates on their shoulders. Silently, they placed the plates in front of each person. Lani smiled and thanked the young woman who placed what looked like a Cobb salad down for her. She waited as Allie and Kai politely thanked their servers and Cameron gave a small nod to his, then watched Cameron as he stared down at his salad, eyebrows furrowed as always. What was up with him? Lani wasn't into the "make the best of every moment" mentality, but they were given the opportunity of a lifetime to be here and Cameron seemed like he'd rather be anywhere else. Or maybe he was just like this all the time, which begged the question of why. But as she thought it, Lani had to stop herself from rolling her eyes. An attractive white guy with a surly attitude toward the world? He was probably realizing for the first time in his life that his looks wouldn't get him everything he wanted and was following the incel pipeline accordingly, angry at everyone who didn't throw themselves at him because of his curly hair and freckles. As if he had read her mind, Cameron looked up and locked eyes with Lani, and she quickly looked away.

Everyone ate quietly. Lani wanted to break the silence, but Allie, Kai, and Cameron all seemed to be focused on something else. She held back and tried to focus on her salad as well. Her mind wandered to her blackmailer. Hopefully, he had gotten her text message and didn't think she was bluffing. Panic suddenly flooded her body. What if he didn't believe her and had already released the photos when she didn't message back? What if there was an email from her school announcing her expulsion sitting in her inbox as she sat here?

Lani was jolted out of her thought spiral by the sound of a chair scraping against the floor. She looked over to see Cameron heading out the door.

"See you later, Cameron," she called.

Cameron gave a one-handed wave without turning around and left the room.

Lani huffed.

"Seriously, what is his problem?" she whispered loudly.

"I think he might be going through something," Kai said.

Lani looked up in surprise.

"What makes you say that?"

Kai was staring thoughtfully at the door.

"I don't think he's a bad guy," he said. "I think he knows when he's being rude, and he feels bad about it."

"And...he does it anyway?" Lani said.

Kai chuckled.

"No, I meant that I think he says and does things that he instantly regrets."

Lani frowned.

"Well, he is an adult. He should know basic manners."

Kai shrugged softly.

"Yeah, that's fair. But sometimes people are dealing with a lot, and I think it's important to give them the benefit of the doubt, at least."

Lani wasn't sure she agreed. Cameron gave her a bad vibe and she had been nothing but friendly to him. On the other hand, Kai seemed to behave the opposite of Cameron in every way, but he didn't mind Cameron's jerk-ish behavior.

"I think that too," Allie said quietly. "About Cameron. We don't need to pry, but it seems like he's working through something."

Kai nodded in agreement.

Lani looked between the two. Did she happen to go on a retreat with two of the most compassionate people on the planet, or was she being unreasonable?

"Okay," she sighed. "I'll try not to be annoyed with him as much."

Kai smiled bashfully.

"I'm not trying to reprimand you or anything," he said quickly. "I just...think he's just as hard on himself. And maybe could use friends right now. But don't tell him I said that because I still wouldn't put it past him to stab me in my sleep."

Lani and Allie giggled. Kai stood up.

"I need to start that essay. I'll see you two later."

After waving to Kai, Lani turned to Allie.

"So, do you want to go try to find that room they were talking about?"

"Actually, I think I'm going to lie down for a little while," Allie said. "I don't feel great."

"Oh, are you okay?" Lani asked. "Do you need me to get someone?"

"I'm fine," Allie said. "I just feel a little nauseous. Regular stuff. I'm going to take a nap. I'll explore with you later, though."

Lani walked with Allie to her room and said goodbye as the bedroom door closed in front of her. She turned and began walking in the direction that the guys had gone when they were first shown their rooms, assuming the mystery room that Kai and Cameron had discovered was this way. Lani began wandering in any direction that felt right. Although she knew her gut instinct wasn't going to be helpful here, she became more confident with where she was going the further she moved down the winding hallways. As the minutes ticked by, she could feel she was close to the room—she was sure of it.

After about ten minutes of walking, Lani came to a T. The hallway extended to the left and a long staircase appeared on the right. Kai hadn't mentioned a staircase, so she knew she had to go left, but she turned in the other direction for a moment to admire the intricately carved banister. It looked like a grapevine that wound down the entire staircase. It was beautiful, she thought, but it probably made it difficult to hold onto when walking down.

Just then, Lani felt something shove her from behind and she felt her stomach drop as she fell headfirst down the stairs. She screamed, but it only lasted a second before the wind was knocked out of her lungs as she hit the first staircase. She continued to fall, hitting every body part on the sharp wooden steps along the way. Pain shot through her and she felt herself panicking more and more, somehow having a clear enough head to pray that she wouldn't crack her skull on the floor below. Somehow, just before she hit the bottom, Lani shot her hand out in desperation and was able to catch a baluster. Her whole body swung to the side and a sharp pain shot through her wrist that made her let go, but the catch had slowed down her momentum enough that she rolled at a much slower speed down the last few steps before landing on her back on the cold stone floor.

Lani lay there trying to catch her breath, tapping her fingers on the floor in an effort to get her lungs working again. Finally, after an agonizing period of time, her breath came back, and she gulped in air so fast that she choked. Once her breathing slowed, the pain started to set in and Lani groaned. Every inch of her body hurt except for her head, which, even then, she recognized as insanely lucky.  She slowly began feeling her arms and ribs.  She'd have bruises later and her wrist might have been sprained, but nothing felt broken. Lani heard what sounded like footsteps running away. She looked toward the top of the staircase but didn't see anything.

Something gripped Lani's heart that made her forget about the pain for a moment. Had someone pushed her? Who would do something like that? Why? Why her? Had she imagined it?  Maybe...maybe she had just tripped.  Maybe she had a concussion and imagined the footsteps.

Now shaking from more than the fall, Lani gingerly felt her legs. They'd probably be bruised as well, but there were no sharp pains or weird bumps that concerned her. She looked back up the staircase, now looking steep and foreboding.  It was a miracle she hadn't broken her neck. She remained on the floor, too sore to sit up just yet. As she stared at the ceiling and felt the cool tile under her body, she thought again about the feeling of two hands pushing her back. Maybe they weren't expecting a miracle either.

# 14

# Cameron

Cameron stared at the ceiling of his room. The bed was surprisingly comfortable for something that looked like it was made in a different century. He had tried to start his assignment after leaving the rest of the group at lunch, but he quickly realized that nothing was going to happen as long as his mind kept going back to the strange room where he ran into Kai.

The room didn't seem unusual at first, just like a boring office or something. Cameron had been intrigued by the large door at the far end and gave in to the sudden urge to open it. But when he started pulling on the handle, an image of Thomas had flashed into his mind, strikingly different from the memories Cameron had been clinging to over the past two years. This vision was so clear and vivid that Cameron knew—he just *knew*—that Thomas was standing behind him in that room. But when he turned around, his brother wasn't there. The disappointment he had felt in that moment was almost as bad as the grief Cameron experienced the day it happened.

Cameron rolled over on his side. He didn't want to think

about that day, but his experience earlier had opened some floodgate in his brain and the memories were rushing back. The first thing that always popped into Cameron's mind when he had to relive everything was the back of Thomas's head as he hiked ahead of Cameron on a dirt trail. It was a hot, sunny day, and Cameron had been sweating profusely, trying hard to keep up with his athletic brother. The hike had been his idea though—he used to love getting out of the city whenever he could. They had found a promising state park several hours away and had borrowed their parents' car for a day trip. After climbing for over an hour, Cameron remembered Thomas pointing into the woods and suggesting they visit an overlook he had read about. Cameron followed him and, sure enough, they were treated to a fantastic view of rolling hills and open skies, bolstered by the sheer cliff below them.

The rest was always going to be a little blurry. After a few minutes at the overlook, Cameron had turned around and taken a few steps back toward the trail when he heard a deep rumbling noise. He looked back and saw Thomas' frame slipping out of view as he scrambled to get a hold of the rolling rocks and dirt falling around him. Without thinking, Cameron dove toward his brother and almost fell off himself as he desperately threw his arms over the edge of the cliff. Somehow, he and Thomas had caught hands. But they were both so sweaty that Thomas's right hand slipped out of Cameron's left almost immediately. Cameron may have screamed or he may have stayed silent the entire time—he couldn't remember for sure. But, whether he wanted to or not, he would never forget the look on his brother's face. Thomas's green eyes were frozen in pure terror and fixated on Cameron. Feeling himself begin to inch toward the edge, Cameron had used his remaining free hand to latch onto Thomas's left forearm, but he could feel his brother slipping. Thomas had dug his nails into Cameron's arm so deeply that Cameron bled as he tried to hold on. Everything happened too slowly and then too fast. Cameron froze in horror as Thomas's last finger slipped out of his hand and he watched his brother fall.

Ignoring his bleeding arm and the intense pain in his side, Cameron had immediately called 911 and sprinted down the trail to try to find his brother. He got to Thomas long before the emergency crew did. Cameron didn't think of it as a merciful event at the time, but Thomas wasn't bleeding badly or splayed in a strange position—he looked like he had fallen asleep in the middle of the woods.  Cameron remembered checking for a pulse and starting CPR after he couldn't find one, his mind blurred and buzzing but focused, like he was shining a flashlight through a thick fog. He didn't know how long he was there, but at some point, someone pulled him off of Thomas while another person began chest compressions. There were flashing lights everywhere and a lot of yelling, and somehow Cameron ended up in an ambulance with Thomas as someone rubbed something on his arm that stung. Someone else began touching his side, and when Cameron looked down, he saw a chunk of wood, a branch maybe, sticking out of it.

The ride to the hospital was too long, and Cameron cursed himself again and again for agreeing to hike in such a remote location. When they got to the hospital, Thomas was whisked away on his gurney and Cameron ended up in a bed nearby. He asked everyone who walked by how Thomas was, but no one could give him an update. A few minutes later, or maybe a few hours, a doctor sat down next to Cameron and told him that Thomas hadn't made it. There was nothing they could do.

Although the day was hazy, there were some parts that Cameron would never forget. The feeling that someone had punched him in the chest so hard he couldn't breathe. Sobbing into his pillow while a nurse held a hand to his back. Seeing his parents rush into the ER and watching his mother collapse to the floor after speaking with the doctor. Speaking with the hospital psychiatrist and the police to explain what had happened. His father staring at the long cuts on his forearm. His mother asking why they had to go hiking that day. The psychiatrist trying to interject something about coming together but his parents getting up and insisting they go home as soon as possible.

The moment he was released from the hospital and got into the car, Cameron no longer felt like a member of the family. His parents had never explicitly blamed him for what had happened that day, but they found ways to make him never forget about it. As if he could forget.

Cameron brushed his wet eyes. He hated thinking about that day. He hated thinking about Thomas at all, but he was even more terrified of the idea of losing memories of him. So when the memories did come back, he let them run through his mind, whichever ones they chose to be.

Cameron jumped off the bed and shook his head. He needed to get his mind off of this. The room immediately jumped to the forefront of his mind. Something in the back of his brain told him it was a bad idea to go back, but an even more powerful urge told him he had to check it out again.

Cameron left his room and began wandering down the hallways, trying to remember how he got to the room the first time. Fortunately, the same feeling that drew him in the right direction initially was back and he could almost feel himself being told which way to turn at every corner. After several minutes of walking, Cameron came to a T that he recognized from the last time he was there. He knew he needed to turn left, but just before he did, he heard a groan to his right. He looked over at the long staircase that led downstairs and saw something move at the bottom of the steps. The hair on the back of his neck stood up, and he crept to the top of the staircase and looked down. Someone was lying on the floor at the bottom of the staircase.

*Was that—?*

He squinted. It was Lani. Her eyes were open and it looked like she was taking deep breaths. Cameron let out a short huff. He knew she didn't like him, and he'd rather be on his way toward the room than hearing her snarky comments about his attitude, but he couldn't leave. He quickly began to walk down the stairs and saw Lani whip her head around. Her eyes were wide and her face was pale, but her expression softened when she saw him.

"Oh, Cameron," she said.

"What are you doing?" Cameron asked as he reached her. "Why are you on the floor?"

"Uh," Lani said.

She looked back up the staircase. Cameron looked back but didn't see anything. He looked back at Lani and noticed she was holding her wrist.

"Are you okay?" Cameron asked, leaning down. "Did you fall down the stairs or something?"

"I—"

Lani tried to sit up and winced. Instinctively, Cameron put his hand on her back and helped her into a sitting position.

"Thanks," Lani said, shifting her back.

Cameron pulled his hand away.

"Uh...yeah," she said slowly. "I fell. I tripped and then couldn't get my footing."

"Do you need me to get help or something?"

"No," Lani said quickly. "No, I'm fine. Really. I'm a little sore, but it's fine. I just need a second."

"Did you hit your head? That can be serious. Can you move everything okay?"

Lani was now looking at Cameron with suspicion. Geez, what did he do to her to make her act like this? Cameron held her stony gaze for several seconds.

"What?" he finally asked.

She looked like she might say something, but then looked away.

"Nothing," she said. "I'm fine."

Lani braced her hands on the floor and tried to get up, but gasped and fell to the side. Cameron grabbed her waist to catch her fall.

"You okay?" he asked.

"My wrist," she grimaced. "I might have twisted it. I'm fine, though."

She twisted her torso and Cameron pulled his hand away.

"I'll get someone," Cameron said, standing up.

"No," Lani said quickly. "No, I'm fine. Really. Please, just give me a minute."

"Whatever," Cameron said, shaking his head. "I tried."

He took a step back, wanting to get back to the room, but Lani stopped him again.

"Don't go," she said. "I mean, can you stay for another minute? I don't want...just, can you stay?"

Her eyes were darting up the stairs nervously and Cameron

followed her gaze again.

"You sure you're okay? Did you see something?"

"No," Lani said quickly. "No, I just...the whole thing just kind of freaked me out. And it was embarrassing. I don't really want anyone else to know what happened."

She giggled awkwardly and flashed a bright smile, but Cameron thought it looked fake. The desire to go back to the room tugged at his brain, but he told himself he could go later. Lani did seem like she was in a lot of pain, and if she was dumb enough to refuse help, he could at least make sure she didn't fall over again.

"Fine," he said, sitting down a few feet away from her.

"Thanks," she said.

They sat in silence for a few moments, which Cameron didn't mind, but Lani didn't seem to like it when people weren't talking.

"Do you like Queens?" she asked.

"It's fine," Cameron said.

"Do you ever visit the city? I've never been to New York. It looks amazing."

"Yeah, I've been a bunch."

"You're close to your family?"

Cameron frowned.

"What's that supposed to mean?" he asked.

Lani looked a little taken aback.

"I'm sorry, you just said earlier that you picked Queens College because it was close to family. I just assumed—"

"Oh," Cameron said, looking away from her embarrassed expression. "We're...whatever. We don't hate each other, if that's what you mean."

"Cameron, I wasn't accusing you of anything," Lani said

with a huff. "It was just a question."

Cameron waited a second before glancing over. Lani was picking at her nails angrily, and a small pit formed in his stomach.

"Sorry," he muttered.

Lani looked at him in surprise.

"Sorry?" she said with a small smile. "Did you just apologize?"

Cameron grunted and looked away. This was why she was so annoying. But Lani seemed to understand that he wasn't in the mood and didn't press it any further, which, Cameron realized, made her bug him a little less. They sat in silence for another couple of minutes.

"I have a little sister," Cameron said finally, surprised at himself for breaking the silence. "I mostly wanted to be close to her when I went to school."

"What's her name?" Lani asked.

"Greta."

"How old is she?"

"She's seven."

"Oh, cute!" Lani said. "I don't have any siblings. But I always thought it would be fun to have a younger one, especially a younger sister."

"Yeah, she's great."

Cameron couldn't help but smile when he thought of Greta.

"She's so fun to be around," he said. "She's always making up these new stories and worlds and stuff. And she's really smart, too. I'm always impressed with the stuff she says. She's way smarter than I was at seven."

"She sounds great," Lani said. "So it's just the two of you then?"

The all-too-familiar feeling of someone grabbing Cameron's insides and twisting them came over him.

"Yeah," he said, hating that his throat was starting to tighten.

Lani must have sensed something, and, to Cameron's relief again, she stopped talking. The two sat for another few minutes.

"I didn't mean to ask too many questions," Lani said softly. "I just like to get to know people before...I mean, I just like to get to know people."

Lani was definitely hiding something. Cameron sighed.

"It's fine," he said. "Don't worry about it."

Lani pushed her hands against the floor gently.

"I think I'm good," she said, slowly lifting herself to a standing position. Cameron put his arm out, but she didn't grab it.

"I'm fine," she said with a smile, although Cameron could tell she was wincing. "See? Told you."

"Okay," Cameron said. "Bye."

"Where are you going?"

Cameron hesitated. He wanted to go back to the room, but he didn't want Lani to follow him.

"Back to my room."

"Yeah, I'd like to lie down for a second. I'll go that way too."

Cameron had no choice but to walk back to his room with Lani trailing behind him. He had to slow down his pace because she seemed to be struggling to walk, but she refused to take his arm when he offered.

"See you later," Cameron said as they reached his room. "Go find a nurse."

He pointed down the hall and Lani rolled her eyes.

"I told you, I'm fine," she said. "See ya."

Cameron went into his room and closed the door before pressing his ear against it. He waited until he heard Lani's footsteps get quieter and quieter. When it had been silent for several seconds, he slowly creaked the door open. The hallway was empty. Cameron quickly slipped out of his room and started walking back to the mysterious room he had been trying to visit in the first place. He made his way through the winding hallways and took a left at the T where Lani had fallen down the stairs. He let his instinct lead him again, and sure enough, in a few minutes, he came across the large mural at the end of the hallway. He ran his hands against the wall until he found the door handle and opened it, his heart starting to pound.

The room was completely dark. Kai must have found the light switch when he first came. Cameron fumbled around for a few seconds, running his hands along the walls until he found a light switch and flicked it on. A single weak bulb hanging from the ceiling flooded the room in a dim light. Cameron thought a billionaire could afford a better lighting situation.

Cameron stood still for a few seconds, looking at the door at the far end of the room. He had the vision of Thomas over there, but nothing was happening right now. Did he have to be near it to see his brother? He walked slowly toward the door, his heart racing in anticipation. It was just a vision. Thomas wasn't actually there. But...

Cameron reached the door and touched the handle like he had done last time. He braced himself, but nothing happened. Cameron turned around and, confirming he was alone in the room, turned back to the door.

"Hello?" he whispered.

He grabbed the doorknob and twisted it, but it was locked, just like before. He yanked on the handle angrily and pounded his fist on the door when it wouldn't budge. He was annoyed at the profound, raw disappointment he felt, and he wanted the feeling to go away. Cameron leaned his forehead into the door and sighed. When he opened his eyes, he noticed a crack at the bottom of the door. A tiny beam of light was peering through it, and Cameron could feel the slightest warm breeze coming from the other side. Did the door lead to a balcony or something?

Cameron got down on all fours and peered under the door, but all he saw was dim, fuzzy light. Suddenly, a strong gust of wind blew into his face and he fell backward in surprise. The breeze was warm and smelled like pine and dirt, exactly like the air had been the day he and Thomas had gone hiking. Cameron scrambled to his feet and backed away from the door. This wasn't a good feeling, like when Thomas had come back smiling. This was just a vivid reminder of what had happened, almost like the room was taunting him. Cameron grabbed his head with his hands and shook it, trying to get the image of his brother out of his mind. This happened sometimes, but Thomas' body lying in the woods wasn't usually so plastered in his brain that he felt like it had been glued there. He rubbed his eyes vigorously and accidentally bumped a bookshelf with his elbow, causing a pile of books to come crashing down onto the floor.

The noise and the pain in his elbow seemed to be enough of a jolt to get Cameron's mind back to normal. Swearing under his breath, he leaned down to pick up the books. He read each of the titles as he placed them back on the shelf. *History of the Universe. Space and Time: The Possibilities and Consequences.*

Cameron glanced over at the remaining books in the bookcase he had bumped. They all had something to do with—

"Time travel?" he murmured.

Cameron shook his head. It was almost laughable. Why would Dr. Fredricksen have an entire bookshelf dedicated to something like this? There were some wild scientific theories out there, but time travel had been debunked more than pretty much any of them. Still, as Cameron finished placing the last book on the shelf, he couldn't help but think about all the times he had wished he could go back to that day. The longing to do it all over again ached in his chest like it never had before, so much so that he had to lean against the wall for support. But that would be impossible. It was stupid to dwell on those ideas—Cameron had been in a really dark place for months after Thomas died, wishing for all the things he had no control over. He didn't want to go back to that.

Cameron took a few deep breaths, shook out his arms, and checked his watch. It was almost time for dinner. He looked around the room again, silently hoping to see a smiling Thomas one more time, but nothing happened. What a crappy visit. He left the room and headed back to his.

# 15

# Allie

"He spent the rest of his life in bliss, having few possessions but everything he needed," Allie read from her notebook. "It was the people around him who truly mattered, and he knew that."

She looked up at Lani, who was lying on her back with her head propped up by a pillow.

"That's really good," Lani said earnestly. "I see why you were picked to come here. That was beautiful."

Allie blushed.

"Thanks," she said. "Do you want to read me yours?"

Lani nodded and sat up but winced in pain and let out a sharp breath. Allie rushed to her side.

"What's wrong?"

Lani had seemed weird when she knocked on Allie's door an hour earlier, but she hadn't said anything before flopping down on Allie's bed.

"I'm okay," Lani said. "I, uh...I fell down the stairs earlier and kind of bruised myself."

"What?" Allie gasped. "Are you okay? Let's go find a nurse,

I'm sure Barbara—"

"No, it's okay," Lani said, cutting her off. "I'm fine. Seriously. I think I sprained my wrist a little, that's all."

Lani gave Allie a sincere smile.

"Really, I'm fine," she said. "Cameron actually found me and helped out. I'll get some ice at dinner and I'm sure it will be better by tomorrow."

"Okay," Allie said, sitting down on the bed next to Lani. "Well, good thing he was there. Did you trip or something?"

Lani hesitated for just a second, but Allie noticed. It was the same way she had hesitated earlier when they were talking about their parents.

"Uh, yeah, I tripped," Lani said, glancing at her wrist. "Fun fact about me—I am incredibly clumsy. Stuff like this happens all the time."

Allie chuckled but felt like there was more to the story. Lani had been on her way to find the hidden room that Kai and Cameron had been talking about, and they had both been acting strange after their visit as well. Did this have something to do with that? And why wasn't Lani telling her everything?

A knock at the door shook Allie out of her thoughts. She walked over and opened it to see Cameron standing in the doorway, holding a clear plastic bag filled with ice. He held it out to Allie.

"This is for Lani," he said.

He turned to Lani, whose eyes were wide in surprise.

"Ice your wrist or I'm telling Barbara to call a doctor."

He turned and left. Allie slowly closed the door and brought the bag of ice over to Lani.

"That was...nice," Lani said, the tiniest smile forming at the sides of her mouth.

"See, I was right," Allie said playfully. "He isn't such a bad guy."

Lani giggled.

"Yeah, maybe."

Allie and Lani sat in silence for a few minutes while Lani iced her wrist. Allie imagined herself reading her story in front of the group and started twirling her hair through her now-shaky fingers.

"You okay?" Lani asked.

Allie nodded.

"Just a little nervous about tomorrow," she admitted. "I hate speaking in front of people."

"You'll be great," Lani said reassuringly. "I'm excited to talk to Dr. Fredricksen again. Well, not excited, I guess, because let's be honest, he's a little weird, but I would like to talk to him more."

"It feels like this story is a test worth 30 percent of my grade," Allie said.

Lani laughed.

"Yes, that is exactly how it feels," she said. "But I don't think mine is worth $100,000, so hopefully there's a lot more that goes into his decision."

Allie looked out the window, wondering if the slight tension she now felt between them was in her head.

"That's so much money," she said softly. "It could change everything, you know?"

"Yeah," Lani agreed.

"No, like, it could change so much for me," Allie said.

She hadn't made many girlfriends since dating Michael, and it felt good to confide in Lani. She peeked over at Lani, who was looking at her curiously.

"It's not just about me and Michael breaking up," Allie said. "His parents have a lot of money and they've been taking care of me since we started dating. My mom left me what she could, but she didn't have a lot and it all went to school anyway. I have a job, but I would never have been able to keep my grades up for my scholarship if I had to work enough to pay for everything myself. Michael paid for my food, and he bought me clothes, and he even covered rent sometimes. He wanted me to spend all my free time with him, so he would pay for anything that got in the way of that. We also—"

Allie felt a stabbing pain in her chest.

"We had talked about getting married," she forced herself to go on. "He was supposed to get a great job in a few months when we both graduated, and we were going to get married right after that. So...he told me I didn't need to get good grades or a lucrative degree or anything because I was just going to become a housewife. And I was excited about that."

Allie sighed deeply and looked back at Lani, whose brows had now furrowed slightly.

"I kind of hate myself for that now. We were going to have this perfect life together, but I needed him for it. And now that he's gone, I'm about to graduate with a degree in music with no career experience or anything other than a couple of years at a coffee shop. I don't have any savings or anything."

The tears that had been teasing her finally appeared in the corners of her eyes.

"I...I don't know what I'm going to do," she said, trying to keep her voice steady. "If I won, I could get back on my feet, you know? Get my master's or, like, go to a trade school or something. Just find a way to make a living."

Allie finally broke down and Lani pulled her in for a hug.

"It's so embarrassing," Allie said, her voice muffled in Lani's shoulder. "My mom raised me to be better than someone who throws her future away for a guy."

"Hey," Lani said, pulling away but keeping her hands on Allie's shoulders. "Don't say that. You didn't throw your future away. You dated an asshole, which is a universal female experience. You still have plenty of time to figure things out."

Allie took a deep breath and forced a smile.

"You're right," she lied.

Lani seemed pleased and hopped off the bed.

"It'll be dinnertime soon," she said. "I'm going to grab a jacket from my room. It's getting kind of chilly."

"I'll meet you down there," Allie said.

After Lani left the room and closed the door behind her, Allie started fiddling with the comforter on her bed. She bit her lip, trying not to cry. She did throw her future away, and this retreat was just making it more apparent. Everyone here had their lives together except for her. None of them, except maybe Lani, had any idea how much the prize money would mean to her. Allie had been happy to see only three other competitors at the beginning of the retreat, but now four people felt like too many.

Allie grabbed a sweatshirt from her suitcase—Lani was right; it did feel colder this evening—and slipped it on. She opened her bedroom door to head to the dining room and let out a startled scream. Barbara, who was standing just outside Allie's room with her hand raised, jumped.

"Oh, Barbara," Allie said, putting her hand on her chest. "I'm so sorry. You scared me."

Barbara didn't say anything. Her hand was still in the air, bunched in a small fist like she had just been about to knock on the door. Her eyes were slowly getting wider and darted between Allie and her room. Allie looked back as well, but didn't see anything unusual.

"Are...you okay?" she asked.

Barbara locked eyes with Allie, and Allie held the gaze of her creased brown eyes uncomfortably.

"I—," Barbara finally said. "I was looking for Lani. I was hoping to talk to her about—"

Footsteps came from their left, and Allie looked over to see Dr. Fredricksen walking toward them. She glanced over at Barbara, who had thrown on a professional smile but wasn't able to hide the look of fear that flashed over her face first.

"Ladies," Dr. Fredricksen said with a small bow. "I was just heading down to dinner. Should we all walk together?"

Barbara's strange behavior made Allie feel even more uncomfortable with Dr. Fredricksen, but she couldn't exactly say no. She nodded and followed the two down the stairs. Just before they entered the dining room, Dr. Fredricksen pulled Barbara to the side and gestured for Allie to go in without them.

"I just need to speak with Barbara for a moment, but we will both be joining you shortly," he said.

Allie shot one last glance at Barbara, whose face now wore a look of confusion, and stepped into the dining room. Cameron and Kai were already sitting down, but Lani was apparently taking her time getting dressed. Kai was talking to Cameron about something in an animated way and didn't notice Allie as she walked to the table. Cameron, who wore a neutral expression, looked at Allie briefly but didn't nod at her until Kai paused his story.

"Oh, hey," Kai said. "Didn't see you, sorry. Where's Lani?"

"She said she was grabbing a jacket from her room. She

should be down soon."

As she was speaking, Allie looked around at the table and frowned. Kai noticed.

"What's wrong?"

"Oh, um...I ran into Barbara and Dr. Fredricksen on the way here, and he said they were eating with us today. But there are only four spots."

Kai looked around the table and shrugged.

"Maybe they decided last-minute."

"Yeah," Allie said.

She thought again about how strange Barbara was acting outside her room and leaned closer to Kai and Cameron, who both leaned toward her curiously. She lowered her voice.

"So right before I came downstairs—"

"Ah, dinner time!"

Allie jumped backward as Dr. Fredricksen entered the dining room, followed by Barbara, who was back to looking like her stern but kind self. Allie tried to make eye contact with her, but Barbara seemed determined to avoid her gaze. Or maybe that was just a coincidence.

"It seems we are two place settings short," the professor said before snapping his fingers.

In a few seconds, a server rushed inside the room carrying two piles of plates, napkins, and silverware. He quickly arranged everything at the end of the table and left the room silently.

"They must have forgotten we were joining you all tonight. But we do seem to be missing someone. Ah..."

He paused as Lani entered the room. She was smiling brightly, but Allie felt like something was wrong. Lani seemed to avoid Dr. Fredricksen and took the long way to the remaining seat at the table. She sat down next to Allie without making eye contact.

"Sorry I'm late," she said. "I was just admiring the house on my way here."

"Yes, it is lovely," the professor said fondly.

As he looked around the room in admiration, he seemed like a normal, kind man, just like he had been when they had all first arrived. Allie looked at Barbara, who was also looking at Dr. Fredricksen while he surveyed the dining hall. But instead of fear or professionalism herself, Allie thought she had pity in her eyes. Allie burned with curiosity.

"I can't imagine ever leaving this place," the professor said quietly. "Of course, I don't have to if I don't want to..."

He trailed off and looked back at everyone, seeming to realize they were all staring at him.

"Oh, don't listen to an old man speak his crazy thoughts out loud," he said cheerfully. "Let's eat, shall we?"

As if on cue, six servers entered the room and placed steaming bowls of stew in front of each guest. Allie took a bite of hers. It was warm and comforting, and felt good in her stomach against the chill of the dining room.

"So, Dr. Fredricksen," Lani asked. "Can I ask why you wanted to host this retreat?"

Dr. Fredricksen looked at her quizzically.

"We're very grateful to be here, of course," Lani said quickly, blushing a little. "I didn't mean to question you. I just meant, like, how did you get the idea?"

The professor smiled warmly, which made Allie feel even more uneasy. Did they all imagine his weird behavior the other day? His eyes seemed so kind right now.

"I'll never forget my first year of college," he said. "I had no idea what I wanted to do with myself. Of course, I wasn't very invested in my future either, so I wasn't trying very hard."

Dr. Fredricksen raised his eyebrows.

"Then I discovered my university's library. An odd teenager like myself had no friends, so I spent hours in there every day. Every time I finished a book, I would find another from a different section of the library. Everything fascinated me, and I realized that there wasn't a single subject I should pursue—it was education itself. Hence, my path to teaching and writing."

Dr. Fredricksen lowered his voice slightly.

"That was also the time I met someone very important to me. She changed the trajectory of my life forever. I didn't understand at first why she chose me, but over the years, it became clear that I was well-suited for it. Perfect, even. I began to wonder how willingly she gave everything away."

Once again, it seemed like the professor was talking only to himself. His face didn't look manic this time, but deeply serious in a way that made Allie hold her breath.

"Does it even need to happen?" Dr. Fredricksen murmured.

Then, quickly, he popped his head up and smiled at the group.

"Apologies, I am reminiscing again," he said. "I've been reflecting on my life quite a bit lately, but you don't all need to hear about it."

The professor seemed to hesitate for a moment, then put his hands on the table.

"I'm afraid I must be off. I have an important call to make."

He stood up quickly and bumped the table, causing it to wobble aggressively. Kai, who was sitting across the table from Dr. Fredricksen, tried to grab his glass but wasn't quick enough, and it fell over, spilling red punch across the white tablecloth.

"Oh dear!" Dr. Fredricksen cried. "I'm terribly sorry. Let me get you another glass."

"Oh, it's okay," Kai said. "You don't—"

"I insist," the professor said.

Dr. Fredricksen walked to a small table close to the kitchen door and grabbed the almost empty pitcher of punch that had been sitting next to a pile of cloth napkins and extra silverware. He drained it into Kai's glass before handing it to Barbara, who placed it in front of Kai. The professor grabbed a towel and placed it on the stain.

"Please ignore the mess until you're finished," he said. "My staff will clean everything, and I will see you all tomorrow after breakfast. I'm looking forward to hearing your stories. Barbara, please come with me."

Dr. Fredricksen gave a small bow and left the room quickly, with Barbara trailing behind. Everyone at the table looked at each other in silence until their footsteps faded away.

"Everyone noticed that, right?" Lani finally said. "How he started talking to himself about...well, I don't even know what that was."

Allie nodded.

"Yeah," Kai said slowly, still staring at the door. "He's...I don't know what he's doing. Maybe he's just...old?"

"He's weird," Cameron said.

"Oh, that reminds me," Lani said, leaning into the table. "The reason I was late is because I overheard him talking to Barbara outside the dining room on my way down here. He sounded really serious and she looked upset. I heard him say something about protecting something, but I couldn't really understand more than that."

"Oh," Allie said quickly, and everyone at the table turned to her. "Lani, after you left my room, Barbara stopped by. She said she wanted to find you to tell you something, but then Dr. Fredricksen came out of nowhere and interrupted her. So we came down together, but let me come in here first while he talked to her outside."

Cameron and Kai were both frowning.

"Are they...hiding something?" Kai asked. "Does it have anything to do with us?"

Allie shook her head slowly. She didn't know what any of this meant, but it didn't feel good.

"I feel like it has to concern us in some way," she said. "Why else would Barbara come to my door about it?"

"Yeah, and why was she looking for Lani?" Cameron asked.

Everyone looked at Lani, and Allie saw her face get red.

"I don't know," Lani said. "That could have been a coincidence."

Everyone glanced around at each other, which made Allie's stomach turn. Did they suspect Lani of something?

"Well, I'm sure this has nothing to do with any one of us specifically," Allie said. "And maybe it doesn't have anything to do with us at all. Maybe he has a stolen painting in Lani's room or something he doesn't want us to see because this retreat is so publicized."

"That's a good point," Kai said, taking a sip of his punch.

Kai didn't seem convinced, though. He kept shooting glances at Cameron, but Cameron seemed so absorbed by his own thoughts that he didn't notice. Allie suspected the guys were hiding something from her and Lani, although she didn't know why.

The conversation stopped and everyone ate their soup quietly.

"Dude, what's wrong with your arm?" Allie heard Cameron ask.

Allie looked up. Kai was scratching his arm, which was now covered in red hives.

"I don't know," he said.

He cleared his throat.

"This is—"

He cleared his throat again.

"Uh, does anyone know if this punch has kiwi in it?" he asked.

Allie shook her head along with everyone in the group.

"Are you okay?" Lani asked. "Are you allergic or something?"

Kai nodded, grimacing slightly.

"Yeah, I'm allergic to kiwi," he said. "But I told them that when I got here."

He cleared his throat again.

"Do you have an EpiPen?" Cameron asked urgently.

Kai nodded again.

"It's in my room on the table by my bed. I don't think I need it, though."

"Give me your key," Cameron said.

"Cameron, you don't—"

"Come on," Cameron said, holding his hand out.

Kai pulled his key out of his pocket and handed it to Cameron, who ran out of the room.

"Is there anything I can do?" Lani asked. "Should I go get someone?"

Kai shook his head.

"Really, I think I'm fine," he said. "I need to eat a lot of kiwi to need my EpiPen. And it would be way worse by now if that happened."

Lani, who was starting to stand up, froze.

"Are you sure?"

Kai nodded.

"It looks worse than it really is. This has happened to me a couple of times before. It's mostly the hives, and my throat gets itchy."

He cleared his throat again.

"Which is annoying but not deadly.  I just need some antihistamines."

"Do you have any?" Allie asked. "Can we go get some?"

"Yeah, they're also in my room. I should have told Cameron. Really guys, it's fine," he said reassuringly.

Allie looked at Lani, who looked as worried as she felt.

"Believe me, if I was having a bad reaction, you would know," he said lightheartedly.

He stood up.

"I'd better help Cameron," Kai said.  "I don't want him freaking out over nothing."

"We'll go with you," Lani said.

"Yeah," Allie agreed. "Please let us know if you start to feel worse or need us to get someone."

Kai smiled and nodded. The three of them left the dining room and started up the stairs, but they ran into Cameron before they had made it halfway.  He had obviously been running toward them and was out of breath.

"You okay?" he panted to Kai.

"Yeah man, thanks," Kai said. "Sorry, I was coming to tell you it's not as bad as it looks. I don't need my EpiPen, just some meds."

"Okay, good," Cameron said, his breathing slowing. "Because I couldn't find the EpiPen."

"Should have just been by my bed," Kai said.

"I know, I looked. I looked in the drawers too, under your bed, everywhere. It wasn't there."

Kai frowned.

"I know that's where I left it. I put it out to remind me to bring it to dinner, which didn't work, but it should have been there."

Kai walked past Cameron and made his way to his room with Allie and the rest of the group trailing behind. They entered Kai's room, which was still unlocked, and Allie watched as Kai search through the desk next to his bed. She took a quick glance around the room while he looked for the EpiPen. It was kind of messy, with several shirts thrown over chairs and a half-unpacked suitcase on the floor in the corner.

"Weird," Kai said. "You're right, it's not here. I wonder if I..."

He began rummaging around his room, pulling up pillows and tossing shirts aside. After a few minutes, he turned to the group.

"It's not here," he said, looking concerned.

"Do you think you left it somewhere maybe?" Lani asked.

Kai shook his head.

"It's pretty important. I usually always have it on me, I just forgot this one time. And I definitely left it here."

No one said anything.

"Do you think someone...took it?" Allie asked.

Everyone turned to her.

"Like stole it?" Lani asked slowly. "On purpose? Why would someone do that?"

"Kind of a weird coincidence that he's exposed to something he's allergic to and his EpiPen just happens to be missing, isn't it?" Cameron asked.

"Yeah..." Kai said, running his hands through his hair. "I mean, maybe I left it somewhere by accident, but I can't think of where. And I did tell them that I was allergic before the retreat started. You'd think it would be easy not to put kiwi in anything."

"That's really irresponsible on their part," Lani said, frowning deeply. "You should tell Barbara about this."

"Well, I do need a new EpiPen," Kai said. "I'll tell her later, though. It seems like she had a hard day."

Lani was right, Allie thought. It was wildly irresponsible for the kitchen staff to serve something with kiwi in it when they had been informed of an allergy. It was more than irresponsible—it was dangerous.

"Well, I'm going to chill for the rest of the evening," Kai said, popping what Allie assumed were several antihistamine tablets in his mouth. "This will knock me out pretty soon. Thank you guys for your help."

Lani smiled at Kai.

"I hope you feel better," she said.

Allie noticed a blush on her cheeks.

"Yeah," Allie agreed. "And let us know if you need anything tonight."

"'Night," Cameron said.

The three waved goodbye to Kai and let his door shut behind them.

"See you guys tomorrow," Cameron said before heading down the hall.

"It is really weird," Lani said quietly as Cameron walked

away. "All of this. Barbara acting strange and Dr. Fredricksen at dinner and the EpiPen and when I—" she cut herself off and glanced at Allie.

"When you what?"

Allie could tell Lani was uncomfortable and didn't want to push anything, but her curiosity got the better of her.

"Uh," Lani hesitated. "Well, when I fell down the stairs. Maybe I was imagining it, but I think...I don't know, maybe it wasn't an accident."

"What?" Allie asked.

"It's a little blurry. I think the adrenaline and everything. I might have just slipped. But I don't know, maybe something else happened."

Allie bit her lip, too nervous to ask any more questions.

"Yeah, maybe."

Lani sighed.

"You know, I think I'll turn in early too. It's been kind of a crazy day."

They walked to their rooms and said their goodbyes. After getting ready for bed, Allie sat on the windowsill and looked out at the starry sky. She felt a chilly breeze and shivered. She didn't want to be here anymore.

# 16


# Kai


Kai jolted awake to his alarm clock blaring loudly. He preferred to wake up to soft music on his phone, but this was the only option he had here. He turned his alarm off and groaned. The antihistamines had helped his hives go away but had made him miserably groggy like usual. He forced himself out of bed and jumped in the shower in an attempt to wake himself up.

After showering and getting dressed, he took off to find someone to talk to about getting a new EpiPen. He had torn his room apart the previous night and hadn't found it anywhere. He figured it was really gone after searching with everyone in the room, but he wanted to make sure. Something was really strange about it going missing—he knew he had left it on the table by his bed before he went to dinner, and only about 30 minutes had passed before Cameron would have made it up there. Someone must have taken it.

Kai didn't want to sound dramatic to the rest of the group, but he could tell that they were all freaked out too. And when Lani and Allie had mentioned how strange Barbara and Dr. Fredricksen were acting...it couldn't be a coincidence. He didn't want to admit it, but Kai was nervous. Why would someone steal something that would be essential for saving his life? And Cameron was right—it was too weird that something at dinner had kiwi in it the one time he didn't have his EpiPen on himself. Kai must have only had a small amount of kiwi based on his mild reaction, but if the punch had been full of the stuff he could have died last night if an ambulance hadn't arrived in time. Was he being targeted? Did he have anything to do with what Barbara was going to warn Lani about? Was Lani in on the whole thing?

No, he reprimanded himself. It was obvious she wanted to win the prize, but she seemed like a genuinely nice person. And what could she possibly gain from participating in a crime? Besides $100,000, Kai admitted to himself. For a brief moment, an image of Lani being sent away in an ambulance flashed in his head, and with the thought came a tiny flicker of hope at the idea of one less person to compete against for the money. He shook his head. That was a horrible thing to think.

A noise in the next room brought Kai back to reality. He entered and saw Barbara at the far end of a fancy living room, dusting above a fireplace mantle.

"Barbara?" he asked.

She jumped and turned around.

"Oh, hello Kai," she said, grabbing her chest. "It's you."

"Sorry, I didn't mean to scare you," he said quickly. "I just, well, last night there was some kiwi in the punch they served with dinner. Anyway, I'm allergic, and I had a reaction. It wasn't that bad, but I'm really allergic, so it could have been."

"Oh dear," Barbara said, her eyes wide. "I am so sorry. I remember you listed that on your intake form."

She frowned and looked past Kai's shoulder.

"I will inform the kitchen staff immediately," she said, her voice sounding stern like the day they had all arrived. "This is completely unacceptable. I am very, very sorry. It will not happen again."

"Thank you," Kai said. "I'm sure it was an accident. And also, I didn't end up needing it, but my EpiPen disappeared yesterday."

Barbara froze.

"Your...EpiPen?" she asked.

Kai couldn't really read the expression on her face. He nodded.

"Yeah, Cameron couldn't find it in my bedroom, and then the rest of us went to look, but we couldn't find it anywhere. I know I left it in there before dinner."

"So, no one was in your room after you left for dinner?"

"No. Well, no one but Cameron, I guess. He went to go get it when I told them I was allergic because I got hives on my arms."

"Hm," Barbara murmured.

Her eyes darted around the room.

"Um, well, I'm going to need another one," Kai said. "I mean, I need to have one on me for emergencies. That was the only one I had."

"Oh, yes," Barbara said, snapping her head back to Kai. "Please, follow me. We have a first-aid closet that is always stocked for events like this. There should be one in there. Follow me."

Kai followed Barbara through several more rooms until they reached a closet door in the middle of a hallway. She opened the door, and Kai could see that the shelves were stacked with white containers. She rummaged through a few until she pulled out a new EpiPen from one.

"Ah, here we are," she said, handing it to Kai. "There you go. Feel free to get anything from here that you need. I will speak to the staff about your allergy, and I promise it will not happen again."

"Thank you," Kai said. "Again, I'm sure it was a mistake. But thank you for your help."

Kai turned to head to the dining room for breakfast but heard Barbara say something behind his back. He turned back around.

"Sorry?" he said.

Barbara was looking at him nervously, wringing her hands together.

"Are...you okay?" Kai asked.

He felt uneasy. Barbara took a deep breath.

"I need...I think..." she stumbled.

Suddenly, her eyes shot down the hallway. Kai looked over too, then felt a surprisingly strong hand gripping his arm. He jumped and turned to see Barbara staring intensely into his eyes.

"Be careful," she whispered urgently.

Kai didn't say anything. His heart was pounding. Barbara looked like she wanted to say more, but a creaking floorboard from another room made her jump and she let go of his arm.

"Let me know if you need anything else," she said, her voice back to its normal volume and tone.

With a curt nod, Barbara left Kai alone in the hallway. He stood there for a few moments, too freaked out to move. What was that? Be careful? About what? He heard another creak and jumped, then made his way to the dining room as quickly as he could. He didn't run into anyone else on the way and saw that the rest of the group was there already by the time he arrived. Allie and Lani smiled at him as he walked in, and Cameron gave him a slight nod.

*So, no one was in your room after you left for dinner?*

*No. Well, no one but Cameron, I guess.*

No way. Just like Allie, Kai knew there was no way Cameron was capable of doing something like that. Sure, he had only known him for a couple of days, but he could tell he was a good guy. Kai wondered if he should tell everyone about what just happened with Barbara. He still hadn't revealed to anyone what he saw in the strange room before running into Cameron, but that was personal enough that he didn't want to bring it up unless he absolutely needed to. He concluded that Barbara probably just told him what she had tried to tell Allie, which meant he needed to let them all know.

Kai sat down and relayed his strange experience to everyone at the table. When he finished the story, Cameron's face didn't change, but Lani looked surprised and Allie looked scared.

"Do you think that's what she was trying to tell me?" Lani asked.

"Maybe," Kai said.

"I don't...do we need to tell someone about this?" Allie whispered.

"Tell who?" Cameron asked dully.

"Cameron's right," Lani said.

Her voice was stiff, and as freaked out as he was, Kai had to suppress a smile. Lani clearly didn't like Cameron, and he could tell she didn't like admitting Cameron was right about anything.

"Barbara knows that something's going on, but she's obviously not telling us anything," Lani went on. "And Dr.

Fredricksen has been acting weird since the beginning, so I don't think he's the right person to talk to. Plus, besides the servers, I haven't seen another person here the whole time, have you?"

Kai shook his head.

"I don't know where they hid our phones either," Kai admitted.

"Do...do we need to leave?" Allie asked quietly.

"And do what?" Cameron asked. "We're in the middle of nowhere."

That made Allie look even more scared, and Kai threw a look at Cameron.

"It's okay," Kai said. "We don't need to get ahead of ourselves. We don't really know what's going on, if anything is at all. This is a very publicized contest and he's a well-known public figure. No one's going to do anything to us."

He wasn't sure he believed that himself, but Allie seemed a little less worried as he said it. Everyone ate their breakfast quickly, and Kai skipped the juice just in case. After breakfast, the four students shuffled quietly to the classroom that had hosted their first lesson for the next meeting. They sat in silence, the room tense, until Dr. Fredricksen entered.

"Good morning," he said brightly. "I'm looking forward to hearing your stories, so let's begin."

One by one, everyone read their short story out loud. Allie went first. She had written about a man who had been given information about the stock market that could have made him rich but decided to use it to help the people around him. Lani wrote about a child who had learned about an embarrassing secret that could have made him look better to everyone around him but chose to keep it to himself to protect his friend.

Kai got through his story quickly. It was short and he hadn't spent as much time on it as he wanted to, considering the allergy fiasco the previous night. He thought of his mom and felt a little guilty, thinking about how she would have felt listening to his weak attempt at the assignment.

Cameron was the final one to share his story. He sounded bored while he read, but his writing was good. He had written a story about a teenager learning a secret that could solve a murder case, but the adults in his life refused to listen. Eventually, the teenager and his friends ignored the advice of the adults and solved the case themselves. It was entertaining and fun to listen to, but Kai couldn't help but notice Dr. Fredricksen's mood shift toward the last half of the story. He looked annoyed and, by the end, a little angry. But when Cameron finished reading, the professor quickly changed the expression on his face back to enjoyment.

"Thank you!" he said cheerfully, clapping with the rest of the group.

Kai looked around, wondering if he was the only one who noticed Dr. Fredricksen's mood swings. No one else seemed worried.

"Excellent work, everyone," the professor said. "I'm impressed with each of you."

His gaze lingered on Kai for a second, and Kai felt another wave of guilt for not trying as hard as he could have. Did he just ruin his chances of winning the prize?

"I only have one more assignment for you today," he said. "I want you to visit my library and browse at least five books. You don't need to read them all, of course, but I would like you to get a good idea of what each one is about. This evening, please write about what you learned. What you read and how much you write is completely up to you."

He paused as if he was anticipating questions, but no one moved.

"I would also like to conduct one-on-one interviews with each of you today," he went on. "These will help me get to know you better. Kai, I would like to see you first, after I dismiss everyone else."

Kai gave a small nod. He tried not to look as uneasy as he felt.

"Allie, I will see you after Kai. Then, after lunch, I'll visit Lani and, finally, Cameron before dinner. We will meet in this room. Any questions?"

The room was silent.

"Then you are dismissed," the professor said. "Please, enjoy my library. And do try to stay out of trouble. You'll know if you end up somewhere you shouldn't be."

Kai and Cameron glanced at each other, but Kai quickly looked away, not wanting Dr. Fredricksen to suspect anything. He watched as everyone left and returned Lani's wave to him as she walked through the doorway. He remained at the table, and Dr. Fredricksen stayed at the front of the room.

"So, Kai," Dr. Fredricksen said, looking at a clipboard in his hands. "You're from Seattle, and you're studying business."

Kai nodded.

"What do you see yourself doing with that?" Dr. Fredricksen asked.

"I think I'm applying to law school next year," Kai said.

"And is that what you want to do?"

Kai hesitated. He didn't know how honest he wanted to be, but he did want to make a good impression.

"I don't know," he said. "It would be a good career path."

"True," Dr. Fredricksen said. "It's what your mother wants, isn't it?"

Kai hesitated. How did he know that? He let out a small breath, trying to stop himself from overreacting. It's not like he was the only person in the world with parents who expected a lot from him.

"Uh, yeah," Kai said. "She just wants me to be able to take care of my family."

"Yes, as mothers do," Dr. Fredricksen said. "It must be even more urgent for her at the moment, considering her condition."

Kai froze and stared at Dr. Fredricksen, who looked unbothered.

"I—" he stammered. "How did—?"

"I can't imagine how frustrating it must be to watch her go through that without being able to help," Dr. Fredricksen said, looking around the room casually. "It must leave you feeling quite hopeless."

Kai felt a chill run down his spine. He didn't respond. He had written about his mother immigrating to the United States from Japan in his application essay, but he hadn't talked about her illness.

"Many doctors are brilliant," Dr. Fredricksen went on. "But sometimes the science isn't there yet. If only it were up to us to decide."

He looked at Kai expectantly, but Kai didn't know how to react. How did he know about his mom? Had he called his parents? What was the point of doing that?

"Uh, yeah," Kai said, trying to regain focus on the conversation. "That would be, I mean, if that was possible, it would be great, obviously."

"Tell me in one word how you feel about your mother's health situation."

Kai paused.

"I think you said it already," he answered honestly. "Hopeless."

"Hm. I imagine you would do anything to help her."

"Well, yeah."

"Anything?"

He looked at Kai urgently.

"Uh," Kai said, leaning back a little.

He wanted to get out of this room and away from Dr. Fredricksen forever, but he thought of his mom lying in her hospital bed, getting more frail each day. He thought of Akiko and Mia spending their afternoons doing homework in her hospital room. He thought of his dad bent over bills late at night. He had to win this thing.

"Yeah, anything," he said, looking into Dr. Fredricksen's intensely blue eyes. "Of course."

"What if it forced you into an ethical dilemma? The world is not a fair place, and those who reap good often do so at the expense of others."

"That's true," Kai said slowly. "I can't answer that for sure, then. If there was something I could do to help my mom but I knew it would hurt someone else, I don't know what I would do. It would depend on the situation."

The professor looked at Kai thoughtfully before turning away, and Kai felt a glimmer of hope in his chest. That must have been a good answer.

"You seem like an honest man," Dr. Fredricksen said. "Of course, the greater good tends to be compromised at the hands of honest men."

"I'm sorry, sir," Kai said. "The greater good?"

Dr. Fredricksen turned back toward Kai, and Kai noticed the same strange look in his eyes from his previous outbursts. Again, the professor's voice lowered a little bit, but this time he wasn't talking to himself. He was speaking directly to Kai.

"Yes, the greater good," he said quietly. "The future of humanity. The world was not meant to remain stagnant, Kai. We have only come this far thanks to those who looked past the suffering of a few to make way for the greatness they knew others could achieve."

"I'm...I'm sorry, what does this have to do with my mom?" Kai asked.

Dr. Fredricksen put his hands on the table and leaned toward Kai.

"The cure for your mother's disease is out there," he said. "Knowing that, wouldn't you do anything to bring it to her?"

Kai's heart pounded.

"What?" he asked. "It is? Are you serious? Do you know something?"

"When given the chance, many people won't take it after they understand the circumstances," the professor said, ignoring Kai's questions. "Would you take it, even if there were consequences?"

Kai desperately wanted to ask more about his mom, but he kept the prize money in his mind.

"I..."

He frantically debated in his mind about how to answer. He thought he knew what Dr. Fredricksen wanted, but he couldn't lie about something like this. Or maybe the whole conversation was a test of his integrity. Should he play the villain or the hero in the hypothetical story? Or should he just be honest? Kai sighed and shook his head.

"No," he replied. "If I knew there was a cure but people would get hurt for my mom to get it, I don't think I could make that choice. I'd have to leave it up to fate or the universe or whatever you want to call it."

The professor didn't say anything, but he looked a little disappointed. Kai's heart continued to pound. Had he just ruined his chances?

"Too many people are content with things happening as they're supposedly meant to happen," he said, turning away from Kai. "But someone always has to make the decision in the end."

He lowered his voice until Kai could barely hear it.

"Why shouldn't it be me?"

A cold draft suddenly swept through the room and Kai shuddered. It seemed to knock Dr. Fredricksen out of a daze, and he threw on a cheery smile.

"Well, this has been a lovely conversation," he said. "It has been wonderful getting to know you more, Kai."

"Oh, uh, you too," Kai said.

Dr. Fredricksen strolled to the door and opened it, which Kai took as his cue to leave.

"Thank you," he said as he reached the doorway.

He reached out his hand and the professor shook it firmly.

"Thank you," Dr. Fredricksen said. "Please, enjoy my library. And do let me know if your opinion changes."

Kai stared at him, but the professor was smiling like nothing he had said in the past half hour was strange in any way. Kai gave a small smile back and let the door close behind him. He stood in the hallway for a few moments, trying to process what had just happened. He was itching to tell the rest of the group about it and see what they thought, and he wanted to know if the rest of the meetings would be conducted in the same way. Even though nothing had really happened, Kai couldn't shake the feeling that something bigger was going on.

# 17

# Lani

Lani stood at the top of the staircase and looked down. She thought she heard something behind her and whipped her head around, but the empty hallway confirmed that she was completely alone. She gripped the banister tightly and darted her eyes across the area. The person who pushed her could have come from the way she had, but that hallway was long. They would have needed to run in order to disappear without her seeing them, and she would have heard their steps, wouldn't she? Maybe not. She wasn't thinking about anything other than not breaking her neck when she was falling down the stairs. The person also could have come from the direction she had been going, which was to the left of the bust on the table. That hallway turned sharply, so it would have been easy for them to slip around the corner quietly.

Lani rubbed her wrist. It was still sore from yesterday, along with the rest of her body, but the ice had helped. She thought again about seeing Cameron at Allie's door holding the bag of ice. It had felt so out of character that it had almost been funny. He must have had some ulterior motive—maybe he was trying to get her to let her guard down so she wouldn't try as hard to win the competition. But even as the thoughts swirled through Lani's mind, she had a feeling that maybe he was just being nice. If he had really wanted her out of the competition, he could have gotten help and she probably would have been taken to a hospital. He had listened when she asked him not to tell anyone.

Lani blinked several times. She needed to stop thinking about Cameron and focus on why she was here: to find the mysterious room she had been looking for the last time. After taking one last look at the stairs, she turned around and took a left at the bust. Kai had told her how to get to this point but hadn't been clear about where to go from here. He said he couldn't remember the rest of the directions well enough, but Lani suspected he wasn't being completely truthful. She could tell that he and Cameron knew something about this room that they weren't telling her and Allie.

Although she was unsure of where she was going, Lani began to wind her way through the hallways with growing confidence. She tried not to think too hard and took her turns based on her intuition. She wasn't sure how much time passed, but after walking a while, she noticed a door on the left side of a wall that seemed to be hidden within a large mural. Something told her this was the place she had been looking for, and her heart started to beat quickly as she pushed the door open.

The room was dark. Lani ran her hands along the wall just inside the door until she found a switch and flicked it. The bulb that turned on didn't provide a lot of light, but it was enough for her to see that she had stepped into a small library. It was warm and cozy here, like someone had left a heater running. It was a nice contrast to the chilly drafts that had been running through the house since yesterday. Something else about the room felt warm and inviting too, although Lani couldn't quite place what it was.

After taking a sweep of the room, Lani noticed a door on the far side tucked between two bookshelves. Curiosity consumed her, and she walked over quickly to open it.  Just as she reached for the handle to twist it open, a clear image came into her mind.  A faceless man was looking at his computer angrily, yelling something that Lani couldn't understand. A notification that read "File Deleted" flashed on the screen again and again as the man pounded his fists on his desk.

It was her blackmailer. The photos had been erased. A wave of relief washed over Lani, so strong that she fell to her knees on the wooden floor. Then, suddenly, the image in her head was gone and the room came back into focus. She sat there frozen, still on her knees, and looked around, almost expecting to see the man in the room with her. But once again, she found herself completely alone.

Disappointment set in as the intense relief faded away. Lani stood up, slightly embarrassed about her reaction, even though no one had seen it. She tried to shake off the feelings that had just rushed through her body and turned away from the door, no longer wanting to open it.

She began browsing the bookshelves that lined the walls, determined to explore the room regardless of what just happened. There were books on every subject imaginable, from geography to cooking to colonization, with an entire shelf dedicated to digital technology and surveillance.

Lani walked to a circular table in the middle of the room. There were a few books stacked on one end and a messy display of papers on the other. She could see the papers were written in English and she picked one up, her curiosity getting the better of her. It was dated thirty years earlier.

*Theo,*

*I was about your age when I was chosen. I know it is a difficult decision for you to make, as it was for me. You will be required to sacrifice your time, career, and even relationships. This must be your priority until your replacement is selected.*

*However, I would hope that you remember what this is all for. You are protecting more people than you can possibly imagine. Although the task itself does not seem that impressive, it is the most important thing you could ever do in this life. The selection process is rigorous, and you were chosen because of not only your intelligence, but your heart as well. I am confident that you will not confuse power with goodness and that you will remain humble and teachable for the remainder of your life. I saw that in you, which is why I picked you.*

*Please reconsider your decision. I am always available to answer any questions. I believe you are the correct choice, and I am pleading with you to accept.*

*Sincerely,*
  *Anita*

Just as Lani finished reading the letter, she heard a noise behind her and whipped around. Cameron was standing just inside the room.

"Oh," she said, her heart pounding. "You scared me."

"Sorry," Cameron said. "What are you doing?"

"Uh, just reading this," she said, holding up the letter. "I found it on the table."

Lani saw Cameron glance at the other door at the far end of the room, but he walked over to the table to meet her.

"What's it about?" he asked.

"I'm not really sure. Whoever wrote it is telling Theo that they should accept a position, I think, and it sounds like Theo doesn't want it."

Lani handed Cameron the letter and watched him as he read it. His expression didn't change.

"Hm," he said when he finished. "Theo? It must be to Dr. Fredricksen."

"Oh yeah," Lani said quickly. "I totally forgot his first name is Theodore. Interesting. I wonder what job this lady is talking about, though. And why would he keep the letter?"

Cameron shrugged and looked at the door again. Lani noticed he was tapping his fingers together, which was something she did sometimes when she was nervous. At second glance, she could tell he was uncomfortable—he was chewing on his lip, and she thought she saw him shiver. Lani wondered what he had experienced the last time he was here.

"Are you...okay?" she asked slowly.

Cameron quickly turned away from the door.

"Yeah," he said, clearing his throat. "How's your wrist?"

"Oh, it's still a little sore, but better today," Lani said. "Thanks for the ice."

"Yeah. Can I see it?"

Lani raised her eyebrows.

"Why?"

The corners of Cameron's mouth twitched.

"I'm not going to do anything. I just want to see if it's swollen."

Lani wasn't sure why he was being so nice to her, but she

held out her wrist. He put one hand underneath it and ran the other gently down the side. She could feel the hair on her arms stand up.

"Okay, doesn't feel too bad," he said. "You probably just sprained it a little. I would ice it tonight and make sure you move it as much as you can to keep it from getting stiff."

"Are you thinking of med school after this?"

Cameron let out a chuckle, and Lani couldn't help but mirror it.

"No, I was really into the Boy Scouts when I was younger. I did it with my brother—"

He stopped suddenly, and the smile that Lani had seen for the first time since she met him was gone.

"I thought it was just you and your sister," Lani said without thinking.

The look on Cameron's face told her that she should have kept her mouth shut. His jaw was clenched and his cheeks had flushed a dark red.

"I'm sorry," she said quickly. "I shouldn't have said anything. You don't have to talk about it."

Cameron didn't answer right away, then, to Lani's surprise, relaxed his jaw and sighed. He looked away from her and back to the door.

"No," he muttered. "I'm sorry."

Lani was quiet. She didn't know what to say. Cameron stood in silence for a few minutes, and she could see him making a tight fist with one hand. Finally, he relaxed it.

"I know I'm an asshole," he said.

"Oh," Lani said. "No, you're not...well, I mean, yeah, you kind of can be. People don't usually self-identify as one though, so that must count for something."

Cameron ran a hand through his hair, and Lani saw a hint of a smile before his face became serious again.

"I didn't use to be," he said slowly, like he was forcing himself to talk.

"Cameron, you don't have to—"

"I know."

He sighed again.

"I don't really...talk about this a lot. And I think that makes it worse."

Lani gave a small nod and leaned back on the table. Cameron put his hands in his pockets.

"I told you about my little sister," he said. "I had a younger brother too. He...died in an accident two years ago."

Lani put her hand over her mouth.

"I'm so sorry," she gasped.

Cameron swallowed.

"It was my fault," he said, looking down.

Staring at his feet, Lani thought he suddenly looked ten years older. His demeanor was so different than how he'd been acting since they first arrived at the house. Lani wanted to say something to make him feel better, but she knew she couldn't. She let him look at the floor in silence and waited.

"Nothing's been the same since then," he finally went on, so quietly that Lani could barely hear him. "My parents blame me for it. My friends stopped talking to me. It was like my whole life was taken away that day."

Cameron walked to one of the bookshelves and ran a finger along the spines of the books.

"So, I don't know," he said. "I started turning into this person, I guess. I don't try to be such a jerk. It just happens."

He paused again, and for a long time, neither of them said

anything. Finally, Lani spoke.

"What was his name?"

Cameron looked at Lani in surprise.

"Thomas."

Another pause. Lani walked over to him and gently placed a hand on his shoulder. She felt him stiffen at her touch, then relax.

"I wish I could say something that would help," Lani said softly.

"Nothing helps," Cameron said with a dry smile. "So it's fine. Anyway, sorry again for being such a jerk. Keep calling me out on it."

Lani laughed.

"Okay."

"This room freaks me out," Cameron said.

"Really?" Lani asked. "I like it. It's so interesting. Although..."

She looked over at the door where the thought of her black-mailer losing her photos had popped into her head so clearly. Even though she had been disappointed after the vision, there had been a growing sense of hope inside her since it happened, like it could happen in real life if she had the right resources. Cameron turned to the door, too.

"Did you...see something over there?" he asked hesitantly.

That surprised Lani.

"Uh, well, I don't really know," she stumbled out.

Lani wasn't sure if she wanted to tell Cameron. What if his nice-guy persona was all an act? Instantly, she felt ashamed at the thought. Like Allie, he had just shared something deeply personal with her, and it seemed like it was way harder for Cameron to do than it had been for Allie. Lani bit her cheek and looked at Cameron for a few seconds.

"Uh, what?" he asked, raising his eyebrows.

"I...I did see something," she said.

"Oh. Okay. So it wasn't just me."

"It was weird. It wasn't like I passed out or anything, but it was so clear that it was like I was dreaming."

"Yeah, that happened to me too."

They both stared at the door for a while, so Lani finally asked what she assumed he was thinking about asking her.

"What did you see?"

Cameron didn't react, continuing to stare at the door. But just when Lani was about to ask the question again, he answered.

"I saw Thomas."

Lani waited for more, but he didn't elaborate.

"Was he...doing anything?" she asked.

Cameron shook his head. He looked sad.

"No," he said. "He was just there."

He turned away quickly and brushed his eyes. Lani wanted to give him a hug, but he seemed embarrassed and she didn't want to make it worse.

"Oh," she said, trying to put the attention on herself. "I saw someone too. But they were doing something, so I guess it was a little more involved than yours."

Immediately, she regretted speaking so quickly. Cameron turned to face her, his eyes a little red but now bright with curiosity.

"Yeah?" he asked. "Who was it?"

Lani hesitated.

"Just this guy I know," she lied.

"Is he important?" Cameron asked. "Do you think there's a

reason you saw him?"

Lani glanced away.

"No, I don't think so," she said, trying to sound casual.

"What was he doing?"

"Uh...he was just, mad about something, I think. I don't know what though."

Cameron didn't say anything. He stared at the door with a serious look on his face, and Lani noticed his right hand twitch.

"What do you think it means?" Lani asked. "Does this have anything to do with the other weird stuff that's been happening?"

"I don't know. Maybe."

"Should we tell someone?"

Cameron shook his head.

"Who could we tell?" he asked. "Like you said, Dr. Fredricksen is the one acting so weird, and we don't really know what's going on with Barbara. And I think he hires new servers for every meal, so they probably couldn't do anything anyway."

So she wasn't the only one who had noticed that.

"Okay," Lani said. "So we just try to get to the end of the week then?"

"I don't think there's anything we can do. We just need to focus on—"

He cut himself off again, and Lani saw him steal a quick glance at her before looking away. Again, Lani suspected he was thinking what she was. Focus on winning. She wondered how much he really wanted the money. Sure, anyone could use $100,000, but she doubted he needed it as badly as she did.

"Are you heading to the library soon?" Cameron asked.

"Oh," Lani said. "Yeah, I will. But I wanted to look around here a little longer."

Did Lani imagine it, or did Cameron look slightly let down? He glanced at the door at the far end of the room one last time.

"Well, I'm heading there now," he said. "I wouldn't stay here too long, though—Kai and I ran into Dr. Fredricksen after we left the first time and I think he doesn't want people back here."

"I'll keep that in mind, thanks," Lani said, scanning the bookshelf beside her.

"Bye."

Lani turned to wave goodbye, but he was already gone.

# 18

# Cameron

Cameron walked down the long hallway toward the library. Just like he could always find that room without really knowing where he was, he was always able to get back without getting lost. Before he turned the first corner, he looked back at the room to see if Lani had changed her mind, but the hallway was empty. A faint pit of disappointment formed in his stomach, and he tried to shake it off. It was probably growing anxiety about telling her about Thomas, which he now regretted doing.

Or maybe he didn't. He thought about how Lani's hand felt on his shoulder and how she had held herself back when he told her about Thomas. Considering how much she talked, it must have been hard for her not to say a lot during that conversation. Cameron had only told a handful of people about Thomas before—mostly professors when they asked why his grades were so bad—and he was usually met with awkward silences and pity, which he hated. But Lani had asked for Thomas's name.

As he turned another corner, Cameron realized why he couldn't stop thinking about his conversation with Lani. That had been the first time he could remember not feeling miserable after talking about his brother. He didn't feel better, really, but he definitely didn't feel worse. That thought alone was comforting whether it involved Lani or not—maybe there was a way for Thomas to stay with him without causing so much pain.

Cameron continued to walk through the winding hallways, taking his time in case Lani was trying to catch up with him. Suddenly, about halfway to the library, he heard a loud crash in front of him, followed by a scream. Cameron immediately ran toward the sound, turned a corner, and saw Allie on the ground with her back to him. A chandelier that had been hanging from the ceiling was on the floor, shattered into thousands of pieces that spread across the dark wooden floors.

"Are you okay?" Cameron asked Allie, moving toward her.

Allie gasped and jumped before turning around.

"Oh," she said. "Cameron. Sorry, I didn't see you. Um, yeah, I think so."

She started to lift herself off the floor, but Cameron put his hand up.

'Wait," he said. "There's broken glass everywhere. You'll cut yourself. Here."

He took a few steps toward her, feeling glass shards crunch under his shoes. Cameron held out his hands and pulled Allie to her feet.

"Were you cut?" he asked, scanning her arms and legs for blood.

She brushed her arm and shook her head.

"I don't think so," she said in a shaky voice.

Cameron looked at the broken chandelier on the floor, then up to see where it had fallen from. The ceiling was still intact, but all that was left was a small chain dangling from a hook.

"Is that all that was holding this?" he muttered. "No wonder it fell."

Cameron could hear Allie breathing hard next to him. He glanced over and saw that she had tears in her eyes.

"Are you hurt?" he asked.

She shook her head but didn't say anything. Her wide eyes were fixed on the broken chandelier on the floor.

"Oh, uh…" he said. "Do you…it's…it's okay."

He thought about his conversation with Lani and put his hand on Allie's shoulder.

"Do you…can I do anything?" he asked awkwardly.

Allie gulped and shook her head again. Cameron watched as she closed her eyes and took a series of deep breaths. After a few minutes, she opened her eyes again.

"I'm okay," she said quietly. "Thanks."

Cameron nodded and took his hand off her shoulder.

"So," he asked. "What happened?"

"I was trying to find that room that you and Kai told us about," Allie said. "And just after I passed that chandelier, I heard it crash behind me. I was so lucky," she finished in a breathy whisper.

"Yeah…" Cameron said hesitantly.

What were the odds that a chandelier would fall off the ceiling just as someone was walking through a hallway that was empty ninety-nine percent of the time?

"What were you doing before this?" Cameron asked.

Allie bit her cheek.

"Oh, I had my meeting with Dr. Fredricksen. It was pretty short. Then I got a sweater from my room and came here."

"How was the meeting?" Cameron asked, sensing a change

in her tone.

Allie began to fidget with the sleeves of her shirt.

"It was fine," she said. "He makes me...kind of uncomfort-able, though."

Cameron frowned.

"Did he do something?"

"No, nothing like that. He just...I don't know. It feels like he knows more about me than he should."

"What do you mean?"

He felt bad for making Allie look more and more uneasy, but this was important.

"Oh, he just...like, he knew some things that had happened recently, and I don't know how he would have found out about them."

"What stuff?"

"Nothing bad or serious or anything," Allie said, her cheeks turning pink. "Just stuff that no one else knows about. It's weird he brought it up."

Cameron didn't know what Allie was talking about, but it wasn't his place to pry more than he already had, and it didn't really matter anyway. Something was off about Dr. Fredricksen. And this house. Three accidents in a day? And to everyone except—

"Are you okay?"

Cameron looked up.

"Huh?" he asked.

Allie smiled.

"You were staring at the chandelier with, like, a really angry look on your face," she said.

"Oh. I'm fine. Just thinking."

Allie giggled.

"Well, just so you know, you look super pissed when you're just thinking."

Cameron smiled.

"Good to know."

"We should tell someone about this so they can clean up the glass," Allie said.

Cameron nodded.

"I was heading back anyway," he said. "You can go to the room if you want. Lani's still there."

Allie's eyes lit up.

"Oh, good," she said brightly. "Yeah, that sounds great. You don't mind finding someone to talk to about the mess?"

"Nope."

"Thank you!" Allie said, heading down the hallway. "I'll see you at lunch."

She disappeared around a corner. Cameron looked back at the shattered chandelier on the floor, then down the hallway in front of him. He didn't want to start getting paranoid, but everyone had been in an accident, or almost been in an accident, except him. Maybe it was all a coincidence, but... there was no way it could be. He slowly crept around the chandelier.

Once Cameron made it past the last remnants of broken glass, he continued to walk down the hallways until he reached the staircase where he had found Lani. He paused at the top and looked around. Lani said she had tripped, but the floor was even and there weren't any rugs or raised ledges. And why would she have been going down these stairs anyway? He looked down the steps. It was a miracle she hadn't been hurt more.

"Hey."

Cameron whirled around. Kai was standing a few feet away from him.

"Hey," he said back, his heart pounding.

"Sorry to scare you," Kai said.

"You didn't scare me," Cameron replied quickly. "This house is just…"

"Weird," Kai said. "Yeah. What are you doing?"

"Lani fell down these stairs yesterday," Cameron said.

Kai's jaw dropped.

"What? Was she okay? I mean, she seemed fine at dinner, I guess."

"She was okay," Cameron said. "She hurt her wrist, but I don't think it was broken or anything. I found her," he explained.

Kai looked down the staircase.

"I can't believe she didn't get a concussion or something," he said.

"She said she tripped," Cameron said.

Kai looked around.

"On what?"

"That's what I was thinking."

Kai paused.

"I mean, she could have tripped, I guess, if she was coming around the corner really fast. But…"

Kai stood in the center of the top of the staircase and spread his arms out. He could easily drape his hands over the railing on both sides.

"You'd think she'd be able to catch herself pretty quickly, too. I always put an arm out when I'm near a staircase."

"Yeah."

Another pause.

"Do you think she lied?" Kai asked.

Cameron shrugged.

"I don't know. Why would she?"

Kai didn't have an answer to that.

"I went back to that room," Cameron said, nodding toward the direction he had come from. "And on my way back here, I ran into Allie. She was going to the room and a chandelier fell off the ceiling and almost hit her."

"What?" Kai asked again, his eyes wide. "Seriously? Was she okay?"

"Yeah," Cameron nodded. "I ran into her right after it happened. She didn't even get cut, so she's fine."

The air was tense.

"So," Kai said slowly. "Lani falls down the stairs, then I lose my EpiPen, and then Allie almost gets hit by a chandelier."

Cameron was glad Kai was thinking it too.

"And the way Barbara was acting this morning," Cameron said, facing Kai. "Something's going on."

Kai nodded.

"Yeah," he muttered. "Yeah, that is all really weird."

"Allie also said her meeting was strange. Like, Dr. Fredricksen knew stuff about her he shouldn't have known," Cameron said.

Kai looked up, frowning.

"She said that?"

Cameron nodded.

"Why?"

"Well, I don't know what he told Allie, but the same thing happened to me."

"What did he say?"

Kai hesitated.

"My mom's been in the hospital a lot for the past year," he said. "We don't know why. Dr. Fredricksen brought it up in my meeting, but I never told anyone here about her. I mean, I talked about her in my essay, but it was for a different reason, so I never brought up the fact that she's sick."

"Could his office have called your family?" Cameron asked.

"Maybe," Kai said. "But he also—"

Kai looked upset—almost angry—for the first time since the retreat started. Cameron waited for him to speak again.

"He told me that the cure for my mom's disease was out there," Kai said dryly.

"What?"

Kai sighed.

"Yeah. Not, like, false encouragement or whatever, but like he actually knew how to treat her."

Kai's jaw was clenched.

"I tried to ask him more about it, but he wouldn't listen," Kai went on. "Then he started asking me all these ethical questions, like if I would do something to help my mom if it meant hurting other people."

"What did you say?" Cameron asked.

"I said no," Kai replied. "Even if my mom's cure is out there, I wouldn't knowingly hurt people to get it."

That surprised Cameron, but he didn't say anything.

"I don't think that was what he wanted to hear because he told me to let him know if I changed my mind. Not that he was telling the truth anyway. It was just a sick ethics test or something."

Kai looked at Cameron with a grimace.

"Anyway," he said. "There are ways he could have found out about my mom, I guess. But the way he talked about her and about me was just...too specific. He shouldn't have known all of that."

The two stood in silence for a minute.

"I'm sorry, man," Cameron said quietly. "About your mom."

"Thanks. She's strong. And if I win this thing, maybe we can figure out what's wrong after we cover the bills. Money talks, you know?"

Frank's face appeared in Cameron's head.

"Yeah."

So what do you think we should do?" Kai asked.

Cameron shook his head.

"I don't know. Do you really think someone is trying to hurt us? How do they think they could get away with it?"

"You're right, which might explain why no one's been seriously hurt yet," Kai said. "But we need to tell someone besides Dr. Fredricksen or Barbara. If I can find where they're keeping our phones, I can ask my roommates what they think about it. I don't think we should tell our parents yet. We don't want to freak anyone out for no reason, right?"

Cameron suspected Kai was thinking the same thing as him—if the retreat were called off, he'd lose his chance at winning the money.

"Yeah, we're probably overthinking it," Cameron said.

Kai nodded.

"Okay, so for now, just be careful," he said. "Do you know where Allie and Lani are?"

"They're both in that room," Cameron said, pointing down the hallway.

"I'll tell them everything," Kai said. "See you at lunch."

"Bye," Cameron said.

He watched Kai turn a corner and disappear. He winded down the hallways for a few more minutes until he came out near his bedroom. Trying to remember how to get there, he finally found his way to the library and felt his jaw go slack as he entered. The room was bigger than his parent's entire house. Every inch of the walls, except for a few windows that allowed rays of sunshine to pour across the floor, were lined with books. Three circular tables were placed in the center of the room, and five or six cushioned chairs were fixed near the windows. He was the only one here, and the room was completely quiet.

Cameron began to look around for the five books he was going to skim through. After browsing through the history section, he pulled a large hardcover about ancient Egypt and a lighter book about ancient Greece off the shelves. He brought both to a chair at the far side of the room that overlooked a side of the house he had never seen before. There was a dense forest outside, so thick he couldn't see more than a few feet into it, even with the sun shining brightly outside.

Cameron flipped through both books, pausing to read captions of images that looked interesting and jotting down notes about what he learned. When he finished with the two history books, he put them away and started searching for more. A different corner of the room caught his eye. Light from somewhere, maybe a lamp, was bouncing off the books and he couldn't help but go over and check them out.

There was nothing written on any of the spines in this section, which he thought was strange. He pulled one out and read the title.

*Grief Is an Ocean, and I Am Swallowed Up in It.*

Cameron gripped the book tightly, too afraid to open it. Grief was a topic he didn't intentionally seek out. He checked again to make sure he was still alone in the library and, unable to help himself, started flipping through the pages. It seemed to be a basic collection of poetry from people he had never heard of. He stopped on one page and started to read the poem.

*I wear my grief like a puffer on a summer day*
  *it wears me*
  *like a freshly skinned fur coat*

Cameron stopped and closed the book. He couldn't do this. Not here. He put the book back on the shelf and pulled out another one. It was a collection of essays on grief. He put it back and opened another. Someone's story of losing their father. He put it back and stepped away from the bookshelf. Everything here must be on the same topic. Who has an entire bookshelf dedicated to dealing with the loss of a loved one? He stared at the books for another minute, a mix of fear and curiosity swirling around his stomach.

"Hi, Cameron!"

Recognizing Lani's voice, Cameron turned around.

"Hey," he said.

"Wow, this is incredible," Lani said, looking around. "Man, to be rich, am I right?"

Cameron was actually happy to see her and tried to smile, but Thomas was fresh in his mind again and blocking all other thoughts. Lani walked over to him.

"How many books have you looked through so far?" she asked.

"Uh, just two."

"Any good ones?"

"History. So yeah."

Lani nodded and scanned the bookshelf in front of them.

"Anything here look interesting?"

Before Cameron could think of something to say to get her away from the shelf, she pulled a book down. It was the collection of poems about grief he had glanced through first. She opened the front cover and read the introduction. Her face turned from playful to serious. Great, Cameron thought. She was probably going to tell him grief was normal and he needed to talk about it more and—

"I'd love to read something about feminism," Lani said, closing the book and putting it back on the shelf.

"I've been trying to learn more about gender equality and I bet there are a lot of good books here about it," she said cheerfully. "I'm going to look over there."

She pointed to the wall closest to the doorway and left Cameron alone. He stared at her as she walked away and felt something warm in his chest. It was obvious she knew what she was doing, and he appreciated it. Cameron hesitated, then reached for the poetry book again and took it with him to the chair he had been reading in earlier. He began to browse the pages, taking in each line slowly. After a few minutes, he heard Lani next to him.

"Mind if I sit here?" she asked, pointing to the plush chair next to his.

"Go ahead."

She placed two books on the table and sat down to read the third one in her hands. They both read quietly and listened as a rainstorm came in to replace the sunshine, sending drops tapping on the windows. After finishing a particularly impactful page, Cameron cleared his throat quietly. It was starting to close up like it always did before he cried, and he didn't want to do this in front of anyone. He could see Lani glance at him out of the corner of his eye, but he avoided her gaze and turned his head in the other direction. Lani didn't say anything, so he looked at the ceiling and took some deep breaths, cursing at himself.

Cameron peeked at Lani again. Her eyebrows were furrowed and her eyes were darting back and forth quickly. The urge to tell her everything he was feeling came over him, which surprised him enough to eradicate his oncoming tears. He barely knew Lani, but this was the first time he had felt like talking about Thomas to anyone but Greta, and he couldn't truly explain what he was feeling to his younger sister. Cameron looked out the window. Lani could always tell him she didn't want to talk, and he could always stop talking when he wanted to. Thomas was outgoing too, way more than Cameron was, and he would have probably been friends with Lani. Was this his way of telling Cameron to bring it up more? Maybe he—

"Do you want to talk about it?"

Lani's soft voice shook Cameron from his thoughts.

"You don't have to," she said quickly. "You just seem like..."

She trailed off, but he knew what she meant. Cameron closed his book and Lani closed hers. He hesitated for a moment but felt himself get calmer as Lani looked at him.

"I haven't...really talked about it a lot since it happened," Cameron said slowly. "I think I told you that. I thought I would get over it, but it's been two years and I feel like...I can't move on."

"You haven't talked to anyone?"

"Not really. Not since the hospital."

Lani leaned back in her chair.

"Well," she said. "I'm here and we have another hour until lunch."

She smiled.

"Tell me as much as you want to tell me."

Cameron smiled back and took a deep breath. He started to tell Lani about the day he and Thomas had gone hiking. He felt himself speaking cautiously at first, like his throat didn't want him to reveal the details, but after a few minutes, he couldn't slow down. It felt like the day had been trapped in his mind for the past two years and it was finally able to breathe. Lani listened attentively but quietly. She only interjected with a gasp when Cameron showed her the scars on his forearm.

"As soon as my mom and dad heard about what happened, I could tell they thought it was my fault," he said, remembering the looks on his parents' faces in the hospital. "You have to talk to a psychiatrist when something like this happens, and I could tell he knew my parents blamed me too. He tried to talk to them about it, but he couldn't change their minds."

Cameron paused and looked up at Lani. Her eyes were watery, but she didn't say anything.

"Hey," Cameron said. "I'm sorry, I can stop."

Lani shook her head.

"No," she said with a sniff. "No, I'm sorry. I'm a crier. It's...oh my god, Cameron, that's just so horrible. And you've been walking around with this on your shoulders for the past two years without any help?"

She wiped her eyes with her sleeve.

"I can't believe you're still here."

"Yeah, well, I haven't made a lot of great decisions since then."

He remembered the day he first started placing bets. The

adrenaline was the first thing since Thomas's death that made him feel anything other than numb.

"Whatever you've done, you're here. You've made it this far."

Cameron thought of Frank again. He might not make it much further.

"I'm sorry," Lani said. "Please finish. If you want."

"That's pretty much it," Cameron said. "I don't really remember the rest of that month, honestly. And my life since then has been...pretty uneventful."

They sat in silence for a few seconds.

"I don't know what to say," Lani whispered. "I can't imagine losing someone like that. They're in your life for so long, and all of a sudden they aren't."

Cameron nodded.

"It's not even just losing who they are to you," he said. "It's losing who they could have been. Whenever I thought about my future, he was always in it. And now I feel like I have to relive that moment again and again because my brain keeps forgetting that he isn't here anymore, and I have to remind it whenever I pull out my phone to text him or think about inviting him somewhere. It's like...constantly pouring salt on a cut every time it starts to heal."

Cameron felt himself choking up, and he wanted to quit talking, but he also didn't ever want to stop.

"I feel like I didn't enjoy our time together as much as I should have," he said.

He looked at the ceiling again and felt Lani next to him. Neither of them said anything for a long time.

# 19

## Allie

"I still think we should talk to Barbara," Allie said.

Kai had arrived about 20 minutes after Lani left the room and told Allie about his strange meeting with Dr. Fredricksen. He didn't share any details, but he looked as uncomfortable as Allie had felt during her meeting when he described how the professor knew more about his life than he should have. Allie shared that the same happened to her, but she didn't mention that Dr. Fredricksen had known about her abortion or that he had mentioned being able to help her locate her father.

Kai shook his head at her suggestion.

"I don't think that's a good idea," he said. "We don't know if she's involved or not."

"Still," Allie said, folding her arms against her chest. "I don't even know if this is worth it anymore."

Kai leaned against the wall.

"Well, we don't want to make a big deal over nothing," he said. "Let's just wait it out. We're probably being paranoid because we all want to win the prize money."

The two made eye contact for a second before Kai looked

away.

"Or something," he muttered.

Allie sighed.

"Maybe you're right," she said. "It's just been a weird few days."

Kai smiled at her, and her stomach settled a little bit. He had a calming presence that Allie liked. She turned back to the door on the far side of the room. She had noticed Lani staring at it before she left for the library and had been getting progressively more curious about it during her time in the room. She glanced at Kai, who was now absorbed in a book near the front of the room, and walked over to the door. She noticed a cool breeze near her ankles as she approached and wondered if it led outside.

Allie reached for the door handle, and an image of someone came into her mind more clearly than any dream she had ever had. It was a man with his arms outstretched toward her, as if he was beckoning her to come forward into his arms. Even though his face was blurred, Allie knew exactly who it was—her dad. He was here, in this room, and although she knew practically nothing about him or why he left when she was a baby, he was ready to embrace Allie and become a solid component of the life she had to restart.

Allie whirled around, fully expecting to see her dad in the room with them, but as she turned, the vision disappeared. The room was empty except for her and Kai.

"You okay?" Kai asked.

Allie didn't respond, her chest rising and falling slowly.

"Hey, are you okay?" Kai asked, moving toward her.

"Yeah," Allie finally said. "Yeah, I—"

She looked around the room again, still half expecting to

see her dad. She hadn't thought about him much for most of her life, but she had started trying to find him after her mom died. She quickly realized how hard it was to track someone down without professional help and dismissed the idea when a private investigator quoted her a thousand-dollar fee. But she had found her father at the forefront of her thoughts since breaking up with Michael and was desperately curious to at least know who he was and why he had left. Right now, she had no family and no friends. Her dad, if he was still alive, was her only real connection in the world.

"Did you see something?"

Kai's question broke Allie out of her thoughts.

"What?" she asked.

"Did you see something?" he repeated.

"I—how did you know?"

"It happened to me too," Kai said. "When I was in here yesterday. I think Cameron also saw something, but I could be wrong about that."

Allie stared at Kai. He seemed so calm about the fact that they were apparently all having visions in this room. She shook her head, trying to shake off the jittery feeling still buzzing through her.

"So, what does that mean?" she asked.

Kai gave a small shrug and shook his head.

"I don't know," he said. "What did you see?"

Allie hesitated, but Kai's eyes seemed kind.

"My dad," she said. "He left me and my mom when I was a baby, so I've never tried to find him. But a few things, uh, changed in my life recently, and I've been thinking about him a lot. Finding him, I mean."

Kai nodded as she spoke.

"Hm," he said, looking at the door.

"What did you see?" Allie asked.

Now it was his turn to look uncomfortable.

"Uh, my mom. She's been sick for a while, and I saw this image of her, like, better."

"Oh. I'm sorry."

Kai smiled and gave Allie a small nod.

"Thanks. It'll be okay. She's tough."

"I'm sure. You seem like a really tough person, too."

Kai laughed and Allie felt her cheeks get hot. This was why she didn't say things without thinking.

"I meant that in a good way," she said quickly. "Like, you always seem so calm and collected. You're really nice, though, too. I didn't mean you were mean or anything."

Kai laughed again.

"I know what you meant," he said. "Thanks. I am a lot like her."

"Are you guys close?"

"Yeah. We went through kind of a rough patch when I came out, but she came around. She's been great, actually, so we've gotten a lot closer over the past few years."

"Oh. Are you...?"

"Oh, yeah, I'm gay. I thought I mentioned it already. I must have told Cameron."

"Okay, cool," Allie said. "But, um..."

"What?"

"Well...please don't tell her I said anything, but you might want to casually mention that to Lani," Allie said with a small smile. "She kind of has a crush on you."

Kai blushed and ran his fingers through his hair.

"Ah, okay," he said. "Yeah, I'll see if I can throw it out.

That's nice of her to think that."

Allie smiled. Kai had a way of never making someone feel uncomfortable for what they said. At the same time, though, her stomach twisted. She thought of all the times she hadn't spoken up when Michael or his parents talked about the LGBTQ community or the kinds of laws they wished the country would pass. She hadn't agreed to any of those things, exactly, but she hadn't stood up against them either.

"Anyway," Allie said, trying to push her guilt away. "I think we might be glossing over how weird it is that everyone is having visions about their parents when they go near that door."

"Yeah..." Kai said. "I really...don't know what to say about that."

He stared at the door but didn't move toward it. Allie was too afraid to head that direction again herself. Her vision hadn't been scary, but she didn't like feeling so out of control of her thoughts.

"I'm going to try to find where they're keeping our phones," Kai said. "After lunch. I'll text my roommates and see if they think the situation is as weird as we do."

"Shouldn't you tell your dad too?"

Kai looked away.

"I don't want to worry him if it's nothing," he said. "And I don't want him to—"

He stopped himself.

"It should be fine," he said. "We just need to be careful. Maybe we should start sticking together more."

Allie nodded. Everything seemed much more concerning than Kai was saying it was, and even he looked like he didn't believe himself when he said not to worry. But maybe she was thinking for him—he didn't seem like the type of guy to let people make bad decisions if he had a say in it. The thought made her relax a little bit.

"I think it's almost lunchtime," Kai said.

"Oh, yeah," Allie said. "We should go then?"

Kai was looking longingly at the strange door again.

"Kai?"

That seemed to snap him out of his trance.

"Yeah," he said, looking like he was in some sort of daze. "Yeah, let's go."

Allie let out a small sigh of relief. She was afraid he was going to want to stay and she'd have to go back by herself. She was tired of being in this room and house, and she was glad for the company whenever she could get it. She quickly walked toward the doorway leading back to the hallway and turned around, waiting until Kai came outside and closed the door. It almost turned invisible as it blended back into the mural on the wall.

The two walked silently down the winding hallways. Allie glanced at Kai a few times, wanting him to say more reassuring things about the retreat. But he just stared straight ahead and looked deep in thought until they turned a corner.

"Oh," Allie said. "They cleaned it up already."

They had reached the hallway where the chandelier had almost fallen on her. Allie's heart started to pound again at the memory of it. Hearing the terrifying crash behind her and realizing in a split second that she had narrowly avoided a horrible injury had been much scarier than she had admitted to Cameron.

"This is where the chandelier was?" Kai asked.

Allie nodded. The floor was now bare, and there wasn't a

speck of broken glass to be seen on the floor. She looked up at the ceiling, which now had a gaping but tidy hole.

"That was fast," Kai said.

"Yeah, Cameron must have told someone," Allie said. "I wonder who did it, though. I haven't seen a single housekeeper here."

"Yeah, same," Kai said.

He stared at the ceiling for a few seconds.

"Anyway," Allie said, starting to walk forward again.

Kai seemed to snap out of another trance and began walking next to Allie, the same concerned expression on his face. She was dying to know what he was thinking about. After winding through the hallways, they finally passed their rooms and walked downstairs to the dining room. It was empty, but the table was already prepared for them. Allie sat down in her usual seat and Kai sat down across from her.

"It's a few minutes past," he said, checking his watch. "Cameron and Lani are late."

He seemed concerned.

"I'm sure they're fine," Allie said. "Lani loves to read, so she probably got caught up in a romance novel in the library."

Kai didn't say anything and stared at the door intently. Allie sat there, waiting for the food to come out, but no one else entered the room. The air felt tense. She looked down at her lap and started picking at her thumbnail.

"Sorry, I'm being rude," Kai said, still watching the door. "I'm just...I dunno, with so much weird stuff happening, I don't know if—"

Just then, Cameron walked into the dining room, followed by Lani. Kai's expression changed from serious to relieved.

"Hey," he said brightly.

Cameron smiled at Kai and Lani waved at Allie. The two walked to the table and sat down.

"Sorry we're late," Lani said. "We were talking and lost track of time."

Cameron didn't say anything, but Allie thought he looked a little less grumpy than he usually did. Immediately, four servers came into the room and placed trays of sandwiches on the table.

"Hey," Kai said quickly to the server closest to him. "Do any of you know where they're keeping our phones?"

The server, an older-looking man, looked surprised at the question. He hesitated for a second, but then quickly left the room with the rest of the servers without saying a word. Kai watched him leave with a small frown. He turned back to the group.

"Was I rude?" he asked.

Lani shook her head. She looked confused as well.

"No, that was weird," she said.

Kai looked back at the door but didn't say anything else.

"Why do you want to find our phones?" Lani asked.

Kai looked around the room and lowered his voice.

"I'm going to text my roommates and ask if they've heard anything about the professor or the contest," he said.

Lani looked a little surprised but nodded.

"Yeah, I think that's a good idea," she said. "I don't think you should ask people where the phones are, though."

"Why?"

"Well, if something is going on and they don't want us to find them, they'll just get rid of them or something, right? I would try to find them on your own without letting anyone know."

"Yeah, good point," Kai said. "I'll look for them after this."

Everyone ate their food quietly for a few minutes.

"Oh, I didn't even think to ask," Lani said suddenly. "How did your meetings go?"

Allie and Kai looked at each other.

"What?" Lani asked.

"They were kind of weird," Kai said.

"How so?"

"He mentioned things about both of us that he shouldn't know," Kai said. "At least, I don't know how he found out about them."

Lani looked between Kai and Allie quizzically.

"Like what kind of stuff?" she asked.

Kai made eye contact with Allie again and cleared his throat.

"Uh, for me, it was about my mom. She's in the hospital and we don't know why. And not only did he know about that, which he shouldn't have, he told me that he knows how to find her cure."

"What?" Lani said. "Why would he...then what happened?"

"Then he asked if I'd be willing to, like, hurt other people or something if I could get access to it? I don't know what he meant by that. I said no, and he ended the meeting."

Kai looked upset for the first time since Allie had met him. Lani huffed.

"What a dick move," she said angrily. "Why would he lie about something like that? Is that some kind of sick joke?"

"Maybe he wasn't lying," Kai shrugged. "But I don't know what he meant by hurting people. And I don't want to know."

He sighed and looked at Allie again. He seemed to remember something and looked back and Lani.

"Oh, yeah, and he knew I'm gay, which was weird because I

never told him," he said casually.

Lani didn't seem as disappointed as Allie thought she would be. Or maybe she was really good at hiding it.

"Oh, you never mentioned that," Lani said. "That is a weird thing for him to know, though, if you had never talked about it."

"What did he say about you, Allie?" Cameron asked.

"He knew I had an abortion a few days ago."

Allie didn't know why she said it, but she didn't regret the outburst. After years of hiding parts of who she was and how she felt from Michael and his family, she felt a small thrill in sharing what would have been an outrageously scandalous secret with two people who were practically strangers.

Kai and Cameron both stared at her, their wide eyes darting to her stomach, then back at her face. They didn't seem upset or shocked—just a little uncomfortable.

"Are you okay?" Kai asked.

"Shouldn't you be, like, lying down?" Cameron asked at the same time.

Allie looked at Lani, who was offering one of her comforting smiles. Allie smiled back at all of them.

"I'm okay," she said. "Thanks. It's been a few days, and the recovery hasn't been too bad, all things considered. I just get bad cramps every so often, but they're starting to go away."

The surprise on Kai's face slowly left and was replaced with concern.

"Did you tell anyone about it?" he asked.

Allie shook her head.

"Just Lani yesterday."

Everyone looked at Lani.

"I didn't tell him," she said incredulously.

"How could he possibly know that?" Kai asked. "Those would be private medical records."

"Yeah," Allie said, biting her lip.

It was so weird. She felt a sudden urge to jump through the window and run down the road.

"He also, um, mentioned my dad," Allie said. "He left us when I was a baby, and I've thought about him a lot since my mom died. Dr. Fredricksen told me he knows where my dad is if I want to find him."

Everyone was looking at her expectantly.

"He didn't ask if I was okay with, like, hurting people or whatever to find him," she said to Kai. "But he did say something about the 'greater good.' I can't remember exactly what, but something to do with moving humanity forward at a faster pace than it is now. Something like that."

No one said anything.

"Is this guy, like, a supervillain who wants to take over the world?" Cameron asked.

Allie knew he was joking, but she didn't laugh.

"I'll do some research on him when I find our phones," Kai said.

They all went back to eating, but Allie had lost her appetite. Why didn't they seem more concerned about this? Why was no one saying they should all walk out the door right now? She glanced at Kai, who was working his way through his sandwich. If his mom was in the hospital for some mysterious illness, her medical bills were probably racking up. She wondered if he was here for the money more than anything. If that were true, going home early would ruin everything for him. She glanced over at Cameron and Lani, and wondered what they could need the money for so desperately that they were willing to stay too.

# 20

## Kai

"I'm going to go look for our phones," Kai said, getting up from the table. "I'll let you know if I find anything."

He waved goodbye to Cameron, Lani, and Allie, who were still finishing their lunch, and left the room. He started to wander down the main hallway on the ground floor, hoping he wouldn't run into anyone. The house was eerily quiet and seemed colder than usual. He shivered and wished he had put on a warmer sweater. Kai paused outside the first closed door he came across. He put his hand on the doorknob and slowly turned it. His heart started to beat quickly and he had to remind himself that he wasn't doing anything wrong. The professor said they could explore if they wanted to.

The room was completely empty except for a couple of tables and chairs on the far side near a window. He looked around for a few minutes, but there weren't any desks or drawers to keep anything hidden. He left the room and searched in the next one down the hall.

Nothing. He went into the next room. Nothing.

Kai paused outside the fourth room in the hallway, starting

to feel stupid for thinking he could find their phones. This was literally a mansion—they could be anywhere. He opened the door and stepped inside. This room was lined with book-shelves, and propped up at the far end was a long wooden table. He quickly walked over and saw four phones plugged into chargers sitting neatly in the middle.

Kai couldn't believe it. He let out a small laugh, then quickly glanced over his shoulder to make sure no one had come in behind him. Seeing that he was alone, he grabbed his phone and switched the screen on. There were no new notifications on the lock screen, which he assumed meant that someone was checking their phones regularly for emergencies as they had promised. The sense of dread that had been compounding inside of him for the past two days began to leave. If something had happened to his mom, they would have told him.

He checked his texts anyway. There was a reply from his dad after he had told him his phone would be taken away.

*Sounds good. I'll let you know if we have any updates on mom. She is doing well today. Good luck, I know you'll do great.*

He had another one from that morning from Mateo.

*How's the writing thing going?*

Kai began typing a message to Mateo, telling him about some of the weird things that had been happening and asking him to look into Dr. Fredricksen. But when he tried to send the text, an error message popped up with an angry red exclamation point.

*Message not sent.*

Kai stared at the screen. He had no service. How had the other texts gotten through? They had been able to send messages on the first day just fine. There was no Wi-Fi signal on his screen either, but that would be the only other way.

Were they turning the internet on and off throughout the day? Disappointed, Kai realized he couldn't look up any information about the professor either. He placed his phone back on the table as he had found it. Other than confirming that his mom was okay, this had been a pointless endeavor.

Kai crept out of the room, closed the door, and started to head toward the library. A few seconds later, Barbara came out of another room in front of him.

"Oh," she said, immediately looking flustered. "Hello, Kai."

"Hi," Kai said.

He felt uneasy too.

"Has everything been satisfactory since this morning?" she asked.

Kai started to nod but stopped himself.

"Actually," he said. "I'm sure you heard because it's been cleaned up, but a chandelier almost fell on Allie today."

Barbara's eyes widened. Kai watched as she quickly tried to compose herself.

"Yes, yes, I heard," she stammered. "I am so glad she wasn't hurt. This old house is falling apart."

She forced a laugh.

"Barbara, is there...something you want to tell us?" Kai asked carefully.

She looked at him for a few seconds without saying anything.

"I—" she started. "I don't—I don't know what's going on either. I have a suspicion, maybe, but I know nothing more than you."

"What does that mean?" Kai asked quickly. "What suspicion?"

Barbara looked worried and stared at Kai like he was her grandson. At least, she reminded him of his grandma. Strict, but kind. Worried about his decisions in a loving way. But the no-nonsense look she had worn when he first arrived wasn't there anymore. Right now, she looked tired and even a little afraid. Kai was frustrated that she wasn't being more honest, but he felt bad for her.

"Barbara, are you okay?" he asked.

She tilted her head slightly and gave him a small but brief smile before placing a hand on his arm.

"Please, I can't say anything more right now," she whispered. "It's too dangerous for all of us. Be careful and stick together."

Without letting Kai say another word, Barbara took off down the hall. Kai stared at her as she left, bewildered at her behavior. If she thought something was going on, why wouldn't she tell him? What did she think? He shivered but tried to calm himself down, assuming that if whatever was going on was really bad, she would do something about it.

Kai waited until Barbara had disappeared before heading in the other direction. He looked at his surroundings carefully so he wouldn't forget where the phones were, planning to return later that day to check for a signal again. When Kai reached the entryway, he paused by the front door. He looked around and waited a few seconds for any sounds, but the house was completely empty. He grabbed the giant brass doorknob and turned it.

It was locked. Kai wrestled with the doorknob for a few seconds, but it wouldn't turn at all. He scanned the door for a lock he might have missed but saw nothing except a large, old-fashioned-looking keyhole. He understood locking the front door to outsiders, but why couldn't it be unlocked by anyone inside without a key?

Kai looked down the hallway to his right. If he walked far enough along, he had to reach another door that led outside. A house this big wouldn't only have one door in and out. He walked quickly in that direction, passing through the drawing room where they had all met each other on the first day, then through another small office, and then into another room. This one was large but mostly empty except for a couple of couches on the far side in front of a window overlooking the backyard. There was a door in front of Kai that looked like it would continue to lead him toward the far side of the house. It was closed, and when Kai tried to turn its handle, he found it locked as well.

Kai quickly walked to the couches on the far side of the room. The window had a latch, which he grabbed and tried to turn. It wouldn't budge. He pulled and twisted as hard as he could, but he couldn't get it to move. Finally, Kai noticed a thin line of what looked like uneven metal around the latch and the window frame. The window had been welded shut. Kai stepped back, an uneasy feeling seeping over him. He began making his way back to the front door, stopping in every room along the way to check the windows. They were all welded, sealed shut, or locked.

When he made it back to the front door, Kai raced up the staircase and bounded to the first window he saw, almost running his nose into it. He pulled at the handle to no avail and looked outside through the glass, which he now noticed was oddly thick. He could check every door and window in the house, but he knew what he would find.

They were trapped.

# 21

# Lani

Lani sat down nervously as Dr. Fredricksen rustled some papers on his desk in front of her. After everything that had happened so far during the retreat she didn't want to be alone with him, but she didn't really have a choice. Allie admitting that he had known about her abortion sent her nerves to a new dimension and made everything seem significantly scarier. To know a few details about someone's family life was one thing— to access private medical information was another. How could he have known that? That was the kind of privilege that even money couldn't get you.

Lani quietly took a deep breath and put on a cheery smile. She had to remove everything—his conversations with Kai and Allie, being pushed down the stairs, the weird vision she had in that room—from her mind. She was still part of a competition that she needed to win. If she wanted any sort of a future, she needed to dazzle Dr. Fredricksen during this meeting and prove that she deserved to win the grant. She also wasn't sure how seriously he was taking the retreat himself considering how little time they had spent with him, so it was clear that every moment with him needed to count.

Dr. Fredricksen looked up and mirrored Lani's smile.

"How are you, Lani?" he asked.

He seemed so normal at this moment. Even kind. She wondered if they had all been overreacting about him from the stress of the competition. Maybe she could use that to her advantage.

"I'm doing well, thank you," she replied politely. "And yourself?"

The professor put the tips of his fingers together and stared down at Lani through his wire-rimmed glasses.

"I have to admit, things have been rather complicated since you all arrived," he said.

He said it matter-of-factly, not like he was upset or accusing Lani of anything, but casually speaking the truth.

"Oh?" was all Lani could think to say.

Dr. Fredricksen sighed.

"Yes. I had a purpose, bringing you here, of course, but things don't always go as you hope they will."

He looked wearied, and Lani felt a little sorry for him. She quickly straightened out her thoughts. *Don't get too comfortable. Make him think you like him, but remember that he might be a psychopath.*

"I know," she said sympathetically. "That's how life goes sometimes. But you just have to keep pushing on with the cards you've been dealt, right?"

Dr. Fredricksen looked up at her and tilted his head slightly.

"Yes, I do suppose that is how your life has been," he said.

Lani paused, the encouraging smile still on her face.

"I'm sorry?" she asked, trying her best to sound polite.

"A father who gambles and a mother who drinks," he said

casually. "Working away at your college fund until there's nothing left. It's a shame, really. Some people shouldn't be trusted with the power of being parents."

He shrugged at Lani like he was expecting her to laugh along at her bad luck. Instead, she stared at him blankly. Her insides twisted the way they only did when she was talking about her parents, which rarely happened because she rarely brought them up. She had mentioned them in her application essay so she figured this was coming, but she still didn't want to talk about it.

"Yeah," she said, forcing a smile. "It's been rough. But I've tried my best to get to where I am today, and I think it speaks for my character. I really try to make the most of everything and not let it drag me down."

*Like I would make the most of $100,000.*

The professor stared at her for a few moments like he was trying to read her mind. Could he read her mind? No, that was silly.

"Yes, you are very...*vulnerable* when you need to be."

The way he said the word made the back of Lani's neck tingle.

"Um, yes," she said. "I think that's an important trait."

Dr. Fredricksen nodded thoughtfully.

"The need to be liked can make us quite desperate," he said. "I've seen many people do things they later regretted in the pursuit of admiration."

Lani's stomach curled again but in a different way. Did he know?

"I've seen people make decisions that change their lives forever," he continued. "Choices that are later used against them."

It felt like someone had poured a bucket of ice water down

her back, but Lani tried to call his bluff.

"Yeah," she said. "It's pretty unfair that people like to take advantage of the naivety of others, isn't it?"

She stared him down, pushing past the feeling of nausea and daring him to address the apparent elephant in the room. If he already knew, he might as well say it.

Dr. Fredricksen raised his eyebrows slightly.

"It is unfair," he said. "It is even more unfair when they use it against you. I find it repulsive."

Lani didn't answer, unable to tell if he was on her side. The professor went on.

"In everything, we must strive for the greater good," he said. "Blackmail can be useful, but it is often a cheap way to receive a small profit. Ultimately unrewarding. Unoriginal."

He looked at Lani directly.

"Yes, I know," he said calmly. "I know about the photos and the person who is using them against you."

Lani's heart began to pound so hard it hurt her chest. He was going to kick her out of the retreat.

"Look, I didn't think it through," Lani started to explain. "I never thought he would—"

Dr. Fredricksen cut her off by holding his hand in the air.

"I know," he said. "I remember what it was like to be in love with someone and want to make them happy. I am not here to reprimand you for your choices."

Lani stayed silent, her heartbeat slowing slightly.

"I am here to tell you that I can find this person," he said, looking directly at her. "And I can expose them before any harm comes to you."

Lani gaped at him. Gone were all attempts to appear professional and poised.

"What do you mean?" she asked quickly. "You know who it is?"

"No," Dr. Fredricksen said. "But I do know how to find out."

He paused and let his words hover in the air. Lani waited a few seconds but couldn't stand the silence any longer.

"How?" she asked.

The professor looked at Lani introspectively like he was deciding whether or not to tell her. She saw him glance at her hands, which were gripping the front of the table so tightly that her knuckles had turned white. After a few moments, he leaned back in his chair.

"There is a new technology," he said softly. "One that can track any phone in the world and match it to any recipient almost instantly."

Lani stared at him, confused.

"I—how?" she asked.

"The camera lens, face scanning, other identification markers," he said quickly, waving his hand like it wasn't important. "I believe it will be quite accurate. Particularly for finding people who don't want to be found."

Lani's heart was pounding. She had no idea this kind of technology existed, but it sounded like it was exactly what she needed.

"Okay," she said. "Well, um, can you use it? Can I use it? Do you think it will work?"

"Would you?" Dr. Fredricksen asked, looking intently at Lani. "Would you use it?"

"Of course. I—it would really help if I could find this person. Not just help, it could literally save me from getting kicked out of school."

"And you would be comfortable with the repercussions?"

Lani frowned. She had been so excited about the idea of catching the creep that she hadn't bothered to think about how they would be doing it.

"Um…is it illegal?" she asked. "Because technology like that feels like a huge invasion of privacy. For everyone. And it seems like it could be dangerous."

Dr. Fredricksen stood up and turned around so that his back was facing Lani.

"This technology has not been made available to the… general public," he said. "You would be one of the first to use it."

"What? How is that possible?"

"So answer me again," the professor said, ignoring her question and turning to face her. "Would you use it?"

Lani thought about what the world would be like if anyone could be tracked in an instant. There could be some good done, like finding murderers and people who have run away. But if technology like that got into the wrong hands…she thought of all the women with jealous boyfriends. Women and children in hiding. World leaders. She shook her head.

"No," she said quietly. "I don't think it would be a good idea."

Dr. Fredricksen looked slightly disappointed, and Lani wondered why. He had no stake in her blackmailer saga.

"This technology could help millions," he said.

"Yeah, and it could hurt millions too," Lani said. "It sounds like the kind of thing that only rich people would have access to anyway."

Dr. Fredricksen sat back down.

"I see."

Lani had a sudden urge to apologize to him. She didn't want

him to be mad at her. Was this going to hurt her chances of winning the prize? She could still fix this mess with the money.

"That will be all, Lani."

Lani didn't stand up.

"But, we didn't talk about my writing at all," she said hesitantly.

"I learned everything I need to know about you in this conversation," he said.

The kindness had left his eyes.

"I'm sorry if I did something wrong," Lani said. "But I can find other ways to deal with the guy blackmailing me. If I win the prize—"

She was desperate and it had slipped out. She held her breath, waiting for him to respond.

"The prize," Dr. Fredricksen said almost absentmindedly. "Yes, there is quite a prize."

He looked up at Lani.

"I must be honest with you, though," he said. "I don't know if you have what it takes to win."

It felt like he had slapped her.

"What do you mean?" she asked, feeling her eyes start to burn. "You've barely looked at our writing at all. How are you even going to judge us?"

Dr. Fredricksen stared down at Lani, looking deadly serious.

"This competition is about so much more than writing," he said quietly. "It is about your character, your strengths, and your weaknesses. It is about who you are and, most importantly, it is about what you are willing to do to become someone even greater. It is about the value you are willing or not willing to bring to the world."

There was a glint in his eyes.

"Our society demands greatness, Lani," he went on. "And greatness requires sacrifice. I'm afraid you aren't capable of making that sacrifice."

The hurt she had felt was replaced with indignation.

"You don't get to tell me what I'm capable of," she said with a huff. "You think I'm weak because I'm not cool with creating a surveillance state? Fine. But I am a good writer, and I deserve to win the prize. Those two things have nothing to do with each other."

To her surprise, Dr. Fredricksen smiled.

"I'm afraid they have everything to do with each other," he said.

The two sat in silence for a few minutes until Lani resigned herself to the fact that the meeting was over. She stood up and walked to the door, but paused as another thought nagged at her brain.

"That technology you talked about," she said, turning around. "Why would you have access to something like that?"

"In time, you may understand," Dr. Fredricksen said. "We will see. It all depends on how the rest of the day goes."

The only thing left on the day's agenda was his meeting with Cameron. Lani bit her cheek and nodded. She put on a smile again, just in case.

"Thank you for your time," she said.

"You don't have to pretend not to despise me right now," Dr. Fredricksen said. "Whatever happens, I do admire your directness."

Lani didn't say anything back and closed the door behind her. She stood there for a few minutes, fighting back tears. How unfair was it for him to decide in a short conversation that she wasn't going to win? Why would he tell her that? What was the point of her being here any longer? She began to walk to her room, wondering if she should go home early or stay for the rest of the retreat. No, she should stay. This could all be a test. Maybe she still had a chance.

Lani flopped down on her bed when she reached her room and let herself cry for a few minutes. Even if Dr. Fredricksen had been bluffing or testing her, the hope she felt going into this retreat was quickly dwindling. After letting herself wallow in her embarrassment, she threw some water on her face and took a deep breath. She wasn't going to let that meeting ruin the rest of her time here. She shivered, surprised at how cold her room felt. Outside, the sun was shining through the trees, so she tried to open the window to let some warm air inside. It wouldn't budge, no matter how much she twisted and turned the handle.

"That's annoying," she muttered.

She could really use some fresh air, and she realized she hadn't been outside since first arriving here. That's probably why she felt so upset right now. Lani glanced down at the garden outside and decided to take a walk. Just as she reached the bottom of the staircase, she saw Cameron heading toward the classroom where she had finished her meeting a few minutes earlier.

"Hey!" she called.

He turned around and his sulky face brightened when he saw her.

"Hey," he said. "How was your meeting?"

"Oh, it was fine," she lied.

He raised his eyebrows.

"Well, no, it wasn't great," Lani admitted. "He basically said I have no chance at winning this. But whatever, no big deal."

"What? He said that?"

Lani nodded, smiling like she thought it was a joke.

"That's rude," Cameron said, frowning. "And we're only a couple of days in. It's not fair to judge you so quickly."

Lani shrugged.

"Nothing I can really do about it," she said.

Lani noticed Cameron's arm twitch like he was going to reach for something, but he held it back and took a step closer to her. He smelled like an airy seaside cologne.

"You're a good writer," he said quietly. "Don't give up on yourself."

His brown eyes were sincere, but Lani found herself unable to hold his gaze and looked away.

"Yeah, well, thanks," she said.

"I'm serious. The more we learn about this guy, the more he seems like an asshole anyway. Don't take him too seriously."

All of this was less about her pride and more about the money she knew she wouldn't win, but Lani didn't tell him that even though she wanted to. She wanted to confide in Cameron right here and tell him about the photos and her blackmailer and how hopeless she felt now that her only way out was gone. She still didn't really know him, sure, but he had confided in her about his brother, and she could tell it was a hard thing for him to do. It would be so nice to talk to someone about this.

But just as Lani opened her mouth, Cameron turned his head toward the classroom.

"I'm going to be late," he said.

"Oh, yeah. Good luck."

Cameron gave her a small smile.

"Do I need it?"

"Maybe. He's weird. Just...be prepared for him to know stuff about you."

Cameron frowned and scanned Lani's face.

"Did he do it to you too? What was it?"

"Um..."

Lani didn't want to get into everything if Cameron was in a rush.

"It's not a huge deal," she said. "We can talk about it later."

"Okay," Cameron said. "I want to hear about it. I'll find you after I'm done."

"Okay."

He turned to leave, and his fingers barely grazed Lani's as he stepped past her. Lani's stomach did a little flip and she watched as he disappeared from her view. Once he had disappeared into the room, she turned toward the front door and reached for the handle.

"Lani?"

Lani turned around. It was Kai.

"Hey," she said.

He walked quickly towards her, a serious expression on his face.

"Are you okay?" she asked.

Kai had seemed a little agitated when he ran into her in the hallway earlier, but now he looked truly upset. When he reached Lani, he glanced at the door behind her.

"We need to talk," he said.

# 22

# Cameron

Dr. Fredricksen hadn't looked up from the papers on his desk since Cameron sat down. Kind of an asshole move. But then again, this is the guy they were dealing with. Cameron was still pissed at him for the way he spoke to Lani—she was the type of person who didn't seem to let things get her down easily, but Cameron could see how much the professor's comments had hurt her.

He glared at Dr. Fredricksen but refused to speak first. Instead, Cameron picked at his fingernails, a bad habit he had developed after Thomas died. One of the many issues he had developed after.

"Cameron."

Cameron looked up. Dr. Fredricksen was smiling smugly at him over his papers. Guess he was finally ready.

"Yes," he said.

He caught his tone and told himself to ease up a little. He still needed to win this competition and couldn't do it if this guy knew how much he didn't like him.

"How have you enjoyed your time here so far?" Dr. Fredricksen asked.

"It's been good," Cameron said. "It's a nice house."

"Thank you. I'm rather fond of it, of course. Plenty of antiques and classic style, although many people have remarked over the years that it is ahead of its time."

He sighed.

"I will miss it one day."

"Are you selling it?" Cameron asked.

This didn't seem like the type of house you would just sell and move on from. Of course, he didn't know what it was like to be a billionaire, so maybe it was.

Dr. Fredricksen looked at Cameron curiously in a way that made Cameron feel uncomfortable.

"We shall see," he said. "Recently, I thought I was, but even more recently, I decided not to. But that again may change."

*What was the point of this meeting?*

"Tell me what you have learned so far," Dr. Fredricksen said.

*Nothing, because all you've done is have us write one essay and freak us all out.*

"Uh..." he said, trying to think of a good answer. "Well, the essay you assigned yesterday was very thought-provoking. It was a good exercise."

Dr. Fredricksen smiled at Cameron, but it didn't feel warm.

"I know you don't believe that."

Cameron didn't respond.

"The truth is, I really haven't been teaching you much about writing," the professor went on. "My goal has been to get to know who you are. Frankly, I don't care that much about your writing abilities, but personal essays and poems are the best way to get to know someone's character. It's much harder to create a persona in those mediums."

Again, Cameron didn't know how to respond. Why was he telling him this?

"I am quite intrigued by you, Cameron. And your story."

Cameron knew that Thomas was going to come up. It was his fault for writing about his brother in his application essay, but he figured it was the surest way to get in. People love hearing tragic stories, and his was up there. And, if he was being honest, writing the essay felt good. He was able to let out feelings that had been trapped inside his chest for the past two years, almost like he was letting some air out of an overinflated balloon.

"Okay," Cameron said.

"Yes, I am referring to Thomas, and yes, I know you don't like talking about it," the professor said. "Your little debacle with your gambling debts is another thing, but let's focus on Thomas for now."

Cameron felt like his heart had stopped. How could he possibly know about that? If anyone found out—anyone—he was dead. Those guys didn't mess around with the risk of publicity.

"How—" Cameron started.

"I told you I want to focus on Thomas for now," Dr. Fredrick-sen interrupted. "I assure you, I will not share your secret, nor are your, eh, *friends* aware that I know anything."

Cameron remained frozen. Maybe the dude had gone through his phone and put two-and-two together. Maybe he was telling the truth. What reason would he have for holding this over Cameron's head or getting him in trouble? He felt the smallest amount of tension leave his body.

"What about Thomas?"

Saying his brother's name still hurt, like it was a thorn he had to touch every time he used it.

"First, let me say that I am so deeply sorry for your loss," Dr. Fredricksen said. "To lose a sibling, and so young, well...I have seen a lot of tragedy in my life, but it is hard to find anything that compares."

Cameron gave a short, curt nod. He could feel his throat tightening, but he was not going to cry in front of this man.

"We are often left clinging to fragments of the past, wishing that we had more to remember them by. Their slow, steady departure from Earth's memory can feel more cruel than death itself."

He was right. Already, Cameron had found himself forgetting small things about Thomas, like the exact hazel shade of his eyes or how his hair curled depending on the weather. Every time Cameron realized he was forgetting something, he would frantically pull his phone out and flip through all the photos he had of his brother, studying each one intensely until he could locate the fading memory. They were a light brown with flecks of gold that stood out in the sunlight. His hair would curl above his ears after it rained, which he hated, prompting him to immediately put on a hat until he could wash and style it again.

"Why are you bringing this up?" Cameron asked.

He didn't want to talk about Thomas. He just wanted to know what he could do to win the money, pay off his debt, and move on with his life.

Dr. Fredricksen didn't say anything. Instead, he pulled a phone out of his pocket and placed it on his desk. For a minute, Cameron thought it was his since it looked to be the same color and model but without a case. He watched as the professor tapped the screen a couple of times before turning the phone so that the microphone was facing Cameron.

"I don't really know why I'm doing this."

Cameron's breath caught in his throat. It was Thomas's voice.

"I had a weird dream last night and, I dunno, I started thinking about, like, what if I died suddenly?"

There was a laugh.

"I know that's really morbid. But stuff like that happens. Like that kid on the news yesterday. So I figured I'd make this just in case. Knock on wood. So here it goes: Mom and Dad, you guys are great. I love you both. Thanks for raising me and Cam so well. Not to brag or anything, but you did a good job."

Another laugh.

"Kenan, you're my brother for life. Really dude, I appreciate you so much. And Cameron—"

Cameron let out a sharp breath. He felt stuck to his seat, every inch of his body completely paralyzed.

"I don't know what to say, dude. You're my best friend. I'd never tell you this in person because you'd probably punch me, but I look up to you so much. I want to be like you when I get older. You're so cool, but you're also just so nice to everyone. You're not one of those popular kids who's really a jackass— people actually like you because you're cool and friendly and just a good guy. You're like, what a man is supposed to be. I know that's kind of cringe, but I don't know how else to say it. I love you, man."

A distant voice said something that Cameron couldn't make out.

"Coming!" Thomas's recording yelled. "Okay, that's it. Hopefully, no one ever listens to this, I guess. Peace."

The phone went silent. Cameron didn't know how long he sat there without moving, but at some point, he felt a tear fall down his cheek, jerking him back to reality. He leaned his cheek into his shoulder to wipe it away. That was the first time he had heard his brother's voice since he died. There were videos out there, he was sure, on friends' phones or old family recordings from when he was young, but Cameron had never even tried to find them. He was afraid if he had access to that, he would spend every free second watching and rewatching them and losing himself more than he already had.

Cameron looked up at Dr. Fredricksen. He was sitting patiently, looking at Cameron with no expression on his face.

"Is that real?" Cameron asked hoarsely.

Dr. Fredricksen nodded.

"Does this phone look familiar?"

Cameron looked at it again. Now, he recognized it as Thomas's phone. They had the same one, but Thomas never used a case, which drove Cameron crazy. That phone was the one thing of Thomas's that was never recovered from the accident. Everyone assumed it had fallen out of Thomas's pocket when he fell and was lost in the forest forever.

"How did you get it?"

Cameron's voice was shaking.

"I am fortunate enough to have a wide range of connections and technology at my disposal," Dr. Fredricksen said. "I was able to track it down just last week."

The emotions swirling in Cameron's chest were intense and blurred, and made it hard to think of anything other than the echo of his brother's voice in his head.

"But," he said, closing his eyes and shaking his head a little, trying to get himself to think straight. "Why would you? Why are you showing it to me now?"

"As I said, it truly is one of the worst tragedies. I can't imagine how many times you've thought about that day and about the things you could have done differently. If only you had held on longer. If only Thomas hadn't stepped so close to the cliff. If only you hadn't gone hiking at all."

All of those thoughts had gone through Cameron's mind every day since the accident. Cameron took a deep breath, trying to compose himself. He hated this weak, shaky feeling and hated it even more in front of people.

"What's your point?" Cameron asked.

"What if there was a way?" Dr. Fredricksen asked.

Cameron's brow furrowed.

"What do you mean?"

"What if there was a way to bring Thomas back? To ensure that it never happened?"

Cameron remembered what Dr. Fredricksen had told Kai about his mom.

"That's impossible," Cameron said.

"Is it?" Dr. Fredricksen asked, his eyes lighting up. "How do you know?"

The absurdity of it all was helping Cameron think more clearly.

"If you're talking about changing the past, you know it's impossible," Cameron said. "It's been debunked a million times. Even if there was theoretically a way, there's the whole butterfly effect thing and all the other potential repercussions. It's just stupid."

Dr. Fredricksen didn't look offended. He actually looked more excited—even a little manic. His eyes had the same red glint that Cameron had noticed during their first lecture.

"Many ideas were considered stupid and impossible in the past," he said. "Flying, space travel, for heaven's sake, even aspirin. But all of those things still came to be. Have you ever thought about why?"

Cameron frowned.

"What do you mean, why? That stuff was invented by smart people who had the resources."

"So who is to say that one day we won't have those same smart people and resources to successfully travel through time?"

Cameron hesitated for a second but then shook his head.

"Even if that does happen one day, it can't right now."

"But what if it could, Cameron?" Dr. Fredricksen asked. "Humor me for a moment. If it could, would you attempt it? If you could save Thomas?"

The vision of Thomas that Cameron had in the strange room the other day flashed in his mind. He thought of hugging his brother again, and the longing in his chest hurt so much that he winced.

"Yeah," he said quietly. "If it was possible, of course I would."

"What about the repercussions?" Dr. Fredricksen asked, looking intensely at Cameron. "The butterfly effect? There would be a real possibility that you would cause harm to someone else's life if you went through with it. Even yours. Would you still do it?"

Cameron thought of the life he had now. His parents, who blamed him for everything, and Greta, who they would tell about Thomas soon, and who would probably blame him too. He thought of the friends who didn't speak to him anymore and all the jobs he'd been fired from. He thought of Frank, sitting in a plush chair while his cronies beat him and Joseph up. He thought of what Frank would do if he went back to New York without the prize money. His brother flashed to the front of his mind again. His life had been great before Thomas died, and it had been hell since. Thomas was such a good person, and Cameron had been a pretty good person before. When Thomas died, he took all of Cameron's good with him.

Cameron realized there were tears in his eyes again as he pictured Thomas next to him like he had never left.

Cameron felt himself nod.

"Yeah."

Dr. Fredricksen smiled, and Cameron could tell there was something off about it, but he didn't care. He didn't care if this was all a joke. He just wanted to keep picturing Thomas clearly and hear his voice again.

"Excellent, Cameron," Dr. Fredricksen said. "That is excellent. I knew there was something different about you. And I assure you, this isn't a prank or a test. I am quite serious about helping you and Thomas find each other again."

The professor stood up and gestured to the door.

"This concludes our meeting. We will speak more tomorrow."

Cameron opened his mouth to protest, but Dr. Fredricksen held up a hand.

"Again, I am serious about this," he said. "But I need some time to prepare everything. You'll understand tomorrow. We will meet again and visit the room you have all been so intrigued by."

He smiled at what must have been a look of surprise on Cameron's face.

"Yes, I know you all have been sneaking back there. All I ask is that you do not go there for the rest of the evening and that you keep the rest of the group out as well."

Cameron nodded.

"Goodbye, Cameron," Dr. Fredricksen said. "This time tomorrow, you may see your brother again."

Cameron's heart began to pound, and he left the room.

# 23

# Allie

Allie looked up from her book about 1970s America to see Lani and Kai walking quickly toward her. Kai looked worried and Lani looked scared, which made Allie assume that something had happened to Cameron since he wasn't with them.

"What's wrong? Is Cameron okay?" she asked, feeling the stress radiate from them as they reached her.

"He's meeting with Dr. Fredricksen," Lani said. "No, this is—"

She turned to Kai.

"We're locked inside the house," Kai said.

Allie blinked.

"What?" she asked.

"All the doors are locked," Lani said breathlessly. "All the windows are sealed. I mean, we didn't check *all* of them, but we tried dozens—"

"There's no way to get out," Kai said.

He seemed less composed than usual, which made Allie even more nervous.

"Um...what does that mean?" Allie asked. "Like, did they

lock us in here on purpose? Maybe it's a safety thing."

"Maybe," Kai said. "I thought about that. But we're adults, for one thing, and the staff still has to get in and out. They must have a door we can't access. I think the four of us, specifically, are locked in."

Allie bit her lip.

"Maybe it's a misunderstanding," she said, hoping she was right. "Did you ask Barbara? Maybe there's a way to open the doors you didn't notice."

Kai shook his head.

"I didn't ask her. I haven't seen her since I found out, but...I don't know. There's something she's not telling us."

"Something's going on," Lani said, her voice shaking slightly. "I know all this weird stuff has been happening, and I just assumed they were all coincidences, but like the chandelier and the EpiPen and being pushed down the stairs—"

"What?" Kai interrupted. "You were pushed down the stairs? You said you fell."

Lani's face turned red.

"Um, yeah, I...I think I was pushed," she said, looking down.

"Why didn't you say that?" Allie asked.

"That's important," Kai said seriously. "Why'd you lie about it?"

Lani shook her head.

"I don't know," she said. "At first, I thought I imagined it, but then the other stuff started happening and...I don't know, it's not like I know you guys very well."

She looked embarrassed and a little annoyed. Allie glanced at Kai, who was frowning at Lani. He opened his mouth, and she braced herself for him to yell at her. She had lied to Michael once about something so stupid she couldn't even remember what it was, and he had gotten so angry that she thought he was going to hit her. He didn't, but she never forgot the look on his face while he berated her for not being truthful.

But to Allie's surprise, Kai didn't yell.

"No, you're right," he said.

Allie was surprised at this statement, and Lani seemed to be too. Kai gave Lani an understanding smile.

"We don't know each other. I'm sorry," he added. "I didn't mean to scold you or anything. I get why you wouldn't trust us right away."

Allie knew Kai was right, but she still felt a little hurt. Lani had seemed so kind and open with her, and Allie had confided in her about some really personal things. It felt one-sided knowing that Lani was hiding something like this from her. Did Lani think that it was one of them who pushed her?

"I, um, wasn't sure who did it," Lani confessed, like she had read Allie's mind. "Not that I assumed it was one of you, but, you know…"

Allie glanced at Kai, who was looking at her.

"It wasn't me," she said to Kai quickly.

"I know," he said. "But I was thinking…"

He trailed off, looking uncomfortable.

"What?" Lani asked.

Kai scratched the back of his head.

"I'm not saying anything for sure, but, well, Lani, you said that Cameron found you after you fell down the stairs, right?"

Lani nodded.

"And Allie, he ran into you right after the chandelier fell?"

Allie nodded slowly. She knew where this was going.

"And Cameron's the one who went to my room to get my

EpiPen."

The three of them stood in silence.

"But he helped Lani," Allie said. "He stayed with her until she could get up and then brought her ice. And he helped make sure I didn't get cut by any glass. And, well, he seemed really worried that your EpiPen was gone, Kai."

"That's true," Kai said. "Look, I don't want to accuse him or anything. He seems like a good guy. But he's also the only person who hasn't had some weird accident. It's strange."

"No," Lani said firmly. "It's not him. He wouldn't do that."

"You said yourself, Lani," Kai said gently. "None of us really know each other."

Lani bit her cheek and looked away.

"I'm not saying it's him," Kai said. "Let's just be careful until we figure out what's going on and how to get out of here."

Allie nodded and looked at Lani, who was still staring at the far corner of the library.

"It's almost time for dinner," Allie said. "Why don't we head to the dining room?"

Kai nodded and began walking toward the exit of the library. Allie waited as Lani slowly turned around and followed him. She walked next to her friend, trying to calm the annoyance bubbling inside her.

"I'm sorry I lied to you," Lani said quietly.

Allie looked over. Lani's eyes were watery.

"Hey," Allie said, trying to sound nicer than she felt like being. "It's okay. Seriously, I get it."

"You told me about your abortion and your mom and all this stuff," Lani said. "And I just lied to you about everything."

She wiped her eyes with her sleeve.

"It's probably why I don't have any friends," she said with

a weak laugh. "I don't know why I do that, I just..."

Allie pulled Lani in for a shoulder hug.

"It's okay, really," she said.

She meant it this time. Lani smiled up at Allie before her expression went serious again.

"I think it's because of my parents," Lani said.

Lani launched into a story about how her parents were wealthy at one point but bankrupted themselves through drinking and gambling, and how they had spent all of Lani's college money, which forced her to attend a small religious school close to her house.

"And now, I'm about to get kicked out if I don't—"

She stopped herself, suddenly turning red.

"If you don't what?" Allie asked.

"Um," Lani looked at Kai walking in front of them. He was close enough that he could definitely hear everything Lani was saying, but he didn't comment or turn around.

"About a month ago, I got a text from a number I didn't recognize," Lani said.

Allie could tell how difficult it was for Lani to share this, and she felt a rush of admiration.

"It was some guy, I think," Lani went on. "I don't know who he is. Anyway, he sent me all these pictures of myself from when I, um, sent them to my boyfriend a few years ago. Like, naked pictures."

Her face turned beet red. Allie grabbed her hand, hating that the first thing to run through her mind was, *Well, what did you think was going to happen?* That's the kind of thing that Michael or his parents would have said. The kind of thing she would have said a few months ago. *No,* she corrected herself. *That's not fair. This is his fault, not hers.* Allie had been trying her best to correct herself internally when those kinds of thoughts came into her mind, and it was frustrating how slow the process was.

"He asked for them," Lani went on. "And he said it was normal and I thought everyone did it. We broke up a while after that and he swears it wasn't him, but I don't know if he's lying or if he sent them to some of his friends or whatever. Anyway, whoever it is has been texting me the photos and told me he'd send them to my school if I don't pay him."

That finally got Kai to whip around.

"What?" he asked angrily.

Lani nodded, her face still red. A tear rolled down her cheek.

"If my school gets those, I'll be expelled. I'm over halfway done with my degree and I can't afford to go anywhere else because I'm on a scholarship and I...I don't know what I'll do if that happens. Plus, like, how humiliating."

Lani broke down. Allie pulled her in for a hug, and she stood there as Lani cried into her shoulder. She looked at Kai as she rubbed Lani's back. He looked livid.

"Have you told the police?" Kai asked after Lani began to calm down.

Lani pulled away from Allie and shook her head.

"My ex's dad is a cop, and he basically threatened to ruin my life if I got him involved with the police about any of this. This guy also said he'd send the photos if I talk to anyone. I don't think they could help anyway—he uses a different number every time. Maybe there's some technology that—"

She stopped herself.

"What?" Allie asked.

"Oh, Dr. Fredricksen," Lani said, wiping the mascara under her eyes. "During our meeting, he said he knew about this guy blackmailing me. I have no idea how he found out, but he also told me that he could find him. With a new technology."

"What else did he say?" Kai asked.

"He asked if I would want to use it, and I said yes, but then he told me that I'd have to deal with the repercussions. And I realized that the technology he was talking about—intense surveillance stuff, very Big Brother—would be so dystopian and a horrible idea for a lot of reasons. So I said no."

"Did he seem disappointed?" Kai asked.

Lani looked surprised.

"Yeah," she said. "That's when he told me I wasn't going to win the prize money."

"He said that?" Allie asked.

Lani nodded, smiling through her tears.

"So overall, I'm having the best day of my life," she joked.

Allie smiled, but Kai remained serious.

"Allie, you said he brought up your dad," Kai said. "Did he say how he could find him?"

Allie shook her head.

"Not specifically, no. But like I said at lunch, he mentioned something about the 'greater good' and all that. It freaked me out, so I said I wasn't interested before he could explain."

"And did he seem disappointed when you said that?" Kai asked.

"Actually, yeah," Allie said. "It was weird because I don't know why he'd care."

Kai crossed his arms.

"It's been the same for all of us," he said. "He knows something about us that he shouldn't, he offers a cure or solution that shouldn't be possible, he brings up ethical questions about it, and he's disappointed when we say no."

"Yeah," Allie said. "Yeah, that's so weird."

She paused.

"What do you think it means?" she asked.

Kai shook his head.

"I don't know," he admitted. "I wonder what he's talking to Cameron about."

Tension filled the room again.

"He should be done soon," Allie said. "Let's go to dinner and we can talk to him."

Kai nodded solemnly. Allie could tell that he and Cameron had become friends, and the idea that Cameron was somehow involved in the bad things that had been happening seemed painful for him. The three of them began walking to the dining room again.

"Sorry for that outburst," Lani said to Allie. "I'm not a big crier normally, so when I do, it's like a dam has burst."

Allie laughed.

"It's fine," she said. "Really. I'm so sorry though. What a psychopathic pervert."

Lani sighed.

"It's so humiliating," she said. "To have stuff like that used against you. It makes me feel so...violated."

She took a deep breath and, to Allie's surprise, smiled.

"I have to say though, it feels good to tell someone. I'm not getting the prize money, so I won't be able to pay him off, and I'll get kicked out of school and never be able to face my parents again, but, I don't know, for some reason I feel a lot better right now."

"That's what happens when you open up to people," Allie giggled. "It's like, a crucial part of human existence."

"Sounds fake, but okay."

Allie laughed and put her arm around Lani's.

"You're a good person," Allie said softly. "Those pictures... don't let anyone make you think you're less of a person for doing that. It's not wrong. Someone using them against you is wrong."

Lani squeezed Allie's arm.

"You're a good person, too," she said. "Really. You've had such a hard life, but you're still so nice."

Allie's stomach twisted a little.

"I'm not," she said. "I was, I think, but the past few years, I've...kind of turned into someone I don't really like."

Lani raised her eyebrows.

"Well," she said slowly. "I mean, at least you recognize it. And you're trying to change, it sounds like. That's all that matters."

Allie bit her cheek, trying not to cry. She gulped a couple of times and nodded.

"Thanks," she said.

It didn't really make her feel better, but Lani was right. She couldn't do anything about the things she had done (and not done) over the past few years, but she could change how she moved forward. Allie made a mental note to look up volunteer opportunities when she got back to New York.

"Hey, let's not say anything to Cameron about the accidents," Kai said quietly as they approached the dining room. "I don't want to accuse him of anything. Or freak him out."

Allie and Lani nodded. The three stepped inside and saw that the table was set but empty of guests. Cameron must still be in his meeting. They sat down and waited in silence for a few minutes. The sound of footsteps approaching caused them all to turn their heads toward the door as Cameron walked in.

"What?" he asked, pausing at the sight of them all staring.

"Took you long enough," Kai joked.

Cameron didn't respond and quickly sat down in his seat. On cue, four people came into the room and set down plates in front of everyone before leaving silently. Allie saw Kai staring at them intently as they disappeared through a door at the far end of the room. He craned his neck before the door shut.

Allie looked back at the table, expecting Cameron to ask Kai what he was doing, but he was staring at his plate.

"How did your meeting go?" Lani asked.

A strange expression flashed across Cameron's face, and Allie thought she saw him take a quick breath before answering.

"It was fine," he said, not looking at Lani.

"Yeah?" she asked. "He didn't ask you anything weird?"

Cameron shook his head.

"No, it was pretty normal."

Lani frowned and took a bite of mashed potatoes.

"Are you sure?" Kai asked. "He didn't know something weird about you and then tell you he could fix it?"

Cameron put a large forkful of food in his mouth and shook his head again.

"No, we just talked about writing," he said.

Allie could tell he was hiding something. She could tell that Kai knew, too. Lani seemed more hurt than suspicious.

"Well, you know how we talked earlier about something being off about this place?" Kai asked. "We're locked in. Lani and I checked a bunch of windows and doors, and they're all locked or sealed."

Cameron seemed genuinely surprised by this, which made Allie feel a little better.

"What?" he asked. "Are you sure? Why would they do that?"

"We don't know.  But we can't leave.  And they have our phones."

Kai lowered his voice to a whisper.

"I found them," he said.  "After lunch.  They're in a room down the hall.  I'll get them after dinner and try calling someone. It looks like there's no service here—they use Wi-Fi, but I think they turn it off a lot—but I might be able to send an emergency message."

Allie's heart rate slowed a little. She felt an immense wave of gratitude for Kai, who was able to remain calm when she couldn't be. She suddenly felt a little stupid for not thinking about using their phones to contact someone. She had been picturing them smashing through the windows with chairs and tables.

"Is there anything else we can do?" Lani asked nervously. "I mean, are we just supposed to sit around and wait for someone else to push us down the stairs?"

Allie glanced at Cameron, waiting for him to act as surprised about that news as she and Kai had. But he continued to pick at his food and didn't even look up. He seemed so deep in thought that Allie figured he hadn't even heard Lani.

"I don't know what else we can do," Kai said.

He looked nervous too, but his voice was steady.

"I can't shake the feeling though," Kai added. "I feel like... that room has something to do with all of this. I think we need to go back. All of us together."

"Yeah, that's—" Allie started.

"No," Cameron said quickly.

They all turned to look at him.

"Uh, not tonight," Cameron said. "It's been a long day. Let's go tomorrow when we're not so tired."

He seemed nervous. But, Allie thought, so was she. Kai opened his mouth to protest, but Lani interrupted him.

"I'm okay with that," Lani said. "I'm tired, too."

She smiled at Cameron, but he looked back down. Kai looked between Cameron and Lani but didn't protest any further.

"Fine," he said finally. "We'll go tomorrow after breakfast unless we have another class."

"No one's mentioned anything, right?" Allie said. "I guess we'll get our schedule at breakfast."

There was a pause.

"I'm going to bed," Cameron muttered.

He got up from the table and walked out of the room. None of them spoke for several minutes, and Allie could tell they were waiting until he was out of earshot.

"Something's wrong," Lani whispered. "I don't know what Dr. Fredricksen said to him, but it must have been bad."

"That doesn't seem like normal Cameron to you?" Kai asked. "A little moodier than usual, sure, but maybe he really is just tired."

Lani shook her head.

"No, this is different," she said, staring at the door. "I wonder if he brought up..."

She shook her head.

"I don't know," she said. "But I'm super tired. I think we'll all be able to think more clearly tomorrow."

She stood up and Allie followed.

"Okay," Kai said, getting up too. "Let's walk together, though."

The three walked to their rooms in silence. Lani gave Allie and Kai a warm smile when they reached her room.

"I'll see you guys tomorrow," she said, grabbing the handle.

"Don't forget to lock the door," Kai said.  "And you should barricade it. Use a chair or something. Just in case."

Lani's smile disappeared and she nodded.

"Goodnight," she said.

Kai walked Allie to her door a few steps down the hall.

"You do the same," he said.

She nodded.

"Thanks," she said.

He grimaced.

"Don't thank me yet," he said.  "We'll see what happens tomorrow."

# 24

# Kai

Kai lay in bed staring at the ceiling. It was still dark outside. He had dozed off occasionally for short periods of time, but a small creak would always jolt him back awake. He rubbed his eyes and looked at the digital alarm clock by his bed. 5:57. Kai rolled out of bed and jumped in the shower. He stayed there for at least thirty minutes, letting the hot water pour over his tired body. He was trying not to get too freaked out by everything—Allie, in particular, seemed really anxious, and he didn't want to make it worse—but things didn't look or feel good.

He just had to get to their phones again and call the police. His dad had told him once that cell phones can call 911 without any cell service, so he had to try. They would be okay. Kai thought of his parents and Mia and Akiko.

He had to be okay.

Kai stepped out of the shower and was hit with a blast of cold air—the steamy shower had made him forget how chilly his room had become overnight. He quickly dried off and got dressed before checking the clock again. 6:35. He could head out now without being suspicious.

Kai crept down the hall and checked each bedroom door as he passed. Nothing looked out of the ordinary. He went down the winding staircase as quietly as possible, freezing whenever an old floorboard creaked, but the house seemed empty. He made his way down the hall to the room holding their cell phones. He turned the handle, half-expecting it to be locked, but it opened easily. He breathed a sigh of relief that was cut off early when he looked inside. The table at the end of the room was completely empty. Kai rushed over and frantically looked for any sign of them—maybe they had been knocked off the table or set somewhere nearby—but he quickly realized the room was empty. Someone had taken them.

Kai ran his hands through his hair. What should they do now? He could start hunting for the phones again, but the odds of finding them weren't good. Whoever took them must have known he had found them in the first place and—

Kai froze. Barbara. Had she moved them? Her behavior the other day had been strange, but she seemed to be on their side, all things considered. Kai let out a huff of frustration, trying not to let the growing sensation of fear overtake him. What was going on? Why were they all wrapped up in this? What was he supposed to do now?

Kai took a deep breath. It was still early. He would look for the phones for another hour and then meet everyone at breakfast, and they could try smashing through a window if they needed to. Kai began opening every door that wasn't locked to check inside. After searching the fifth room with no luck, he decided to move to the second floor. If someone tried to hide the phones on purpose, there was a good chance they would keep them far from the original location.

Kai walked as far down the second floor hallway as he could before stopping outside the last door on the left. He jiggled the handle. It felt stuck, but not necessarily locked, so Kai twisted it back and forth until he heard a loud click and was able to push it open.

Intrigued, he stepped inside the room. It looked like another bedroom, similar to his upstairs, but it didn't seem to be occupied. He scanned the room for places where the phones might be hidden. The room was empty except for a bed, a desk, and two plush chairs. Kai walked over to the bed and crouched down to check underneath.

"Hello?"

Kai jumped, the back of his head slamming into the bed frame. He stood up and blinked away the stars in front of his eyes.

"Hello?" the voice said again. "Please?"

"Barbara?" Kai asked, recognizing her finally.

He turned to a door located to the right of the bed.

"Yes!" Barbara said quickly. "Kai, is that you?"

Kai walked over to the door and grabbed the handle. It was locked.

"Are you okay?" Kai asked. "What's going on?"

"It's Dr. Fredricksen," Barbara said from behind the door.

Her voice sounded hoarse, like she had been yelling or maybe crying.

"I'm so sorry," she said, her voice cracking. "I suspected it was him earlier, but I...well, you work with someone for so long and you think only the best of them, I suppose. And he seemed to be fighting it. I know I could see the good in him. I never thought he could...Kai, something is very wrong."

Goosebumps erupted on Kai's arms.

"What do you mean?"

"I don't fully understand it," Barbara said. "He hired me not long after he moved into this house. There is…some sort of power here. A power that he can access. It has always been good, I think. He has always been good, at least. But over the last several years, he has become consumed with something. Since you all have arrived, it's gotten worse. Up until this two days ago, he had never so much as raised his voice at me."

Barbara paused, and Kai could hear sniffling.

"I'm sorry," she whispered. "He is such a dear friend of mine. Was."

She paused again.

"I know there is still good in him," she said. "Please remember that."

Kai wasn't sure about that.

"Does this have something to do with the room by the huge mural on the third floor?" Kai asked.

Barbara didn't seem surprised he knew about it.

"I suspected at least one of you would find your way over there," she said, now sounding less hoarse and more nervous. "Yes, that is where he spends most of his time. I don't know anything about it though, except that there's an odd door on the far side of the room. I went near it once…"

She trailed off.

"Barbara, what do we do?" Kai asked urgently. "All the doors are locked. The windows look like they're too thick to break. How do we get out of here?"

"I didn't know he was locking everything," Barbara said quickly. "When you first arrived, nothing seemed out of the ordinary. I don't leave very often. I didn't realize we were trapped until last night when I tried to go for a stroll through the garden."

"How do we get out of here? How are you going to get out?"

"There is a master key that can unlock any door in the house," Barbara said, lowering her voice. "Dr. Fredricksen keeps it on his bedside table. His room is on this floor at the other end of the hall."

Kai hesitated.

"In...his room?"

"I would go, but—"

Barbara gave a small knock on the door.

"I don't believe he's there, though," she said. "He hardly ever sleeps these days. When he locked me in here this morning, he was heading outside himself."

Kai nodded, then remembered she couldn't see him.

"Okay," he said. "I'll find it. And I'll come back to get you."

"No," Barbara said quickly. "If you find it, get everyone and get out of here. I'll be fine, but you all need to leave as quickly as you can. Then call the police. I can't imagine a world where he would...but to be safe, you need to get out."

Kai hesitated again but understood.

"Okay," he said. "I'll do my best. Are you sure you'll be okay?"

"Yes, I'll be fine," Barbara said. "Thank you, Kai. Good luck. Stay safe."

Kai turned and rushed out of the room back into the hall. He paused for a moment, listening for any sounds of movement. It was completely still. No one else seemed to be awake yet. He crept as quickly as he could down the hallway, eventually making it to a large set of double doors with ornate decorations. It had to be Dr. Fredricksen's room. Kai held his breath and slowly turned one of the doorknobs. To his surprise, the door wasn't locked and it shifted open. Kai pushed it slowly and paused as it creaked, his heart pounding in his chest. He waited a few seconds before peering through the two-inch gap in the door. The morning light had begun to pour into the room and lit it up just enough for Kai to see that no one was inside. Cautiously, Kai opened the door the rest of the way and stepped in.

The room smelled musty, like no one had opened a window in weeks. Moving to the bedside table, Kai noticed a fine layer of dust on all the wooden surfaces illuminated by the sunrise. Barbara seemed to be right—the professor didn't spend much time here.

Still jumpy, Kai began rummaging around the bedside table for a key. The table was covered in loose papers in various languages scattered on top of a thick notebook. Ignoring the papers, Kai opened a small drawer and saw a key ring with a single large key dangling from it. He breathed a sigh of relief. They could get out. They would be okay.

Kai closed the drawer and turned to leave the room, but he saw something out of the corner of his eye that stopped him. He quickly grabbed one of the pieces of paper sticking out from the pile. Written on the top in a scratchy cursive was the word "students," and immediately underneath the title was his name.

*Kai, 21*

*Mother ill, no treatment*
*Medical bills with compounding interest*
*Possible treatment, but out-of-pocket expense*
*Application: Writing is decent. Clearly a compassionate person. May get in the way, but family situation could change that.*

Kai frowned. His compassion could get in the way? Get in the way of what? He thought back to the odd questions Dr. Fredricksen had asked him in their meeting yesterday about finding and using his mom's supposed cure. He put the paper down and rummaged through the stack until he found notes on the other contestants.

*Lani, 20*
   *Blackmailer w/ explicit photos, $10,000 ransom*
   *Could lose scholarship*
   *No help from parents*
   *Application: Writing is good. Independent and relies on no one. That + desperation may work.*

Kai felt nauseous. Lani hadn't mentioned that her blackmailer wanted $10,000. That was an impossible amount of money for a college student, and it made sense why she was so upset about Dr. Fredricksen's comments earlier. She needed to win the money to pay the guy off.

*That + desperation may work.*

Kai gripped the paper tighter. He didn't know what the professor was planning, but he was clearly taking advantage of their situations.

*Allie, 21*
   *In an abusive relationship*
   *Mother died three years ago*
   *No father*
   *Application: Writing is concise. Obviously caught: either the relationship will end & she will be left to fend for herself with nothing, or she will remain abused wishing she could leave. Ideal*

*for an escape route.*

Kai's stomach twisted again. He felt like he shouldn't be reading this. It felt too private, like he had opened Lani's and Allie's own diaries. He didn't know Allie was, or had been, in an abusive relationship. He assumed the abortion had been after a one-night stand or something. He stopped himself. He shouldn't be speculating about her dating life—it didn't matter. He turned to the last page.

*Cameron, 22*
  *Unpaid gambling debt with threats to pay back soon*
  *Brother dead in accident two years ago*
  *No parental support (they blame him)*
  *Application: Writing is gut-wrenching. Outstanding trauma that has not been addressed. Seems likely to do anything to see brother again. Can use?*

Kai stared at the page with wide eyes, his hands starting to shake slightly. Cameron had mentioned a sister but nothing about his brother. Not that the topic ever came up, but...Kai suddenly understood why Cameron was so reserved. He didn't blame him. He didn't think he'd ever smile again either if something happened to one of his sisters. And an unpaid gambling debt? With threats to pay it back soon? Who had Cameron borrowed money from?

He put the notes back down, but a small mark on Lani's caught his eye. At the bottom right corner of the paper were two red X's. He looked at Allie's, which also had the same red marks. Cameron's paper had a single black question mark. He looked at his paper. Like Lani and Allie, there were two red X's at the bottom, but his also had a single word scribbled underneath them.

*Kiwi.*

Kai's throat started to burn the way it did when he had his allergic reaction. He had assumed it was a mistake by the cooks. Barbara had seemed genuinely shocked when he told her about what had happened. Why would Dr. Fredricksen need to note it here when he had nothing to do with their meals?

Immediately, everything became clear. It wasn't Cameron who had taken his EpiPen, or pushed Lani, or tried to hurt Allie. It was Dr. Fredricksen. He had selected them because they each needed the prize money, and he thought he could convince them to do something—what, he still didn't know— in order to get it. The red X's must have been for times that they indicated they wouldn't go along with his plan. Since Cameron didn't have any X's and nothing had happened to him, Dr. Fredricksen must have picked him for...whatever he was going to do. Kai remembered how Cameron was acting more reserved than usual last night, right after his meeting with the professor. Did Cameron agree to something? What had Dr. Fredricksen said to him?

Kai put the notes down and grabbed the key. They had to get out of here. He didn't know what Dr. Fredricksen was planning on doing with them now that he had obviously selected the contest winner. He had almost killed each of them once already, so Kai wasn't confident in the idea that they would be able to just walk out the door now. But first, he had to find Cameron. Whatever Dr. Fredricksen planned to do to them, Cameron was probably in even more danger.

Kai grabbed the key, slipped it into his pocket, and ran out of the room.

# 25

# Lani

Lani stared at the staircase again. She couldn't help but pause whenever she passed it now. She thought about the feeling of two strong hands on her back and inadvertently whipped her head around. She was alone. She thought of Cameron's hand on her waist when he had found her. Had he pushed her and then come back once he realized she was okay? Is that why he was there so quickly?

She didn't want to believe it. She had seen a different side of Cameron yesterday, and she couldn't picture him hurting all of them just to win a contest. A contest with a $100,000 prize, sure, but he could have killed her here. He could have killed all of them if he was behind what happened to Kai and Allie too. Still, she reminded herself, she didn't really know him. It had only been a couple of days. He could have lied about everything to get her to trust him. People did that.

Lani turned away from the staircase and began walking down the hallway, letting her feet take her where they wanted to go. She had been to the room several times now and somehow never got lost on her way. After waking up early that morning and not being able to get back to sleep, she decided to visit the room one more time by herself before they all met together, if that happened at all. If Kai found their phones and was able to call the police, they might be driven away before they all had a chance to meet like he had suggested. She couldn't stop thinking about the room all night and knew she had to visit again. She liked how it made her feel—powerful in the way you only can when you're helping someone achieve something they wouldn't have been able to on their own. She hadn't done anything, of course, but that was how the room made her feel each time she was there, and she needed it. She also wanted to get near the door again and imagine life without her blackmailer, which was another sensation that would probably never happen again. As soon as she got her phone back, she would have to tell him that she didn't have the money, and he would email the photos to her school and she would be expelled. She'd have to start over with nothing. Her life wasn't over— she wasn't that melodramatic—but it would really, really suck. It would be nice to feel like she was ahead of this one more time before it all came crashing down.

Lani reached the mural at the end of the hallway and slowly opened the door. The room was warm and cozy, just like she remembered. She turned on the small light and let it cast a shaky glow over the space. She walked over to the door at the far side and confidently placed her hand on the doorknob.

She waited eagerly for something to happen, but the vision didn't come. Disappointed, Lani pulled her hand away, but as she did, she felt the door give a little. A warm rush of air came out and poured over her. It smelled like freshly printed paper and lilacs. She grabbed the handle again and tried to pull the door open, but it wouldn't budge more than the two inches it had already given her.

Heart pounding, Lani moved to the side and tried to peer into the crack. All she could see was a blinding white light. The feeling she had thought about earlier, the feeling of having the power to do good, flooded her body. She felt confident. Proud. Eager. Happy. The emotions were so strong that tears came to her eyes. She hadn't felt like this in years.

In high school, before she knew about her parents blowing her college fund and their fortune, Lani had volunteered at a women's shelter. Seeing those women every day was heartbreaking, but she had spent every second of her free time there helping as much as she could. She had also spent several thousand dollars—the last money that was ever really hers— to invest in security measures, cleaning, and healthcare for the people staying at the shelter. She never told anyone about the volunteer experience, except for Dr. Fredricksen in her application essay, because it was impossible to explain how it had made her feel. There was always a sense of injustice that these women were in these situations and living in a country that could readily help them but chose not to. Her position came with pain for those people every day, as well as a deep sense of guilt over the privileged life she had been brought up in. But it also made her feel better than anything had ever made her feel before. She could only do so much, but every day, she was able to help make someone's life a little better. She wished again and again that she had the power to enact real change for these women, and had to remind herself that she could only do the best with what she had. That was not enough, but it was enough.

Those feelings came flooding back to Lani as she gripped the side of the door. But this was different. This time, she felt like she actually could do something. She didn't know how, but she was confident that the answers to fixing the women's shelter, fixing the homelessness crisis, and fixing all the other problems in the world, were out there. That clear and overwhelming sense of possibility physically threw her backward from the door.

As soon as Lani's hand left the door, it slammed shut. The light disappeared, and with it, the emotions she wasn't ready to let go of yet. Lani stood there, feeling her chest rise and fall with deep breaths. A new realization was coming over her—she had been so self-absorbed for the past few years. Her problems were real, sure, but so many people in the world had things so much worse. There were people out there with problems no one could fix. Situations that really were ruining their lives. She thought of Kai, and how Dr. Fredricksen had told him his mom's cure was out there. Here in the room, something told her that he was right, but she still felt sad for Kai. Even if it existed, who was to say that it would be approved? Or his family could afford it?

Lani slid down to the floor and put her head in her hands. Her thoughts were spinning so fast that she felt dizzy. Was this what a panic attack felt like? No, probably not, she thought. She didn't feel bad or hopeless—the opposite, actually. It was just too much for her to handle at once.

After closing her eyes and breathing for several minutes, Lani felt her mind begin to calm down. She opened her eyes and looked around the room again, not ready to leave yet. Her eyes landed on some loose papers that had fallen to the floor. She picked them up, stacking them before placing them on the table in the middle of the room. Just before turning away, she paused as she saw her name on one of the sheets.

*April 4*
*Spoke with all four.*
*Kai - no (firm)*
*Lani - no (hesitant, but committed)*
*Allie - no (not worth my time)*
*Cameron - yes (any mention of Thomas)*

*Next step - tomorrow*
*Explain everything to Cameron, mention Thomas frequently until he agrees & we can move forward*
*TT will be leverage. Must seem tangible*
*Remaining students must be taken care of — Cameron may do it*

Lani reread the notes several times. Cameron said yes to what? An uneasy feeling settled in Lani's stomach as she reread the sentence about Thomas. She didn't know what Dr. Fredricksen was going to do, but he was clearly taking advantage of how Cameron felt about Thomas while doing it.

*Remaining students must be taken care of.*

A chill ran down Lani's spine. They were all locked inside. Kai couldn't get a cell signal yesterday. What did he mean by that, exactly?

*Cameron may do it.*

Did this mean Cameron had been in on whatever was going on the entire time? Anger flared inside Lani's chest. Even if it was a plan they had developed together after they arrived at the house, would Cameron really hurt them? Kill them? Tears pricked the corners of her eyes, and she cursed herself for starting to care about him. She was glad she hadn't told Cameron about her blackmailer—at least that was one less thing he could use against her.

A small voice nagged in Lani's brain, telling her that maybe Cameron was a victim here too. She pushed it aside. Everyone had free will. There was nothing Dr. Fredricksen could say or do that would justify Cameron 'taking care of' them.

Lani put the piece of paper back on the table. As she straightened up the papers that had fallen off, she noticed a small metal tray on the far side of the table. There were five clear glasses on it: four small and one large, each filled halfway with water. She walked closer and examined them. They didn't look particularly unusual, but she wondered why they had been set out so early. They must all be meeting here later, but no one had announced a schedule yet, so the meeting wouldn't happen until after breakfast at the earliest. What was the point of putting them the night before?

Lani checked her watch. It was 7:35. Breakfast wasn't for another 25 minutes. Lani took a deep breath and walked back toward the strange door. She wanted to see if she could open it again.

# 26

# Cameron

Cameron awoke with a start as his alarm blared. He rolled over and turned it off, rubbing his eyes until he saw spots. He hadn't slept well, and when he was asleep, his dreams had been filled with memories of Thomas that always ended with the accident. Dr. Fredricksen's voice echoed in his head.

*"I can't imagine how many times you've thought about that day. The things you could have done differently."*

Cameron knew there was no way to change what happened on the hiking trip. It was stupid to think there was. Still…last week, he would have thought the idea of having visions of his brother and other people having visions of their family members was stupid, too. He would have thought it ridiculous if someone told him a random person could find Thomas's lost cell phone. Or that the same person could find out about his under-the-table gambling debts.

There was something off about this house. Cameron didn't know what it was or what it meant, and he didn't know if Dr. Fredricksen could really do anything that would let him see Thomas again. But if there was even a chance, whatever it looked like, he had to take it. What other options did he have? Go back to New York to get his finger chopped off and try to explain it to his parents, who hated him for killing their son? The longing Cameron had felt in his chest since hearing Thomas's voice message had only grown stronger overnight, and he couldn't pass up on a chance to make it go away. He didn't care if it was all some big prank. It scared him how little he cared about what could happen—a feeling that made the decision that much easier.

Cameron checked the time and jumped out of bed. He was supposed to meet Dr. Fredricksen in 20 minutes while everyone else was at breakfast. A note had been slipped under his door the previous evening from the professor, telling Cameron that they would meet at 8:00 outside his room. Then, Dr. Fredricksen would explain everything to him about how to see Thomas again.

After taking a quick shower and brushing his teeth, Cameron heard a knock on his door while slipping his hoodie on. He ran to the door and opened it to see the professor standing outside. His hair was slightly disheveled, and Cameron noticed a small tear in his right shirt sleeve.

"Are you ready?" Dr. Fredricksen asked.

Cameron nodded and followed him outside. They walked silently toward the strange room. Cameron glanced at Dr. Fredricksen once or twice along the way and couldn't help but notice that something felt off about the way the professor's eyes were wide and blazing as they raced down the halls. He forced the feeling away, thinking of Thomas and feeling his anticipation grow with every passing second.

Cameron saw Dr. Fredricksen's hand twitch violently as they passed the long staircase where Cameron had found Lani after she fell. Something in his brain started questioning it, but he shut it down again immediately. He couldn't do anything to ruin whatever was about to happen.

When they reached the room, Dr. Fredricksen stepped inside and turned on the weak light bulb. He looked around and seemed satisfied with what he surveyed before stepping toward the circular table in the middle of the room. Cameron watched him pick up a small stack of papers on the table, fold them, and place them next to a tray with five glasses of water.

"How many times have you been here?" Dr. Fredricksen finally asked.

"Uh, three, I think," Cameron said.

He looked toward the door on the far side of the room.

"Yes, that is quite an interesting door," Dr. Fredricksen said, sounding nonchalant. "I assume you've tried to open it?"

Cameron nodded.

"And you saw something? Thomas, I assume?"

Cameron nodded again, his heart starting to pound as he remembered what it had been like to see Thomas that day. Maybe it could happen again, but this time, his brother would actually be in the room with him. Was that possible? Was that what was going to happen?

"Yes, I remember the first time I tried," Dr. Fredricksen said. "It wouldn't let me in, even though I had already been chosen. It takes some time for everyone, I believe."

"What do you mean 'chosen?'" Cameron asked, confused enough to be pulled from thoughts of his brother.

Dr. Fredricksen smiled like he had been waiting for Cameron to ask.

"Do you remember when we spoke yesterday about ground-breaking discoveries? You said they were created by 'smart people who had the resources.'"

"Yeah."

"Have you ever wondered what it takes to reach that point?" Dr. Fredricksen asked, taking a step toward the door. "There are many intelligent people in the world, and many resources. Why does it take so long for some discoveries to be made? And why do they happen at such precise times?"

"I don't know."

Cameron didn't know where he was going with this. He wanted to see Thomas. Dr. Fredricksen didn't seem to notice his impatience and continued.

"Many people have attributed it to miracles or divine intervention. That scientist or doctor was given a gift; if they had not been on the earth to receive it, the discovery may never have been made."

Dr. Fredricksen paused and looked at the door.

"That is true, I suppose," he said quietly. "But it does not happen the way people think."

Cameron could feel his palms sweating. Dr. Fredricksen turned to look at him with a wide, slightly frightening smile.

"Behind that door lies the secrets to all the knowledge that ever has existed and ever will exist," Dr. Fredricksen said, pointing to the strange door. "It is...well, I don't quite know what it is," he said with a humorless chuckle. "Another world, perhaps. I have never been allowed inside."

The last sentence sounded bitter. Cameron wanted to take a step back, but he felt like his feet were glued to the floor.

"I've tried, of course, more so in the past few years, but it seems to be closing even more tightly for me."

His eyes darkened, and the same unsettling feeling that Cameron felt in the hallway slithered down his spine. But something else was happening that he couldn't ignore—Cameron could feel Thomas nearby. It was like he knew his brother was in the room; he just couldn't see him yet. Cameron was terrified of breaking whatever connection that was—afraid of sending Thomas away—so he remained silent and let the professor talk.

"Thirty-five years ago, I was selected to become the keeper of this house," Dr. Fredricksen said. "I was quite young, just a few years older than all of you, and I couldn't fathom why the previous owner had picked me. I thought I was completing a standard job interview, only to find that the job was maintaining the knowledge of the world."

"I'm sorry," Cameron said, his desire to see his brother growing by the second. "I don't understand. What does this have to do with me? And Thomas?"

His heart was beating wildly. He could smell the cologne his brother used to wear.

"This door, this world," Dr. Fredricksen said, pointing at the strange door again. "Is a gateway that allows crucial knowledge to enter Earth. I do not fully understand how it happens, nor has any previous keeper of this house. Every few years, or every few hundred years, the door opens. During that brief moment, the knowledge is sent to whoever is deemed worthy to hold it, and the door closes again. The final model of the printing press, Penicillin, modern-day optical lenses—these discoveries all occurred shortly after the door opened."

Cameron was so intrigued that his thoughts left Thomas momentarily, but he couldn't fully understand what Dr. Fredricksen was saying.

"It is hard to grasp, yes," the professor said, apparently noticing Cameron's confusion. "Whoever or whatever is over there seems to determine when the world needs a little push to finish through with an idea. From the writings I've been given, it seems that the keepers of the house are not involved in any way."

He sounded bitter again.

"We are simply here to protect the portal from harm. We are gifted with basic temporal knowledge, I suppose, and given comfortable means to live by, but we have no say in the information that passes through. A handful of ideas may come to us, but nothing extraordinary."

Dr. Fredricksen glared at the door.

"It is frustrating to sit around while the world stays stagnant," he said quietly. "I often wonder if they really care. Our world could be so much better if they let it."

Cameron tried to think of any groundbreaking discoveries in the last forty years, but he couldn't place any.

"The door has not opened once since I was appointed keeper," Dr. Fredricksen said, seeming to read Cameron's mind. "Even as tragedy upon tragedy occurs around the world. We could do so much more if they simply let us. The lives we could save. The mistakes we could fix."

He looked at Cameron.

"It is time that I appoint a new keeper," he said. "That is why I brought the four of you here. I must choose someone who will challenge them to move the world forward at a better pace."

"Does anyone really have control over that?" Cameron asked.

"I have found old records," Dr. Fredricksen said, almost in a whisper. "Ancient texts that indicate a select few keepers have been able to open the door and enter. If they can get in, I believe they would have access to the knowledge and would be able to open that knowledge to the world. I believe, Cameron, that you may be able to do that one day."

Cameron stared at Dr. Fredricksen, more shocked at the professor's confidence in him than everything else he had said.

"What?" he asked. "Why?"

"It doesn't matter why. What matters is that I can help you do it. I will continue to live here and help you find ways to open the door. Even if you can't open it, the door may open itself soon, and we can go inside then. Together."

His eyes were wide and lit up.

"Imagine the things we could do, Cameron," he said, his voice rising. "Find cures for diseases, locate anyone in the world with the touch of a button, start wars and end them."

He paused.

"We could discover how to save Thomas."

At the mention of his brother's name, the feelings he had turned away from while Dr. Fredricksen talked came rushing back. Cameron could feel Thomas growing nearer, like his brother was closing in on him from every angle. The faint light behind the door seemed to grow brighter, as if it was telling Cameron it had been protecting Thomas this entire time, waiting until the two were ready to be reunited.

"The secret to time travel is in there, Cameron," Dr. Fredricksen said eagerly. "I'm sure of it. We can go back and make sure that day never happened."

Red flags were going off in his brain like fireworks, but Thomas shrouded any clear thought of them. Maybe this was crazy, but what if Dr. Fredricksen was right? If this place held all the knowledge in the universe, it was the only way he could ever find out if it were possible to see Thomas again. Cameron blinked, trying to clear the fog that was building in his brain. Was this really the right thing to do? Would he regret this? But he couldn't think with Thomas's face so clearly plastered in his mind. It was the only thing he could see clearly, which, maybe, was reason enough.

"Okay," Cameron said quietly. "I'll do it."

A large smile stretched over Dr. Fredricksen's face. It wasn't friendly, but Cameron couldn't muster enough energy to care. The speech made his head hurt, and all he could think about was his brother.

"Excellent," Dr. Fredricksen said. "This is a very intelligent decision, Cameron. You and I will do so much good for the world."

Cameron nodded, not meeting the professor's eyes. He wasn't sure if he should feel better than he did.

"I must note, however," Dr. Fredricksen said slowly. "This retreat has not gone quite as planned. The remaining contestants...well, I'm afraid that due to their curiosities and partly due to my, eh, temper, they know more than they should. More than they can."

"They don't know anything," Cameron said quickly. "We've all talked about the, uh, weird stuff that's happened here. But no one knows what's going on."

Dr. Fredricksen gave Cameron a sympathetic smile, but his eyes were cold.

"I brought four of you here because I believed I could choose an heir to my position and let the others go home. I was wrong about that. I got a bit carried away early in the week, I'll admit, but even with everyone still intact, I'm afraid they all know too much. They'll call the police as soon as they leave the house, and the door may be compromised."

Cameron frowned and opened his mouth, but Dr. Fredricksen interrupted him.

"If anything happens to this door, you will never see Thomas again."

The sentence felt like a stab in the chest, and Cameron closed his mouth. Sick, deep guilt settled in his stomach as he thought of Lani, Allie, and Kai, but the image of himself hugging Thomas pushed it away. He gave a small nod, not meeting the professor's eyes.

"Good," Dr. Fredricksen said. "I will call for them to meet us here after breakfast and we can settle everything. Then you and I can start discussing how to open the door. I have a few theories that I would like you to test out, as they haven't worked for me. But in the meantime—"

Dr. Fredricksen pulled out a piece of paper.

"I will need you to sign this contract to claim responsibility for the house. It is a modern-day formality to protect the ownership of the property. Once you sign, it is all yours. You will also receive a large inheritance that will allow you to settle your debt back home."

Cameron's body moved on its own as it took the pen from Dr. Fredricksen. He felt like he was in a trance, unable to think clearly through the swirling mist of Thomas, Lani, Allie, and Kai fighting for space in his mind. His ears were ringing.

*Just sign the paper. Forget about them. Sign it and your life can start again.*

Was he thinking those thoughts? Was it Thomas, waiting somewhere in the room with them? Was it Dr. Fredricksen, hovering over Cameron like a parent watching a child open a present? Cameron felt something in his eye and blinked, allowing a tear to roll down his cheek. Why was he crying? This was the best thing that had ever happened to him. Everything was about to be okay again. He should be jumping for joy and laughing and celebrating that the impossible was about to happen. So why did his arm feel so heavy?

With shaky hands, Cameron placed the pen on the page.

"Cameron, no!"

Cameron turned around. Lani was standing in the doorway, panting heavily, with Allie and Kai behind her.

# 27

## Allie

"Ah," Dr. Fredricksen said lightly. "You are all a bit early."

He was smiling, but Allie thought he looked as cold as she had ever seen him. He seemed disheveled and wild, with his eyes blazing and his beard sticking up in various parts. Cameron looked the opposite—there were dark circles under his eyes, and he seemed like he couldn't quite place who they were.

"Cameron, don't trust him," Lani said frantically. "Whatever he told you, don't trust him."

Cameron held Lani's gaze for a moment before looking away. Dr. Fredricksen laughed.

"My dear, you can't possibly understand what we've discussed," he said.

"Time travel," Lani said firmly.

Cameron's eyes jumped back to Lani's and Dr. Fredricksen looked slightly taken aback.

"I saw it," Lani said, keeping her eyes locked on Cameron. "On a note he had written. He also said it was impossible. He's lying to you, Cameron. Did he..." Allie saw Lani's jaw clench. "Did he tell you that you could go back to that day and stop

Thomas from falling?"

Allie didn't know what Lani was talking about. She didn't know who Thomas was, but his name seemed to have the same impact as a slap on the face to Cameron. Cameron didn't answer, but his wide eyes seemed to grow darker.

"It's impossible," Lani said, her voice strained. "I'm sorry, but you can't go back.  He's using you to get control of something. He's not going to help you."

"What do you know?" Dr. Fredricksen snapped. "I know more than you could possibly fathom. Who are you to say what is impossible? Cameron has already made his decision. You could have had this too if you weren't so concerned about the strangers around you."

Surprising herself, Allie let out a laugh. She was so terrified that the whole thing suddenly seemed funny.

"Concerned about other people?" she asked. "That's such a bad thing? All you people care about is yourselves. It doesn't matter what you do and how it hurts other people, as long as you're rewarded at the end of it."

Lani and Kai stared at her.

"I'm sick of you!" Allie spat.

Tears welled in her eyes as she thought of Michael and his family and all the things she had done because of them. How little she had cared about people for years.

"You child," Dr. Fredricksen said coldly. "You, of all people, should understand what Cameron is going through. You think I'm being selfish for giving him a chance to get back someone he's lost?"

Allie hesitated, but Lani jumped back in.

"You're lying," Lani said again.  "We know you're lying. You're not going to let him see Thomas again. You know it's not possible. You're just using him."

"He's been using all of us, Cameron," Kai said quietly. "I found notes in his room. I don't know what he's planning, but he's using bad situations we're all in to try to get us to do something for him."

Kai took a step forward.

"He pushed Lani down the stairs," Kai said, nodding toward the professor. "He put kiwi in my drink and stole my EpiPen, and he knocked the chandelier down to hit Allie. He tried to kill us, and the only reason we're okay is because we got lucky."

Cameron looked at Dr. Fredricksen. The professor was staring at Kai with pursed lips.

"As I said, Cameron," Dr. Fredricksen said. "They know too much."

Allie looked back at Cameron. He was staring at the door on the far side of the room. His face was tense, and he looked like he was holding back tears.

"I'm sorry," he muttered to them before turning away.

Allie's heart started to pound as she saw a smile stretch across Dr. Fredricksen's face.

"What do you mean we know too much?" she couldn't help but ask.

"This house holds many secrets," Dr. Fredricksen said, turning toward the table in the center of the room. "This room holds many more. You were never meant to discover this place, but you all got nosy and had to keep coming back. If you've been in my room, I can only imagine it was because you were looking for a key to get out, a fact that only Barbara knew, which means you also discovered her."

Allie glanced again at Cameron, but he was still staring at the door with his fists clenched.

"That doesn't leave me in a very good light when you leave, does it?" Dr. Fredricksen asked. "I can't have you compromise the integrity of this house.  It is more important than you will ever understand. Only Cameron and I understand. Only Cameron and I know the true power this place holds."

Cameron's eyes were now closed, and he seemed to wince when the professor said his name.

"I'm afraid," Dr. Fredricksen said, touching the tray sitting on the table.  "You cannot leave this house alive."

Allie's feet felt glued to the floor.  She wanted to run, but where would she go? He was going to kill them. She glanced at Cameron again, expecting this to be the trigger that broke him out of his trance. His eyes were back open, but they looked watery and lifeless. Instead of feeling sorry for him, Allie felt rage boil up inside her.

"You coward!"  she screamed.  "You're okay with this? You're going to watch us die?"

She lunged at him but felt Kai holding her back.

"Something's wrong with him," Kai whispered in her ear.

"No," she said, pulling harder. "He knows what he's doing. Your brother is dead, Cameron, just like my mom is dead. And there's nothing we can do about it, okay? You just have to learn to live with it and move on."

She stood there panting, letting Kai hold her up by her arms.

"Even if there was a way to see Thomas again, would it really be worth killing three people for it?" she asked.

Cameron finally looked up at Allie. His eyes were bloodshot and filled with tears. His face was stricken with pure agony, and it was so shocking that Allie actually felt herself soften for a second. He looked the way she had felt the moment her mom had taken her last breath in the hospital. She would never forget the feeling, and she was willing to bet it was how he felt when his brother had died.

"What if...it's true?" Cameron croaked.

His voice sounded weak and pleading. He seemed so different from the moody guy she had met a few days ago, like he had been beaten down into a new person.

"It's not," Allie said, trying to keep her voice steady. "You know that. I'm so sorry, Cameron, but you have to know that."

"They don't know what they're talking about," Dr. Fredricksen said.

He put his hand in his pocket.

"Think about your brother, Cameron," the professor said. "Think about what it's going to be like for him to be a part of the last two years of your life."

Cameron turned to Dr. Fredricksen, his face strangled. A tear was running down his cheek.

"Thomas wouldn't want you to do this," Lani interjected.

Allie held her breath, expecting Cameron to get mad, but his face seemed to grow less angry and more sad as he turned to Lani.

"Those moments you talked about," she said. "You won't get them back."

Allie could tell Lani was fighting not to cry.

"And even if you could, they wouldn't be the same if you knew what you had done. Keep the memory of Thomas pure. It's better than this will be."

Cameron's gaze lingered on Lani for a few more seconds, then darted between Allie and Kai. Allie saw him glance at the door and take a quick, deep breath. He seemed to collect himself before turning to walk back to Dr. Fredricksen.

"You guys don't know what you're talking about," he said

quietly over his shoulder.

Allie's heart sank. Her anger was gone and replaced with fear. If Cameron was on the professor's side, there was no way they were getting out.

"Cameron—" she started.

Before she could get the next word out, Cameron grabbed a large hardcover book from the table and swung it around, cracking it into Dr. Fredricksen's head. The professor let out a grunt and fell to the floor. Allie stood there frozen and heard Lani gasp.

"Come on, we have to go," Cameron said, running toward them.

Allie wanted to hug Cameron, but Lani beat her to it.

"I knew it," she said through tears. "Thank god, I knew it."

Cameron pulled her close, wrapping both arms around her shoulders. Allie held back and let them have their moment.

"I'm sorry," Cameron said as he pulled away from Lani, his cheeks red. "I don't know what...it's so stupid. I don't know how I can ever—"

"It's fine," Kai interrupted.

He was smiling.

"Seriously, it's fine, dude," he said. "You made the right decision in the end."

Cameron smiled gratefully at Kai, then turned to Allie.

"Thanks," he said.

"For what?"

"You said what I needed to hear. I felt like I was in a trance or something. My brain was so foggy, and this room was making me think of...Thomas so much that I couldn't focus. When you started screaming, it kind of broke me out of that."

Allie blushed a little.

"Well, in my defense, I did think you were about to let us all die," she said.

"That still will happen, I'm afraid."

Allie whirled around. Dr. Fredricksen was back on his feet and leaning on the table with one hand. The other held a gun pointed at the four of them.

"To the corner," he said, motioning the gun away from the exit door.

Allie hesitated and glanced at the group, but everyone else seemed as frightened as she was. They slowly moved toward the far corner of the room, close to the strange door.

"I was afraid Cameron would be too weak to continue," Dr. Fredricksen said hoarsely. "So, of course, I factored this into my plan. One by one, come and take a glass."

He motioned to the tray of glasses near him on the table. They each shuffled forward slowly, picked up a glass, and brought it back to the far side of the room. Allie was the last to get hers. She kept her eyes locked on the gun as she walked toward the table, too afraid to look away from it. She grabbed her glass and held it with two hands as she brought it back to the group, nervous that she would drop it, considering how badly she was shaking. It looked like a plain glass of water. She looked up and caught eyes with Lani, who was teary again. Cameron and Kai were exchanging worried glances.

"No need to worry," Dr. Fredricksen said. "I'm not as cruel as you think I am. My little concoction will be quick and painless. It should work in seconds, and it will be like you're falling asleep."

So it was poison. Allie wondered how Dr. Fredricksen thought he could explain four dead students to the public after all of this, but he didn't seem to care. She looked at everyone again. They all shared silent glances with each other, and Allie felt a deep sense of love for everyone in the circle. They had only known each other for a few days, but this was the best group of friends she had ever had. Allie sniffed as tears stung her eyes and felt Lani's arm around her shoulders.

"It'll be okay," Lani whispered.

Dr. Fredricksen raised his large glass, which also seemed to be filled with water, although Allie presumed his wasn't poisoned.

"And drink," he said. "If only you had believed in the power of the greater good. Life is unforgiving in the face of weakness."

He pointed the gun back and forth between the four of them. Allie hesitated like everyone else. Was this really happening?

"Drink!" Dr. Fredricksen yelled, waving the gun wildly.

Allie jumped, then raised the glass to her lips and took a sip. She braced herself for something foul, but it tasted like regular tap water. Whatever the professor used must have been odorless and tasteless, which, she supposed, was a silver lining if she had to find one. She continued to drink, thinking that the one mercy she was offered was that no one would be affected by her death. The only people in the world who cared about her were in this room.

Allie had only thought about dying one other time, when her mom was taking her last breaths in the hospital. Even though she was pumped full of drugs and barely conscious, Allie could tell that her mother's last moments were uncomfortable. It was the worst feeling to sit there and watch the most important person in her life struggle to leave it. All the doctors and therapists talked about the peacefulness of death and how it was just another step in the journey, but it didn't seem peaceful at all. Was her mom kicking and screaming the whole way, or was death just this careless with every soul?

As death pulled the last shred of life from her mom's cancer-ridden body, it pulled a piece of hers away, too. Since that was Allie's only real experience with someone dying, it was how she had imagined it would be for her as well, so she tried not to think about it from that moment forward.

But here she was, facing it much younger than anyone would have expected, and she was surprised to feel a hint of excitement. Allie believed in some form of an afterlife that would allow her to see her mom. Not necessarily the heaven that Michael's family preached about, but she had always believed that loved ones would be reunited after death. She wasn't happy or even content—she was still shivering furiously and felt her throat tightening up—but there was a sense of anticipation and longing for this moment to be over so she could run into her mother's arms and lean into her shoulder again.

Then, Allie realized with a crushing feeling in her stomach—or maybe that was the poison—that she was not proud of her life. Who had she been, really? A doll for a boy to dress up and strut around? A voice for things she didn't really believe in? She knew that the person she had turned into was someone that her mom wouldn't have been proud of, and that thought pushed away anything good she had been feeling. She was suddenly afraid to face her mother. Michael's parents had alluded more than once that her mom wasn't going to heaven because she had a baby out of wedlock, and while Allie never let herself believe that, she never criticized their thinking either.

Allie would be seeing her mom again soon—in a few minutes, maybe—and she didn't know what she would say. That she was sorry? Ashamed? Embarrassed? She suddenly felt for Cameron and longed for the ability to go back, but there was no more time to make up for it. To create a life she was proud of. That was the whole reason she came here, wasn't it? To win the prize money and start over. How ironic it was that she had ruined her chances forever by showing up. She was so silly for thinking last week that money was the only thing stopping her from starting over—she should have done that the first time she realized who Michael was.

Allie finished her glass and turned to her friends, whose glasses were empty as well. Kai's eyes were closed and he was leaning his head back toward the ceiling. He actually did seem peaceful, which was something that Allie's tumultuous emotions couldn't comprehend. While she was staring, Kai opened his eyes and caught Allie's. She felt herself blush, but he gave her a kind smile. She wanted to bring up his sisters and his family, to ask him how he felt, but she couldn't bring herself to do it.

Her eyes moved to Cameron. He was also staring at the ceiling, but his eyes were open. They were still red but no longer watery, filled with fear and hopelessness. Watching him take deep breaths, Allie realized another point of irony in all this—Dr. Fredricksen was going to help Cameron see his brother again after all.

Finally, Allie turned to Lani. She felt hot, fresh tears flow down her cheeks as she thought about the friendship they had been building. Lani was nicer to her than anyone ever had been, and Allie knew that she meant the things she said and did. Lani was strong and fearless, and maybe not perfect, but she seemed like she tried really hard to be a good person. Or maybe it came naturally to her. Either way, Allie knew that

Lani could have done so much good in the world if she had been able to. Allie opened her mouth, wanting to say something to Lani in her last moments about how much she appreciated her and how unfair all of this was, but she couldn't catch Lani's gaze.

Lani was staring intensely at Dr. Fredricksen.

Allie looked over at the professor, who was finishing his own glass of water. He let out a refreshed sigh when he was done.

"Now we wait," he said with a smile. "I am terribly sorry, but this was the only way."

They stood there for a few minutes in silence, and Allie began to shake, waiting for a horrible feeling to creep into her body as it shut down. But nothing happened. She glanced at Kai, who was starting to look confused as well. Lani's eyes remained fixed on the professor. Allie opened her mouth to ask Lani what she was doing, but she was interrupted by a groan. She looked to the side and saw Dr. Fredricksen slumped over the table, holding his stomach. He dropped to the floor, the gun still in his hand.

"What—" he said, breathing heavily.

He looked up at the students, who all looked between each other and Dr. Fredricksen, except for Lani.

"I was in here this morning," Lani said quietly, keeping her eyes locked on him. "I found the glasses. I had a feeling something was off, so I poured what was in ours into your glass and replaced ours with water."

"You little—"

Dr. Fredricksen groaned again, clenching his stomach even harder.

"Caring about other people isn't weakness," Lani said, her eyes blazing. "Caring about power is."

Allie couldn't quite comprehend what was going on. There hadn't been any poison in their drinks? They weren't about to die? She didn't breathe as she watched Dr. Fredricksen fall on his side and squirm on the ground for several seconds before going completely still.

No one moved.

"Is he...dead?" Allie asked, her voice barely above a whisper.

Kai crept toward the body slowly and nudged the professor's leg when he reached it. There was no movement. Kai quickly grabbed the gun and locked it before slipping it into his pocket. He turned back to the group, his face white.

"I think so," he said. "Either way, we need to go."

Allie turned to Lani, who was breathing heavily, and after a moment's pause, she and Kai wrapped her in a tight hug. Allie felt tears streaming down her face as the relief of what had just happened swept over her. She looked over her shoulder to see Cameron, who had slid down the wall and was staring at the professor with a white face. He looked up at Allie and let out a strangled noise. The three broke apart and looked at him.

"I'm sorry," Cameron choked out. "Oh my god, we almost died. I almost killed you all."

He looked like he might throw up. Allie wiped her face and laughed.

"But you didn't," she said.

She was surprised at her own cheeriness—she knew Cameron had played a role in this to some degree. But she also didn't care. He had made a mistake driven by grief, something she understood, and he had made the right choice in the end. She forgave him, and she knew everyone else did too.

Cameron looked up at her. Their eyes met and something

clicked between them. Minutes ago, she thought she was about to see her mom again, and he thought she was about to see his brother. She could tell that he had felt it too—fear, but also excitement and anticipation. Something also told Allie that he, too, had evaluated his life when he believed it was over, and was now unsure how to move forward. Allie took a step toward Cameron and held out her hand.

"It's okay," she said softly. "We're still here."

Cameron hesitated, then placed his hand in hers. Kai stepped forward and offered his hand, which Cameron took with his free one. They pulled him to his feet and Allie moved forward to embrace him. Allie felt Cameron brace himself as she wrapped around his shoulder before he relaxed slightly.

"We'll see them again," Allie whispered into his ear so only he could hear her.

Cameron pulled away and nodded. He took a deep breath and gave the first small smile she had seen out of him.

"Yeah," he said.

Kai gently hit Cameron's shoulder.

"We're all good, man," he said. "It'll get weird if you keep moping."

Cameron let out a small laugh and Allie knew he'd be okay. She watched as he turned to Lani, who had been watching quietly from behind. His green eyes locked onto hers, and he suddenly moved past Allie to wrap Lani in a tight hug. She wrapped her arms around his torso, and he placed one hand on the back of her neck, pulling her even closer. Allie exchanged a smile with Kai, but neither of them said anything.

Cameron finally pulled away, his and Lani's cheeks a little pink. He let out an embarrassed chuckle and ran his fingers through his hair. As he was looking away, his eyes landed on the body of Dr. Fredricksen in the far corner of the room. His eyes widened, like it had just hit him what happened. He shook his head and looked at Lani in amazement.

"How did you…?"

Lani blushed and gave a shaky giggle.

"I didn't trust him."

# 28

## Kai

"We need to go," Cameron said.

Kai nodded and stepped back to let everyone out of the room before himself. He turned and gave one final look at Dr. Fredricksen. He hadn't moved and was still sprawled on the floor in an awkward position, his eyes open and lifeless. Kai shivered and, with shaking hands, stepped outside and closed the door behind him.

"We need to get Barbara first," Kai said, walking down the hallway.

"What happened?" Cameron asked.

Kai explained how he had found Barbara locked in the room that morning. He also took the time to fill Cameron in on everything he had told the girls during breakfast before they decided they needed to see if Cameron was in the strange room before they tried to escape.

"You guys could have gotten out?" Cameron asked.

"Well, yeah," Kai said. "But we weren't going to leave you."

Cameron looked a little stunned, then a frown crossed his face.

"You should have just left," he said, looking down. "I almost got you all killed."

Kai shook his head.

"You're our friend. No one wanted to leave without you."

Cameron didn't respond.

"What did Dr. Fredricksen tell you about the room?" Lani asked.

Cameron told them everything the professor had said, which included some bizarre explanation about a portal of knowledge that let important ideas into the world whenever it decided the time was right.

"So, Dr. Fredricksen, like, guards the portal? That's why he's here?" Lani asked.

Cameron nodded.

"He has to pass it on eventually, and he wanted me to be the next keeper," Cameron said. "If I agreed to work together with him. He wanted to try to go inside the portal, I guess. I don't know what he wanted to do, but it probably wasn't good."

"That must have been what he meant with all those questions about the greater good," Allie said. "I bet he wanted to control what ideas came here first. Can you imagine how powerful you would be if you could control new technology and inventions and medical discoveries?"

"Maybe the idea of time travel isn't so crazy after all," Lani said.

Cameron felt his face get red, but he gave Lani a small smile. She knew how to talk to him. They continued to hurry down the hallway until they reached their rooms, following Kai as he led them to where Barbara had been trapped.

"Barbara, are you there?" he asked when they reached the door inside the large empty room where he had left her.

"Yes," Barbara said from behind the door. "Are you all okay?"

"Yeah," the four of them said in unison.

"And Theodore?"

They exchanged glances. Lani opened her mouth, but Kai held up a hand.

"We'll explain everything once we get out of here," he said.

*Not right now*, he mouthed to Lani. Kai didn't know how Barbara would take the news of Dr. Fredricksen's death, and he didn't think this was the best place to share it. He needed to make sure they were all safe before dropping that on her.

Kai fumbled with the key, realizing his hands were shaking. He finally got it into the lock and opened the door to see Barbara standing there, looking intensely relieved.

"I'm so glad the four of you are okay," she said in a shaky voice. "When he locked me in here, I thought..."

She shook her head and smiled at them. Kai noticed her eyes were red, and he wondered if she had been crying.

"It doesn't matter now. What matters is you're safe."

"We should go," Kai said. "Does Dr. Fredricksen own a car?"

Barbara nodded.

"Yes, there is one in the garage. I know the code to get in."

Everyone followed Kai downstairs and stood behind him as he unlocked the front door. He pushed one of the massive doors open, and a rush of fresh air blew into the house. It smelled sweet, and Kai realized he hadn't breathed any outside air in several days.

"The garage is this way," Barbara said, leading them to the right.

Kai waited as Barbara opened the garage door, glancing nervously at the house. When the garage was open, they all clambered into the vintage-looking vehicle. Kai took the driver's seat and began to drive off, checking in his rearview mirror as they tore down the driveway. But the road behind them remained clear. Slowly, the house grew smaller and smaller until it was gone.

No one said anything for several minutes, not even to ask where Kai was driving. He knew from the ride here that there was a town several miles away, and he was planning to take them to the police station there. Slowly, Kai began to feel safe for the first time in several days. He didn't care that his phone and clothes were still at the house—they would get those back eventually. Letting his guard down also provided room for what had just happened to settle over him. He tried his best to focus on the road through his now foggy eyes.

Kai had been thinking about his family when he was drinking what he thought was poison. After closing his eyes, he had pictured his mom, physically frail but stronger in spirit than anyone he knew. He had pictured his dad beside her hospital bed, one hand on hers, doing his best to smile bravely for the family. And he had pictured Mia and Akiko, large grins on their faces with their long black hair in pigtails, swinging with their never-ending movement. Thinking about them shouldn't have felt weird because his view of them always excluded himself, but that time had felt emptier. He really wasn't going to be there anymore. Kai had felt so guilty for the pain he was about to cause his parents and his little sisters, and so guilty that he couldn't have even solved their financial problems first. Guilty that he wouldn't be giving Jenny from work any of the prize money, and guilty for knowing that no one else knew about her debt because he had kept it a secret.

In what he thought were his last moments, Kai had been

praying. He didn't know if he believed in God, but he knew his ancestors were always connected to him. He had been asking them to send his love to his family and to help them get through what would happen soon.

But that was over now. His family wouldn't get a phone call later today that their son had been found dead alongside three other students in a tragic accident. The relief of that fact, the pure joy of it, made Kai's body go weak, and he had a hard time holding the steering wheel straight. He wondered what everyone else had been thinking about as they drank from their glasses. He glanced in the rearview mirror at Lani, Cameron, and Allie in the back seat. Lani and Cameron were each staring out their windows, and Allie was gazing at her knees. They all looked a little shell-shocked, and Kai assumed the aftermath was hitting them, too.

A few minutes later, with some help from Barbara's directions, Kai pulled the car into the police station parking lot. The rest of the day was a blur. Kai explained what happened to someone at the front desk, and the five of them were taken to a back room. They repeated their stories again and again, sometimes together and sometimes alone. No one mentioned seeing their own visions in the room with the strange door. They hadn't discussed it, but if they were thinking the same as Kai, they didn't want to be labeled as crazy alongside Dr. Fredricksen. When Barbara found out that Dr. Fredricksen had died during the first conversation with the police, she slumped into a chair and stared at the floor for a long time without speaking. Police must have been sent to the house, because at some point, they came back with confirmation that a body had been found. Someone gave Kai a blanket and a cup of coffee.

Eventually, someone handed him his phone. This finally

perked him up, and he began checking his messages frantically. There were a couple of "how's it going" texts from friends and just one from his dad.

*The specialist in New York officially accepted mom. We agreed to do it. We aren't flying out until Monday, so you should be back and we can talk more. We'll make it work. He seems to think he can help. Sounded very positive. Mom's doing better too. We're all excited to hear how it was.*

Kai couldn't help but worry about how they were going to pay for this treatment, but money was less of a pressing issue now. A doctor was actually hopeful about helping his mom. He hadn't heard positive news like that since she started getting sick. Kai looked up at the nearest police officer.

"Can I call my parents?" he asked.

She nodded.

"You all should," she said, looking at the other three students. "We're going to send you to the hospital in a few minutes to run a toxicology test to make sure you didn't accidentally ingest any poison, so now's a good time to update family. Unless something new comes up, you should be able to fly home tomorrow."

Kai's dad picked up on the first ring.

"Kai!" his dad said on the other end of the line. "How are you?"

"I"m okay," Kai said. "Is mom there? I need to fill you guys in on the last few days."

Kai told his parents what had happened, downplaying the attempted poisoning the best he could. There was a shocked silence from the other end of the phone, and he did his best to assure his mom that he was fine once she started crying.

After several minutes of promising he was okay and would

update them on his travels home, Kai hung up. He looked around the room. Lani, Cameron, and Allie were all sitting close to each other, seemingly done with their phone calls. He walked over and gave a small smile.

"My mom was really freaking out, understandably," he said. "How did yours handle it?"

There was an awkward pause, and Kai immediately remembered that no one else in the room had a good relationship with their parents, or even had parents to talk to. He felt his face get hot.

"I'm so sorry," he said quickly. "I forgot."

To his surprise, everyone smiled.

"It's okay," Lani said. "I told my parents, but all they cared about was whether I won the money or not. They seemed pretty eager to get off the phone once I told them I hadn't. I don't know if they even heard me when I said I had almost been poisoned."

Her voice sounded bitter, which Kai thought was refreshing in a way. It was better than her pretending everything was okay.

"Mine actually seemed like they cared a little," Cameron said. "We'll see if that lasts."

Everyone turned to Allie.

"I don't really have anyone to call," she said softly. "But that's okay. I have you guys."

She blushed.

"I don't mean that in a creepy way, I just meant—"

Lani interrupted her by throwing her arms over Allie's and Cameron's shoulders and pulling them together for a group hug. She smiled and raised her eyebrows for Kai to join. He did.

"We're your family now," Lani said to Allie.

They all let go, and Kai noticed that Allie's eyes were watery again. He tried to change the subject.

"It does suck that none of us won the money, though," he said. "It would have been nice if at least one person could have used it."

They all nodded. Allie seemed unbothered by the comment, but Lani was suddenly picking at her nails, and Cameron was looking at the floor. Kai remembered Lani's blackmailer and felt awful again about bringing up the money. How was she going to pay him back now?

"We are in a police station," Kai said to Lani. "Is there any chance you want to—"

But she was already shaking her head.

"I mentioned it to one of the cops already," she said. "They said they can't do anything about it if he's using burner phones. And that I shouldn't have put that stuff out there in the first place."

"What?" Kai asked furiously. "Who said that?"

Lani gave him a painful smile.

"I'm not going to tell you for your own sake," she said. "But there's nothing anyone can do. It's okay," she said as Kai opened his mouth again. "Really. I'll figure it out one way or another. I hate that school anyway."

"If there's anything we can ever do," Kai said. "Please, let us know."

Lani nodded, her eyes a little brighter.

"I will," she said.

Kai turned to Cameron.

"You okay?" he asked.

He knew Cameron really needed the money as well, considering Dr. Fredricksen's note earlier about a gambling debt and how Cameron was reacting now. Cameron looked at Kai stiffly for a few seconds, then relaxed his face.

"I'm in some debt," he muttered. "I was hoping to pay it off."

"Oh," Kai said, pretending this was news to him. "I'm sorry."

Cameron gave a small nod but avoided eye contact. Kai could tell there was more to the story, but he didn't want to press further.

"Okay, I think we're done for today."

A tall police officer had walked into the room.

"Barbara has offered to pay for you all to stay in a nearby hotel before your flights home tomorrow," she said. "And she has arranged for your things to be taken from the house to the hotel. They should be there soon."

Kai looked around. He realized he hadn't seen Barbara in a while and wanted to thank her.

"Where is she?" he asked.

"Back at the estate," the police officer said. "Talking to lawyers, probably. I think she's the beneficiary of the home. Anyway, we have a car outside to take you to the hotel."

Kai followed the officer to a black car parked outside the police station. He didn't see any reporters, so he assumed the story hadn't gotten out yet. They all rode in silence to the hotel. Someone checked them into their rooms, and they walked silently upstairs to the second floor, where their rooms were all next to each other, just like they had been in the house.

Kai said goodnight to the others and stepped into his room. It was smaller than it had been at the estate but still larger than anything he would normally stay in. He suddenly felt exhausted. He took a quick shower and ordered a sandwich from the room service menu, a perk they had been told was included in their stay. While he waited for the delivery, he turned on the television. The first channel was news, and he was startled for a moment to see a video of Dr. Fredricksen's estate splashed across the screen.

"Breaking news tonight," the anchor on the screen was saying. "We are just receiving reports that professor and author Dr. Fredricksen has been found dead in his home. The incident occurred this morning during what was supposed to be a week-long writing retreat he was holding for four college students from around the country. All four of those students are safe, although their whereabouts are unknown. We turn now to a press conference being held outside the home."

A police officer Kai recognized from the station came on the screen, standing in front of a pulpit surrounded by microphones.

"This is an ongoing investigation," he said gruffly. "The details are very fresh, and we are still gathering evidence, so we cannot make a statement about the cause of death at this time. We ask for the public's patience as we work to get to the bottom of this, and we ask that no one speculates about what happened, especially regarding the four students involved. We have good reason to believe that they are victims as well. I will not elaborate further."

Kai was surprised to hear the officer mention them as victims and breathed a sigh of relief. It hadn't occurred to him before now that it could look like they had been responsible for Dr. Fredricksen's death. Technically, Lani had been, but only in defense of their lives after he had tried to kill them. It was a wild story that would be hard for the public to believe, which made Kai nervous. He hoped there was enough evidence to prove they weren't murderers.

There was a knock on the door, and Kai jumped. He walked over and looked through the peephole. It was Barbara. He opened the door and let her in.

"Thank you," she said. "I've brought your suitcase with all of your things."

She rolled a large black suitcase toward him and he moved it to the side of his bed.

"Thank you," he said. "How are you doing?"

Barbara sighed.

"I'm as well as I can be, I suppose," she said.

The lines on her face looked deeper than they had the day before.

"I don't mourn for who he turned into," she said, looking directly at Kai. "I hope you know that. But I do mourn for the person he was for most of my time with him. You don't forget that person, you know."

She shook her head.

"I still can't believe he tried to..." she trailed off. "I can't believe I didn't see it. Or do anything about it."

Kai gave what he hoped was a warm smile.

"It's okay, really," he said. "We didn't think he was a killer either. He was manipulative and calculating to all of us. None of us blame you for anything," he added.

Barbara finally seemed to feel a little better after he said the last part.

"You have every right to," she said. "But thank you. I appreciate that. I hope to make it up to all of you somehow, which brings me to my next point."

She held out an envelope to Kai. He took it hesitantly.

"It's a check," she said. "For $100,000. I was left in charge of Dr. Fredricksen's estate in the event that he died, and I believe that you all earned what one of you was supposed to win. I know it does not erase the trauma you endured or what you will continue to experience for who knows how long, but it is the least I can do."

Kai stared at the envelope. He felt his jaw go slack, and he looked up at Barbara.

"Are you for real?" he asked.

Barbara chuckled.

"I hope it helps," she said. "I'm sure we'll speak again at least once before the case is closed, but please feel free to reach out anytime. I've grown to...well, I really respect and admire the four of you. You all seem like wonderful people."

She tilted her head and gave Kai a gentle smile.

"You remind me of my grandson," she said. "He lives abroad, so I don't get to see him very often, but you have his same demeanor. I wish you and your family well."

Kai didn't know what to say.

"Thank you," he finally got out. "Thank you, for every-thing."

Barbara smiled again.

"Get some rest," she said. "And safe travels tomorrow."

She turned and left. Kai waited until he heard her footsteps fade before tearing open the envelope. He didn't think she had been lying, but he had to see the check for himself. And there it was. A warm feeling spread through his chest. He put the check on his bed, afraid he would accidentally tear it with his shaking hands. His family was going to be okay. They could pay off their hospital bills and maybe even cover the specialist. He could help Jenny. He thought of Cameron, who could now pay off his debt, of Lani, who could pay off her blackmailer, and Allie, who seemed like she could use the money for a fresh start.

Kai lay down on his bed and smiled at the ceiling. He hadn't felt this happy in years. He would tell his family tomorrow when he got home. Right now, he just wanted to eat and go to bed, knowing he wouldn't be tossing and turning all night for the first time in months.

# 29

# Lani

Lani heard a knock on her door. Her heart began to pound, but it slowed down when she saw it was Barbara on the other side. She opened the door.

"Hi, Barbara," she said hesitantly. "Is...everything okay?"

The last time Barbara knocked on a door looking for her, it was bad news that she never got to tell.

"Yes," Barbara said. "I just have a couple of things to go over. May I come in?"

"Oh, yeah, of course."

Lani stepped aside and let Barbara walk past her, noticing she was pulling Lani's pink suitcase behind her.

"Oh, thank you," Lani said. "I can take that."

She moved the suitcase to the side. Barbara pulled two envelopes out of her pocket. One was thin and the other was thick, like it was stuffed with multiple pages of paper.

"I have several things I need to discuss with you," Barbara said. "First, I need to apologize again. I knew Theodore was falling apart, but I believed in the good part of him too much. I was naive, and you all almost died because of that. I will never forgive myself."

She choked up, and Lani felt a pang in her chest. She had been a little frustrated with Barbara at a point, sure, but she didn't blame everything that had happened on her.

"None of us hold anything against you," Lani said earnestly. "Really. We could tell that you were in just as much danger."

Lani hesitated, then asked, "What were you going to tell me that night you came to Allie's room?"

Barbara smiled wearily, and Lani wondered if she had beaten herself up over it already.

"I was going to warn you," she said. "I didn't know exactly what was going on, but something told me that you all needed to get out of the house. You seemed like the person to tell."

That surprised Lani. She thought Kai was the most leader-worthy person in the group.

"Me?" she asked.

Barbara nodded.

"You are all wonderful people," she said thoughtfully. "I can tell. But you, Lani, have a rare combination of love and fire inside you. I don't completely understand how the knowledge portal works, but it has sent a few intense impressions my way over the years, and it has never been wrong. I had one of those impressions the moment you arrived at the house."

Lani didn't know what to say, so she smiled awkwardly.

"I don't want to take up too much of your time," Barbara said. "This is for you."

She handed Lani the flat envelope. Lani opened it, and her mouth fell open when she saw the check.

"As the official owner of the estate now," Barbara said. "I felt it was only fair to reward each of you with the prize money. You deserve much more than this, of course, but this is what I was able to do on such short notice."

Lani felt tears of relief sting her eyes. She could pay her blackmailer off, and the nightmare would finally be over.

"I don't..."

Lani couldn't finish her sentence. She threw her arms around Barbara's bony shoulders and hugged her tightly.

"Oh," she heard Barbara say behind her ear. "Yes, well, I hope it can be of good use."

Lani pulled away and wiped her eyes.

"You don't know what this means to me," she laughed. "This is seriously life-changing."

Barbara smiled warmly.

"I am so glad. As I told Kai, please do not hesitate to call me if you ever need help with anything in the future. You all saved my life as well, I think."

Lani nodded, not able to keep her eyes off the check.

"There is one more matter I would like to discuss with you, Lani," she heard Barbara say.

Lani looked up. Barbara was holding out the fat envelope and Lani took it from her hands.

"Lani, did you experience visions in the room where Theodore died?"

Lani was taken aback.

"Um, yeah," she said, feeling like she could be honest with Barbara. "Yeah, one time. The first time I went in and tried to open that door at the end, the portal door, I guess, I saw a guy from my life who has...done some bad stuff. But it was like I saw a way to fight him, almost. It's hard to describe."

Barbara nodded, not acting surprised at all.

"Did you have any other strange experiences in the room?"

"Yeah. This morning. I went there really early because I

wanted to see it one more time. I touched the door, and it actually opened a couple of inches. I tried to look inside, and I couldn't see anything, but I felt something weird. Like... profound responsibility and happiness at the same time. Purpose, maybe. I don't know really know how else to explain it."

Barbara was watching her intently but still didn't look surprised.

"Did Theodore explain to you all how the room worked?"

"Cameron told us what Dr. Fredricksen told him. Something about a portal that sends knowledge to Earth. And that Dr. Fredricksen was in charge of protecting the portal and that he wanted to pass it on to Cameron."

"Yes, that is a very concise summary," Barbara said. "The portal has existed since the beginning of time, and one person at a time has always been chosen to protect it. For the most part, those chosen are intelligent, kind, and patient. They allow the portal to exist and do its job without interfering. There have been a few times in the past when important discoveries were not released soon enough to prevent tragedies, and these incidents have only occurred when the keeper has become corrupt and greedy."

She grimaced, and Lani realized Dr. Fredricksen had probably been a good friend of hers. Since she lived at the house, he might have been her closest friend.

"If something happens to a keeper before they have chosen an heir, someone like me—an assistant or close confidant— steps in. Now, there is much I do not understand about the portal, but there was much that Theodore did not understand either."

She furrowed her brows in thought.

"I believe the most important thing is that you believe the portal exists and understand its importance. And that you don't try to interfere with its decisions."

Lani nodded. She didn't understand why Barbara was telling her all of this.

"I am the keeper now," Barbara said. "Temporarily. I am old, after all. I need to choose an heir myself very soon."

She looked at Lani.

"I believe it should be you."

Lani's eyes widened.

"What?" she asked. "I don't think—"

Barbara interrupted her by holding up a hand.

"This isn't really a discussion we can have right now. There is too much to say, and I'm sure you are exhausted from the day. It is your choice, of course, and you should feel no remorse if you do not want to accept the responsibility. Everything you need to know is in here."

She pointed to the envelope in Lani's hands.

"This explains everything we know about the portal and contains letters and diary entries from previous keepers. You would inherit the house, as well, and receive enough money to live comfortably. Many keepers choose to have careers, often as writers or teachers, although you are free to do whatever you want."

Barbara paused and gave Lani a kind look.

"I've met many people in that house since I started working there 40 years ago," she said. "No one has given me the same feeling as you. I truly believe that you are meant to be the next keeper."

Lani didn't know how to answer, so she just nodded. Barbara squeezed her hand and stood up.

"I still need to talk to Cameron and Allie before they go to bed," she said. "We will be in touch. Take all the time you need."

"Thank you," Lani said. "I'll let you know."

Barbara closed the door behind her and left Lani alone in the room. Lani sat down on the bed. Her, the next keeper? She wasn't even sure if she believed the portal was real. But as she thought it, she knew she did. The things she had seen and felt were undeniable, and she had experienced a pull within the house from the moment she arrived. Was this what she was meant to do with her life? She pulled the stack of letters from the envelope and began to read through them.

All anyone talked about for the next month was the death of Dr. Theodore Fredricksen, the reclusive billionaire professor who had gone mad and tried to poison four college students during a writing retreat. Somehow, he had ended up poisoning himself (the details of how that happened had somehow been kept secret after Lani convinced the police it wasn't a pertinent detail), and the students, along with his long-time housekeeper, were able to escape.

Lani became a local celebrity on campus for a while, and she couldn't deny that she liked the attention at first. But it got old after a while, and people started asking too many questions about the poison, so she tried to downplay it as much as possible. She didn't regret what she had done, but she was worried that someone out there would find a way to spin the story to make her look like a killer.

After depositing Barbara's check, Lani transferred $10,000 to her blackmailer, and to her surprise, he cut contact completely. She was fully prepared for him to ask for more money, but he didn't. She still hoped that he burned in hell, but hey, he wasn't as despicably evil as he could have been. She still kept all of the texts, though, with the hope that one day she might be able to track him down. Her photos were never sent to the school, and Lani was able to finish the semester without any meetings from the school board.

It was early June, and Lani was sitting in a cafe near Bryant Park. They had all agreed to meet up after school was out for the summer, and New York was the easiest destination for everyone. Lani smiled brightly as she saw Allie glide into the cafe.

"Allie!" Lani squealed, jumping up and pulling Allie in for a tight hug.

Lani and Allie had kept in touch since the retreat and texted or talked almost every day. Lani had loved seeing the person Allie was turning into—she was more confident in herself by the day and had even started trying to track down her father. Allie had told Lani a few weeks earlier that she had applied for a graduate program to get her master's degree in social work.

"It doesn't pay much," Allie had said on the phone. "But I can do a lot of good with it. Sort of to pay back for who I was."

Allie sat down in the chair across from Lani.

"You're the only one here?" she asked.

Just then, Kai walked up to the table.

"Hey guys," he said.

Lani and Allie hugged him at the same time.

"How are you?" Lani asked. "We haven't talked in forever."

Kai didn't post much online and never added too much personal information in their group chat.

"Really good," he said. "I just came from visiting my mom, actually. She's doing a lot better. They think they might know what's wrong, and they might be able to treat it for good."

He said the words breathlessly like he had been holding them in all day.

"Oh my gosh, that's such good news," Lani said. "Wow, I'm so happy for you guys!"

"Thanks," Kai said.

He wore a goofy smile, and Lani could tell he was giddy. She was thrilled for him.

Lani heard the door open again, and looked up to see Cameron walking toward the table. She couldn't help but smile. They had kept in touch, too, and were planning to spend some time together now that she was in the city for the week. He looked as grumpy as ever with his dark leather jacket and curls falling over his eyes, and Lani felt her heartbeat speed up. Cameron had confided in her about his gambling debts and the mafia guys who had threatened him for not paying them back. She wasn't going to lie—it was pretty hot, especially since he had been able to pay them off and cut ties with them for good. How many people had a good mob story?

"Hey," Cameron said, sitting down in the free chair next to Lani.

"Hi," Lani said.

They shared a brief glance before looking back at Kai and Allie.

"I mean, you don't have to pretend to hide it," Kai said.

Allie laughed and Lani blushed.

"We're not dating," she said quickly. "We're just...getting to know each other."

"I bet," Allie coughed.

Lani hit her arm. She could feel Cameron looking at her, and she was afraid she'd blush again if she met eyes with him, so she avoided his gaze and fought a smile.

"Anyway," she said. "How are you guys?"

They all chatted and caught up for a while, sipping coffee and snacking on croissants.

"Have you thought more about taking over for Barbara?" Kai eventually asked Lani.

Lani had told them about being picked as the next portal keeper in the airport as they waited for their flights. It felt good to confide in them, and she was surprised at how helpful their advice had been.

"Yeah," she said, taking a deep breath. "I think I'm going to do it."

"Really?" Allie asked. "That's the right move. It's supposed to be you."

Lani smiled. She had poured hours of thought into the decision, and it just felt right. She would tell Barbara after flying home from New York.

"I agree," Kai said.

"Yeah," Cameron said, running a finger along Lani's thigh under the table.

"Thanks," Lani said. "You guys have to come visit me all the time, okay?"

They all nodded and laughed. After more conversation, Kai checked his phone.

"Yikes, I have to go," he said. "Sorry, I'm meeting some-one."

"Ooh," Allie said. "Like a date?"

Kai's cheeks turned pink.

"Yeah, a date. We met online and have been talking for a couple of weeks, so it was good timing."

"When do we get to meet him?" Lani asked.

"I'll let you know if there's even a second date," Kai said. "Then I might show you a picture. I'll see you guys around."

He waved and left the coffee shop.

"I have to go too," Allie said. "I'm meeting some friends for dinner."

She stood up and hugged Lani.

"We're still on for breakfast tomorrow?" she asked.

Lani nodded.

"Of course. I'll text you later."

Allie left too. Lani turned to Cameron, who was staring at her with his deep brown eyes.

"I missed you," he said softly.

Lani smiled.

"Same."

She paused.

"Do you really think I can do this?"

"Yes," Cameron said firmly. "I'm not just saying that. None of us are. I think it's what you were meant to do."

Lani pulled out her phone.

"I'm going to tell Barbara right now," she said, standing up. "Wait here."

Lani walked outside and dialed Barbara's number. As she waited for Barbara to pick up, she watched the people around her strolling by. Every one of them had their own story that was intricately woven with the stories around them, even if they didn't know it. She felt a new sort of kinship with them all. People were better than she had thought, including herself. They were all just getting by and hoping things would work out for them. She couldn't control that, but she could help to make sure that things happened when they were supposed to. And maybe that was enough.

# About the Author

Anne Taylor was born and raised in Spokane, Washington. After graduating college with a BA in journalism, she began a career as a freelance writer and has been working in digital media every since. She published her first novel, What it Takes to Lose, in 2021. When she isn't writing, Anne loves to spend time with family, travel around the world, and hang out with her dog, Pepper.

You can follow Anne's work on TikTok & Instagram @annetaylorwrites or contact her through her website at annetaylorwrites.com.

**You can connect with me on:**

- https://annetaylorwrites.com
- https://www.tiktok.com/@annetaylorwrites

# Also by Anne Taylor

**What it Takes to Lose**

When Eve Allred, a high school junior, loses some weight for the first time, she is intoxicated by the compliments and praise she receives.

Then Ana shows up.

Ana, the beautiful and strikingly skinny girl who seems to come out of nowhere, insists Eve isn't done losing weight, and for reasons she can't comprehend, Eve feels an uncontrollable urge to obey her. Ten pounds quickly turns to twenty, which turns to fifty.

Months of hospitalization and rehab later, Eve is ready to get better. But even the smallest tasks prove difficult when Ana, the friend Eve wishes she never had, has other plans. Trying to transition back to her normal life, Eve struggles with repairing broken relationships with friends and family while trying to get back to the normal life she used to know.

Eve's struggle to balance everything—trying to recreate her old life, vicious Ana, and a mysterious boy who can't look at her—provides a raw look at what recovering from an eating disorder is really like and proves nothing is as simple as it seems.

9 7989 89 5 1 7008